A ... ...ight ...inn, right through her heart.

She'd heard of such things. Arranged marriages happened all the time. She couldn't allow such a wicked life to be imposed upon Fern and Ivy. Could not.

The chaos inside her hit a boiling point. She not only could not let that happen, she *would not* let that happen. Her charges would not be forced to marry—

Her thoughts paused, and everything around her went quiet, even though they weren't. Luke was still shouting, and Mr. Watson was attempting to calm him down. She could see all that, hear all that, even as her own thoughts battled against each other in her mind.

One side of her was telling her she couldn't. The other side was saying it was their only chance. Their only hope.

His only hope. Luke had traveled halfway around the world to fulfil a promise to his brother. He'd left behind a ranch, a life full of adventures, a life that he loved, but he loved his brother more. Loved him so much that he was here, fighting, doing everything he could for Rowland's final wish to be granted.

Before the other side of her could challenge her idea any further, she stood. "Luke and I are getting married as soon as possible."

Author Note

Every so often, characters become so real, I can't type fast enough to get their story written. That's what happened with Luke and Aislinn. She had such a big and genuine heart, and Luke, well, he'd already become a legend in his own time, so I just couldn't wait for them to get their well-deserved happily-ever-after.

When I told my husband that I had finished this book, he said that I must have really enjoyed writing it because I was smiling every time he walked into my office. He was right, and I hope you enjoy their journey that traverses Victorian England to the American West as much as I did.

Happy reading!

A lover of fairy tales and history, **Lauri Robinson** can't imagine a better profession than penning happily-ever-after stories about men and women in days gone past. Her favorite settings include World War II, the Roaring Twenties and the Old West. Lauri and her husband raised three sons in their rural Minnesota home and are now getting their just rewards by spoiling their grandchildren. Visit her at laurirobinson.blogspot.com, Facebook.com/lauri.robinson1 or Twitter.com/laurir.

Books by Lauri Robinson

Harlequin Historical

Diary of a War Bride
A Family for the Titanic Survivor
The Captain's Christmas Homecoming

Southern Belles in London

The Return of His Promised Duchess
The Making of His Marchioness
Falling for His Pretend Countess

The Osterlund Saga

Marriage or Ruin for the Heiress
The Heiress and the Baby Boom

Twins of the Twenties

Scandal at the Speakeasy
A Proposal for the Unwed Mother

Sisters of the Roaring Twenties

The Flapper's Fake Fiancé
The Flapper's Baby Scandal
The Flapper's Scandalous Elopement

Visit the Author Profile page
at Harlequin.com.

Dedicated to one of the sweetest
women I know, Phyllis Nees.

Chapter One

1885

Aislinn Blaydon held one hand over her mouth to muffle her sobs as she stood in the doorway to the nursery for the last time. Fern and Ivy were sound asleep, looking like the little angels that they were, and the idea of never seeing them again was doing more than breaking her heart. There wasn't any part of her that wasn't hurting, aching, and her heart itself had been completely shattered.

'I'm sorry, Aislinn, but it's time,' Christopher said.

'I know,' she replied, with a sniffle and sob that she couldn't smother. Percy Carlisle and his wife, Hazel, the new Duke and Duchess of Havenbrook, had ordered that she leave the house before sunrise. Christopher was only doing his job. The kind-hearted, grey-haired man had been the main butler at Havenbrook long before she'd arrived four years ago, shortly after the twins had been born.

It had been her first job, her only job, having been sent there as a temporary governess, because twins had been a surprise for the late Duke and Duchess, and they wanted to make sure the girls had equal care.

'I expressed it would be proper to provide transport,' Christopher whispered. 'It was declined.'

'It's all right.' She had no idea where she was going, so a ride wouldn't do her much good. No one would hire her as a governess. She'd been told that she would not be provided with a recommendation, and that Mrs Hall, who had trained her to be a governess and still oversaw the orphanage, would be informed that she was not fit to be around children.

Pushing the burning air out of her lungs, Aislinn closed the nursery door and picked up the single tapestry satchel that held her meagre belongings. For four years, she'd been provided uniforms, but had been instructed to leave them behind. Ella, the housekeeper, had given her the black skirt and white blouse she wore, and provided one other set of clothing, as well as the satchel. Otherwise, she'd be walking away in her under-things.

'You will send word?' Christopher asked as he took her elbow, walked her down the hallway.

Talking was hard. Her throat felt clogged. Her nose was plugged and tears were dripping from her eyes. 'I will...' she got out. She was going to add *try*, but hadn't been able to say more.

'I will see to their welfare, I promise you,' he whispered.

She nodded, knowing he would. That was her only saving grace—if she had one, she wasn't overly sure— that all of the servants were wonderful, caring people. Well, most of them, less those that had been brought to Havenbrook when Percy and Hazel had arrived. She would never fully embrace the fact that they were now the Duke and Duchess.

They were nothing like their predecessors, who had tragically died three months ago. If she hadn't witnessed their illnesses and deaths, she wouldn't have believed it possible. They had all been in London. The Duke and Duchess had attended a ball and came down sick shortly thereafter. Other guests of the ball did, too. It was determined to be food poisoning, but that conclusion came too late. A total of twenty people had already died.

'They are waiting at the bottom of the stairs,' Christopher whispered. 'I can say no more, other than, stay close to the hedge.'

She nodded, understanding that he wouldn't be allowed to speak to her in front of the Duke and Duchess. He'd probably been told to make her walk around the hedge to keep her away from the front of the house.

Percy Carlisle, with his narrow, squinting eyes, and his wife, Hazel, with her permanently pursed lips, were standing at the bottom of the servant stairs. They glared at her as Christopher escorted her off the steps.

A not-so-subtle clearing of a throat made her kneel into a passive curtsey. Even though her entire being wanted to defy them, she knew her place and remained like that, head down, until the sound of an insufferable sigh told her she could move.

She straightened, and Christopher continued to escort her down the hall to the back door.

The crisp, fresh morning air provided no relief to the pain consuming her, and the closing of the door behind her echoed through her as if she'd been struck.

She let out a shaky breath and kept walking, past the vegetable garden and clotheslines. As she approached the hedge, which was trimmed tall enough to hide the clothesline from anyone coming up the long driveway, the tears gushing from her eyes blurred everything.

At the sound of her name, whispered quietly, Aislinn quickly wiped one eye, then the other, to clear her vison. Dawn was barely breaking, and it took a moment before she spied Victoria hiding in the leaves of the hedge. The dark-haired kitchen maid was close to her own age, and the two of them spent their free time together whenever possible. Although, free time for any of the staff had practically disappeared since the new Duke and Duchess had arrived.

'Open your satchel,' Victoria whispered, holding a bundle in her arms. 'It's food. Enough to last a couple of days.'

Aislinn hadn't given food a single thought. She truly didn't care if she ate or not.

'Hurry,' Victoria whispered.

The maid would be in terrible trouble if discovered, and that alone was enough to make Aislinn quickly open her bag for Victoria to drop the towel-wrapped bundle inside.

'We are all so sorry,' Victoria said. 'Caldwell deserved to be scolded.'

Aislinn shook her head. 'It wasn't my place to scold him.' Percy and Hazel's son was very troublesome and at seven, was too old to be constantly picking on Fern and Ivy. She was so afraid that one day he might seriously hurt one of the twins. She shouldn't say anything, but what more could happen to her? 'Please warn the new governess about how devious he can be to the girls.'

'We all will,' Victoria replied, 'and we'll keep an eye on him, keep him away from the girls until your replacement arrives. Go now, they are probably watching from a window and will expect you to step onto the road any minute.'

'Thank you,' Aislinn said and hurried away, walking fast to the hedge, then slowing her pace as she left the shelter of the bushes and crossed the lawn to the driveway.

She sincerely hoped that a new governess would be hired, but feared that might not happen. The new Duke and Duchess had arrived at Havenbrook with a tutor to see to their son's care, although they called him Caldwell's man. Mr Horton was a portly man, with dark bushy eyebrows, who touted his tutoring members of the royal family.

Fern and Ivy were afraid of him, and the idea of him taking care of them had the tears gushing forth again, blinding her. Not that it mattered. There wouldn't be anyone on the road for at least four miles.

Lying on his back beneath an umbrella of tree branches, fingers laced behind his head, Luke Carlisle watched the sun come up, signalling a new day.

The day.

The day he arrived home. Although, he no longer thought of this as home.

He hadn't stepped foot in Havenbrook for over eight years.

He could have arrived at the house last night, slept in a bed instead of on the ground, but he hadn't wanted to. Truth was, he didn't want to arrive at all.

Strike that.

He wasn't *ready* to arrive there.

He would be one day, when he'd amassed a fortune,

a diverse fortune, that would make his brother Percy squirm.

No, Percy had always been a squirmer. A sneak, too.

Luke's fortune would *enrage* him.

Luke sighed.

Strike that, too.

Percy had been enraged at him for years.

His success would make Percy green with envy.

Luke grinned, letting out a satisfied sigh. Percy had always been jealous, but his face usually turned red. Seeing it green would be a sight.

Another sigh escaped. One that held no satisfaction. Not because he hadn't amassed his fortune—not all of it yet—but because the reason he was stepping foot in Havenbrook again was that his brother, his oldest brother—the good one—Rowland, was dead.

That was still so hard to believe.

Rowland was—*had been*—as different from Percy as night and day. His oldest brother had been the salt of the earth. A man liked by everyone, other than Percy. Percy hated everyone except himself, and perhaps his wife, Hazel. The two of them deserved each other. Two peas in a pod, they were.

Actually, they were like two snakes in a den.

Rattlers.

There had been times when he and Percy had got along while growing up, their headbutting nothing more than sibling rivalry. But once Percy had married Hazel, it was as if his lifelong resentment about being born second had increased tenfold. Marriage changed men, that was a given, and it certainly had brought out the worst in Percy.

Luke's stomach growled and, giving it a rub, he sat

up, looking around. He was on Havenbrook property, so if he found anything to eat, it wouldn't be stealing. There used to be a couple of plum trees along the road. Big, purple plums that had been juicy and sweeter than sugar itself. He'd eaten plenty of them back in the day, however those trees were closer to the house.

He had stopped here yesterday evening after turning off the main road, knowing the road beside where he sat was nothing more than a four-mile-long driveway.

The spot that he'd chosen to spend the night was next to a little pool formed by the stream, which is where he'd caught a fish before the sun went down last evening. While doing that, and cooking his catch on a stick over a fire, he'd thought of Rowland. How the two of them had gone fishing, more than once, over the years. Caught a fish, cooked it over a fire. They'd done things like that together, because Rowland knew that Luke liked being outside, having adventures. Even simple ones.

Though his oldest brother had been eight years older than him, a mere thirty-four years old at the time of his death, Rowland had been his best friend growing up.

Luke slapped the ground. Rowland would still have been his best friend if he was alive.

Death was a part of life. He knew that. His parents had tragically died within months of each other shortly after his eighteenth birthday, eight years ago.

But that was also when his life had begun. A life that he was in charge of, one he created for himself. Full of adventure and freedom. None of which he'd had here. Nor would he have had, if he'd stayed.

He wouldn't be here long. Once he got things in order, he'd head home. His home. The ranch in Montana Territory that he'd purchased three years ago. The place where he'd found a life he loved, because he never knew what adventures a new day would bring.

That wasn't the case here. Every day had been the same, and it had driven him crazy. He had no doubt it would do so again.

After giving his head a good scalp scratching, he grabbed his hat—not an English one, an American one, with a wide brim and indented crown—and plopped it on his head. He also pulled on his boots. Again, not wellingtons. His leather boots were American, too. They had heels created to hook onto wide wooden stirrups, helping a man stay seated in the saddle while chasing down an errant cow—a maverick—or herding cattle up by the dozen.

Luke stood, stepped out from under the canopy of the ash tree where he'd taken shelter for the night and, while stretching his arms and legs, gave the expansive driveway a good, long look.

A look that grew even longer when a small dot far ahead began to take shape. The sun had yet to chase away the morning haze rising up from the ground, but that was a person on the road. Walking. He folded his arms and watched, waited, until he could make out more.

From where he'd tied him to the next tree over, in order to give each of them a bit of privacy for the night, the horse he'd acquired in Portsmouth let out a nicker.

'You see her, too,' Luke said aloud. 'Good to know that I'm not hallucinating, because that is a woman, walking down the road. Alone.' Letting out a sigh, he continued, 'And that, my friend, does not make any sense.'

The horse snorted, then took a few steps towards the

creek to have a drink of cool water, to go along with his breakfast of lush green grass.

It didn't make any sense for someone to be walking on this road. Woman or not. If their carriage had broken down, they would have walked back to Havenbrook.

Luke waved a hand, just to let whoever it was know that he was a friendly sort.

She didn't wave back.

He couldn't say if that was because she was pretending not to see him, or if she truly hadn't yet. Wearing a black skirt and white blouse, and carrying a travelling bag, she kept walking towards him, head down as if she was looking for something amongst the gravel.

Luke stood still, knowing sooner or later she'd sense him and look up.

When they were little more than four yards apart, she finally lifted her head and saw him. She didn't really appear startled, just simply stopped walking and stared.

He didn't know how he'd expected her to react to him, but he was perplexed by her unruffled state almost as much as he was by her mere presence.

She could be stunned, having not expected to see anyone, and might start screaming and running at any moment. 'Don't worry,' he said. 'I'm not some nefarious highwayman.'

Without moving anything but her lips, she asked, 'Is that your opinion, or someone else's?'

He removed his hat. 'Mine, and I'm usually correct.'

'In your own opinion, again?'

'Yes.'

With a quick glance, she took note of the horse, before asking, 'May I ask what you are doing on private property?'

'Sure,' he replied. She was pretty, except that her big brown eyes were puffy and her face was red. All in all, it looked like she'd been crying. 'And I'll ask the same.'

She pinched her lips together, then with a little nod, said, 'This property belongs to the Carlisle family. Havenbrook is their country estate.'

'I'm well aware of that,' he said. 'I'll be heading up to the house directly, to take care of some family business.'

'Family business?'

He nodded. 'What about you?'

'I—' She let out a broken sigh. 'I'm leaving.'

Before he could ask why, she gasped for air and covered her face. She barely made a sound, but the way her shoulders shook told him she was crying. Damn. Women were a breed he'd never understand. They were downright confusing most days.

He mulled over whether he should touch her, just her arm, or if that would cause her to cry harder, louder. Choosing to stay put, he asked, 'Have you walked all the way from the house?'

She nodded.

'Well, then, I'd say it's time for a rest.' He stepped forward and held out a hand. 'Here, I'll carry your bag. Come sit under the tree, the grass is soft.'

She shook her head. 'I can't. I've been ordered off the property.'

His back teeth clamped together so tightly that his jaw stung. When he was sure the curse that had almost come out was under control, he said, 'Percy's throwing his weight around now that he's got the keys to the kingdom.'

Blinking, she wiped at her eyes and stared at him. 'You know the Duke?'

'I know my brother.'

'Brother?'

He nodded.

'Oh!' She dropped the bag and knelt into a deep curtsey, with one knee bent and her head down. 'Forgive me, my lord. I didn't know.'

An old frustration rose up inside him. 'I'm no one's lord. I gave that up when I left eight years ago. Name's Luke.' That was just one of the things that had always irritated him, how a station in life dictated how people should be treated—respected—even though the elite themselves held very little respect towards others. Especially those they considered beneath them.

Nevertheless, meeting this woman might make today rather exciting. Depending upon her reason for being on the road alone.

He stepped closer and picked up her bag. 'Let's sit down. You can tell me why good old Percy ordered you off the property.'

Aislinn's feet were stuck to the gravel by the same invisible force that had her heart racing. Up until a few moments ago, she'd been numb from the encroaching pain of leaving Fern and Ivy. She'd barely reacted to seeing a man on the side of the road, because she truly did not care who he was, nor what happened to her.

Now she could barely catch her breath. Tales of the infamous youngest Carlisle brother's escapades from around the world—and of his extraordinary handsomeness—from those who had known him when he'd lived at Havenbrook, were legendary. The Duke—the old Duke—had read the letters from his brother aloud, speaking about Luke with humour and fondness, and the staff had genuine affection for him. However, the current duke insisted his younger brother was an insufferable rabble-rouser, who would eventually end up in prison in some foreign land—if he wasn't already.

Even though the letters had fascinated her, she'd assumed that the accounts were exaggerated on both sides, and they very well could have been. Contrary to that, though, there had been no exaggeration when it came to his handsomeness.

He truly was extraordinary. It could be, in part, due to the manner of his dress. He was the spitting image of the pictures she'd seen of an American cowboy, complete with the pointed-toe boots, wide-brimmed hat and leather vest. Tall, with broad shoulders, he was also muscular, like men who performed physical duties regularly.

If she hadn't been so awestruck, she might have considered that part of his appeal was the way the morning sun was casting him in a golden glow, like some angel who had just descended to earth. Still, even if that were to be the case, it was impossible to deny that his face was quite remarkable. His eyes were deep blue, thickly lashed, and hosting a notable twinkle, and his lips appeared as if they held a permanent grin.

Just then, that grin grew, giving her a glimpse of straight, white teeth, and she was hit with the mortifying sense that she'd been caught staring at him. Out of habit, and obligation, she dipped into another curtsey and bowed her head. 'Forgive me, my lord.'

'I just told you, the name's Luke,' he said. 'The rules of so-called society grated on my nerves long before I left here. They still do.'

A firm, yet gentle grip took a hold of her elbow and tugged her upwards, out of her curtsey. Standing there, she had no idea what to do or say. She'd never been told not to curtsey, or to address someone by their first name—other than servants, like her.

'There's not much chance that we'll get run over, but let's move off the road,' he said. 'I truly want to know why you've been ordered off the property.'

It might have worked out better for her if he *had* been a highwayman. If the new Duke and Duchess found out she told him anything, she'd be…

What? They already sent her away, ordered her off the property. Left her with absolutely no place to go. No matter what happened, she'd never be able to see Fern and Ivy again.

He was standing beside her, waiting. Now that he was closer, she saw a resemblance between him and his oldest brother. It was the shape of his eyes, and his chin, more square than oval. A sigh built in her chest. He was by far the handsomest Carlisle man. The most handsome man she'd ever seen.

His arrival was going to upset the new duke.

She almost wished she could see it, despite knowing she shouldn't, because this man had something Percy didn't. He had a personality, a likeable one, and the confidence to match.

If only she had that.

'Ready?' he asked, nudging her forward slightly, before releasing his hold on her elbow.

She walked beside him, off the road and across the green grass to where a saddle and other tack lay beneath a tree.

He set her bag on the ground, lifted the blanket off the saddle, and flipped it onto the ground. 'You can sit on that. The grass is still damp with dew.'

Torn, she bit her lip, trying to decide what to do. It was highly inappropriate for her to be in his company, whether he liked the rules of society or not.

He sat, crossed his legs at the ankles, and leaned back, with his hands planted on the ground near his hips, and looked up at her. 'You know my name, but I don't know yours.'

'It's Aislinn,' she said. 'Aislinn Blaydon.'

'Well, Miss Blaydon, what was your role at Haven-brook? I am assuming you worked there—please correct me if I'm wrong.'

Feeling uncomfortable looking down at him, she lowered onto the small blanket. 'You are not wrong. I was a governess to Fern and Ivy.'

'Rowland's daughters.'

'Yes.' It was difficult, but she stopped herself before saying 'my lord' again.

'Tell me about Fern and Ivy. I have yet to meet them.'

The ache in her heart renewed. 'They are adorable, wonderful children, who fill a room with happiness. They are very well behaved, and very smart.' A warmth was entering her heart, chasing aside a small bit of the pain. 'They are identical in looks, except that Ivy has a small mole—' she touched the side of her nose '—right here on the left side of her nose. But their personalities are very different. Fern is curious about everything. Ivy is more cautious and waits to follow Fern's lead until she's sure it's safe.' A tiny giggle rumbled in her throat. 'Which means she doesn't follow at all once in a while.'

'You care a great deal about them,' he said.

'I love them,' she admitted. 'I've been with them since shortly after their birth.'

'Why are you not with them right now?'

She looked down at the ground, ashamed at what she'd brought upon herself. 'I made a terrible mistake.'

'Everyone makes mistakes.'

'This was more than a mistake. I knew better. I just—' she sighed heavily, frustrated by her own foolishness '—lost my temper.'

'With the girls?'

'Oh, no, never. They never try a person's patience.'

'Then who did try your patience? Percy? His wonderful mate, Hazel? The two human spiders entangled in their silky wed of matrimony?'

The giggle his words caused slipped out before she could stop it. Befuddled by her unacceptable behaviour, she covered her mouth. 'Forgive me, m—'

'Luke,' he interrupted.

Knowing that calling him by his first name would be far too inappropriate, she refrained from saying more and tore her gaze off him. The way he had wiggled his fingers, imitating spider legs, had clearly described her own comparisons of the new Duke and Duchess. Still, she should not have giggled.

'That's what Percy always reminded me of,' he said. 'A spider, creeping around, staying hidden, then dropping down on a silken web when you least expected it. Hazel was just as bad, and I can't believe they've changed.' He shook his head. 'Strike that. I can believe they've changed.' His voice turned cold. 'I bet they are touting their tail feathers like peacocks now that they both have what they've always wanted—the titles of Duke and Duchess of Havenbrook.'

Despite the years he'd been gone, he clearly knew his family well and wasn't happy. She held her silence as he picked a blade of grass and stuck it between his lips.

'So, Aislinn,' he said, sounding normal again, 'tell me, what did you do to receive the ire of my brother and his not-so-dear wife?'

'I scolded their son, Caldwell,' she admitted quietly.

'I can only imagine that, considering his parentage, the kid needs more than scolding.'

'Nonetheless, it was not my place to do so.'

'Why did you?' he asked.

Anger at what had happened last evening, and fear of what the outcome could have been, flared inside her. 'He pushed Fern, and she nearly fell down the staircase. Would have if I hadn't caught her.' Her hands trembled at the memory, and she clutched them tightly together. 'We'd stopped at the top of the stairs so I could straighten the bow in Ivy's hair and, out of nowhere, Caldwell came running by and shoved Fern. Forcefully, on purpose, shoved her straight towards the staircase.'

Indignation, raw and strong, was creeping about inside her. She knew better than to defy the decision of the Duke and Duchess, but not being able to defend her actions was catching up to her. 'I was so scared. Had to act so fast, that I couldn't stop myself. He's so wicked to them all the time. I told him that he was a bad boy and needed to learn to behave.' Still needing to defend herself, to someone, she continued. 'It's true. He does. He's so naughty.'

'That's it?' he asked. 'That's all you said?'

She nodded and shrugged, not sure what more he thought she should have done. 'I was concerned about Fern.'

'I don't doubt that,' he said. 'Nor do I doubt that Caldwell ran straight to his parents to tell on you. Percy was always good at that, telling on others, and has no doubt taught his son to do the same.'

Caldwell did plenty of that, but she shook her head. 'Caldwell didn't have to tell them. His man was there, saw it all.'

'His man?'

'Yes, that is what the Duke and Duchess insist we call Mr Horton. He's Caldwell's tutor and was quite incensed that I'd taken it upon myself to discipline his charge.' Her anger was growing. 'Discipline is exactly what Caldwell needs, but it wasn't my place to do so.' Frustrated, she huffed out a sigh. 'After I put the girls to bed last night, the Duke and Duchess ordered that I leave the residence by sunrise this morning.'

'On foot?'

A wave of embarrassment washed over her. She was being far too forward for a servant, speaking this way with a member of the family. What she'd already told him was enough to incite the Duke and Duchess even further. Planting her hands on the ground to help her rise, she said, 'I need to go.'

Chapter Two

Luke's mind had become a tornado of thoughts, and like the black, tail-twisting storm funnel he'd once watched race across the Kansas prairie, the twister was picking up debris with every revolution. Memories, opinions, and a whole lot of questions. While others who had been with him had been afraid of the tornado, leaping off their horses to take cover, he'd sat astride Buck and watched as the rotating column dropped down out of the dark and stormy clouds, causing mayhem to everything in its way.

He'd been mesmerised by that funnel cloud and its destruction and, truth be, he had that same feeling right now. He wasn't unaccustomed to seeing beautiful women. He'd pursued a few of them over the years, gained their affection. All in fun, and only when the attention was welcome on both ends. His and theirs. And only when there had been no expectations on either side for a blossoming romance or future together.

The silken web of matrimony was not something he'd ever allow himself to become trapped in. Even in his youth, before he left home, he'd known that the life being laid out for him wasn't what he wanted. Marrying a woman of good standing, producing children in order to guarantee the continuation of the Carlisle family, had never been a goal that he could sink his teeth into. It was superficial to believe that all a man needed to do was marry. No man should want to live off an inheritance others had worked diligently to obtain—it was *lazy*. Of course, he would never fault a woman for seeking a man like that. Women wanted stability and security. But that alone was reason enough for him to stay clear of them, other than for some mutual fun now and again.

Deep in his soul, he'd always known that he needed adventure, needed to create something on his own. A life that he could grasp with both hands, building it in ways that created more adventures. The thrill of the unknown is what attracted him and held his attention.

That's what was happening right now. Miss Aislinn Blaydon had definitely captured his attention. Not just her looks, for she certainly was a pretty thing. Her face was round, framed by strands of dark brown hair that had slipped from the bun at the back of her head, and her features were soft, delicate. The swelling around her big, brown eyes had lessoned, and her true beauty had shown itself when she'd spoken of his nieces, Fern and Ivy. Her entire face had lit up, her eyes sparkling, but it had only lasted a moment before everything had dulled again.

There had also been a flash of anger in those brown eyes when she spoke of Caldwell and *his man*. Leave it to Percy to find yet another way to increase just how pompous and egotistical one man could be. A seven-year-old doesn't have a need for his own personal man-servant. It sounded like Caldwell needed a disciplinarian above all else.

But that, right there, was the other reason she held his attention so fully. He and Rowland had shared letters ever since he'd left home, but their correspondence had become far more regular since he'd settled on his ranch in Montana. In part, because mail could reach him on an unvarying basis. Prior to that, he'd never known where he'd be next.

He was here now for a reason. A very important reason. To fulfil Rowland's request of him. He laid a hand atop one of hers. 'Not yet. Please. I will proceed to Havenbrook shortly and would prefer to not be blindsided the moment I walk in the door.'

She had barely lifted her seat off the ground before he'd spoken and slowly lowered it back down. 'Blindsided?'

He nodded, grinned, and winked. 'I want to be the one to do that.'

She frowned. 'I don't understand, m— sir.'

Wanting to get one thing straight, he said, 'For the last eight years, I've been Luke. Once in a while, it's Mr Carlisle. I washed the use of titles from my life when I left this country. A man's title in society should not give him the right to demand respect. It's his actions that should be respected. That's how it is in America.' Being honest, he shrugged, 'In some of the larger cities, society still makes certain demands, and children all over are still taught to respect their elders, but men...'

He had paused, wanting to choose the right words. For he knew, as a servant, she would have a different understanding of things than he did. 'Men from all walks of life have opportunities to succeed. Men have that here, too, but I feel that aristocratic society quells it. Some people, not all, in certain echelons of society, do not believe that others should have the opportunity to obtain a station without it being handed down from a prior generation.'

Rowland had been the only one that he'd shared this perception with, and that had mainly been via his letters. Telling Aislinn was different; he wanted her to fully understand his beliefs. To know that things could be different from what she knew. That she shouldn't be satisfied with a life of servitude, because there were other options. They may not come easily but, in his mind, they were worth it, for everyone.

'In America they have wagon trains. Men and women, families, ride in covered wagons, up to a hundred of them at a time, following each other across the nation. They load up everything they have room to haul and head west, into a vast unknown. A wilderness one can't imagine until it's experienced, all in the hope of a new life, a better life, for them and their loved ones. For the future generation. Armed with little more than determination. That takes courage. Stamina. Bravery. To me, that generates more respect than sitting in a manor house, being served tea every afternoon while awaiting rent payments on properties and farms you never step foot on.'

'I've heard of the wagon trains there, of many things there. But here, you are a Carlisle. Your brother is a duke, that alone—'

'Demands respect,' he finished for her. 'You're right, I am a Carlisle.' Which left him stuck in the middle, and he hated being stuck anywhere as much as he hated having to depend on others. He'd given that up, too. His birthright had given him the means to leave, to seek out adventures, and as soon as he'd earned enough of his own money, he'd repaid the family coffers the amount that had been in his pockets when he'd left England. That hadn't changed anything, except inside him. However, money wasn't what he owed his family now.

She was still frowning, and he figured it would take more than some rambling by him to convince her of anything. Furthermore, it was time he got off his own high horse. He'd come to love his new life, and truly didn't want to re-enter his old one. But he would, for Rowland's sake. His nieces' sakes.

He gave her a nod, silently putting an end to his self-induced lecture, before saying, 'I'd still prefer if you'd call me Luke.'

She gave a slight nod, and he went on to the subject at hand. 'I was hoping Percy hadn't heard about my arrival.'

She was silent for a moment, then shook her head. 'I don't believe he knows. You never responded to his letter about the death of the Duke and Duchess.'

Disgust rose up inside him. 'Percy never wrote me a letter. Not about Rowland and Leslie's deaths, or anything else.'

'But Christopher said that he'd given him your address right after the Duke and Duchess died.'

Glad to know the old butler was still in residence, Luke replied, 'Christopher may have, but Percy never wrote to me. Rowland's solicitor in London, Mr Watson, did. Rowland had already been dead for six weeks.'

She gasped and put a hand over her mouth.

'I didn't see the letter for another two weeks, because I'd been up in the high country, conducting our spring round-up.' A stab of guilt struck his stomach at leaving his men to complete the round-up, calving season, and spring branding without him, but Raf Swanson was fully capable. The two of them had several adventures together, before they'd settled on the ranch. 'As soon as I arrived home, I had a transatlantic telegraph sent, asking Mr Watson to have a barrister submit a petition on my behalf, and to not inform Percy that I was on my way to England. He had a message waiting for me in Portsmouth when I arrived two days ago, assuring me that Percy had not been informed that my petition had been accepted, or of my impending arrival.'

'Petition for what?'

'Guardianship of Fern and Ivy.'

'You?'

'Yes, me.' He couldn't blame her for being shocked, and wanted to know her thoughts. 'Having lived in the household, having been in charge of Fern and Ivy, do you believe their guardianship should be granted to Percy?'

There wasn't a moment of hesitation in her reply. 'No, but I assumed they had already been granted custody.'

'They haven't.' He pointed a thumb at his chest. 'Yours truly has. Mr Watson's letter stated that he assumed I hadn't heard about Rowland and Leslie's demise, because of Percy's petition for guardianship of Fern and Ivy. Rowland wrote to me a couple of years ago, informing me that he'd put me in his will as guardian of the girls. Even sent me a copy of it.' He patted the pocket of his shirt beneath his vest. 'Mr Watson's letter said that Percy's petition claims that attempts to find me have failed, therefore guardianship should revert to him.'

'But he didn't attempt to find you.' Shaking her head, she whispered, 'They don't even like the girls.'

'They don't want guardianship because they care. They want it because of the amount of money Rowland left for the care of his children.'

Her frown increased. 'Is that why they wanted to get rid of me?'

Luke's spine stiffened. 'What do you mean?'

She shrugged. 'Ever since the Duke and Duchess died...' Letting out a sigh, she said, 'It's felt like they wanted me to leave. Leave the girls.'

He contemplated that. Knowing how Percy worked, his brother would have thought that if he did return, he wouldn't want guardianship over the girls without a nanny in place. Figured the more barriers he erected, the less likely Luke would be to fight them. Percy had been wrong. Was wrong.

Curious, he asked, 'Besides scolding their son, what else has happened?'

She sighed, shook her head. 'Nothing of importance.'

Instinct told him there *had* been things of importance, but before he could respond, his stomach growled too loudly for anyone to ignore. He rubbed it with one hand. 'Sorry. The fish I caught and ate last night is long gone.'

'I have food,' she said, sliding her bag closer to her side. 'I'm not sure what it is. Victoria, a kitchen maid, was hiding in the hedge when I left and gave this to me.' She pulled a bundle from the bag, set it on the ground and untied it. 'There wasn't time for me to see what's in it, the Duke and Duchess were watching to make sure that I didn't dawdle.'

The sibling rivalry and his loathing over Percy's actions had waned over the years, mainly because he'd been far away and too busy to think about anything but the tasks at hand. That loathing, though, had returned in full force upon reading the letter from Mr Watson, and had plenty of time to fester during the long weeks of travelling from Montana to England.

However, upon meeting Aislinn, a gentle, kind woman, who was at this moment neatly arranging food items on the cloth to share with him, and discovering that she had been ordered off the property on foot, before sunrise, his loathing had reached an entirely new level.

A level he was finding hard to control.

'Please,' she said, gesturing to the food in offer. 'I'm not hungry.'

There was bread, cheese, fruit, a small piece of ham, and a sealed jar of brewed tea. Altogether, it was less than he ate at a single seating, yet he assumed the absence of any larger amounts of food would have been hard for the cooking staff to explain. He could imagine that Hazel ran the household with an iron fist. She was as selfish as Percy. The two of them, like Rowland and Leslie, had been married before he'd left home, so he knew Hazel. Knew that she and Percy were a single snake with two heads. He was also ninety percent sure the real reason this nanny had been sent packing was because of him. Percy knew he'd arrive home sooner rather than later.

'Please,' she repeated.

'I can't eat alone.' Luke picked up the chunk of bread, broke it in two, and held half of it out to her. 'You must eat some, too.'

She took the bread and tore off a tiny piece.

He waited until she chewed, swallowed, before asking, 'Where will you go? Do you have family near?'

Aislinn licked her lips to moisten her mouth after eating the dry bread. For a moment, she'd been so caught up in listening to him, to his explanations of people in America, and then his plans to claim guardianship of the girls, that she'd forgotten her own plight. 'No, I have no family. I don't know where I'll go.'

'Where did you live before coming here?'

'An orphanage,' she admitted. 'In London. I don't remember my mother—she died when I was a baby. My father delivered flour from the mill to bakeries, and there was an accident one morning when I was seven. I stayed with a neighbour for a while, then I went to the orphanage.' Not wanting him to feel sorry for her, she continued, 'It was a good place. Everyone cared deeply about all of the children. I was too old to be adopted, but old enough to help care for the younger children. Later, I received the education required of a governess, and began working at the orphanage.'

She truly had thought she'd spend her entire life living and working there, and had been satisfied with that. She was happy there. It was the only life she'd ever known, until being hired by the Duke and Duchess. That's when she'd discovered the true meaning of family. The love one could feel for others. If possible, her love for Fern and Ivy had grown upon the death of the Duke and Duchess. Having lost her own parents, she wanted the girls to know that they were still loved. Still had a family.

'How did you come to be at Havenbrook?' he asked.

She took the slice of apple that he'd cut with his

Lauri Robinson*33*

knife. 'Mrs Hall had been informed that the Duke and Duchess were looking for a second nanny. They had been surprised by having twins and feared their nanny might be overwhelmed with two babies. Claire—Miss Shaw—was an excellent nanny. Very good with Fern and Ivy. When they were a year old, she told me that she'd fallen in love with John Moore, the stableman at the Duke and Duchess's London home. She and John were married, and she works as a maid in the London home now. Fern and Ivy still enjoy seeing her.'

'You haven't fallen in love with anyone working at Havenbrook, or the London home?'

'Oh, no, sir,' she replied instantly while putting a hand over the racing of her heart. 'Fern and Ivy have been my only focus. I love them. I would never...' She wasn't sure how to explain the devotion she felt to the twins.

'I didn't mean to fluster you,' he said. 'It wouldn't be unreasonable for you to fall in love, to want a life and family of your own.'

She pressed her fingers against her lips in order to remain silent. To keep from telling him that Fern and Ivy were her family. That's how she saw it. *Had* seen it. When Claire said she was leaving the girls to get married, Aislinn had been shocked. Truly couldn't understand how Claire could love someone, anyone, more than Fern and Ivy. She still felt that way.

'Will you return to the orphanage?' he asked. 'Work there again?'

Dread pressed down on her shoulders. 'I can't.'

'Why? You don't want to go back? Or have them help you find another governess position?'

'That's not an option.'

'I don't understand why.'

She avoided looking at him, because she'd already made enough disparaging remarks about the new Duke and Duchess.

'They told you that you couldn't, didn't they?' he asked. 'Percy and Hazel. What did they threaten?'

'It's not important,' she said.

'Yes, it is.' He opened the jar of tea and took a drink. 'It's very important, Aislinn. You are my first, and perhaps only, ally in this mission I'm about to embark on, and I need your help for it to succeed.'

She hesitated in taking the jar he was holding out to her. 'What do you mean?'

'Have a drink.' He gestured to the empty cloth lying between them. 'I've eaten all your food, the least you can do is drink the tea.'

'I wasn't hungry,' she reminded him, but took the tea and had a sip before handing it back. 'I don't see how I can help you.'

'I need a governess for Fern and Ivy.' He patted his chest. 'The papers I have in my pocket give me guardianship of the twins. Percy will fight me, and I'll fight back, as long and as hard as it takes for the courts to confirm that. During that time, and beyond, because I *will* win, Fern and Ivy will need a governess. One hired by me.' He leaned closer to her. 'There is no one more qualified for that position than you.'

Her gasp was so hard and deep, it made her cough. Several times.

'Here,' he said, holding out the jar, 'have some more tea.'

She accepted the jar and took a long swallow, then sucked in a much more controlled gasp of air. It would be a dream come true to be with Fern and Ivy, to know that they weren't under the new Duke and Duchess's control. More than that, because she hadn't even dreamed it. Hadn't imagined there was a single possibility that she'd be reunited with the girls. Could it be true?

Her hands were shaking and she folded them together, held them beneath her chin as she sought the courage to ask, 'Why?'

'Because you've been their nanny since birth,' he said.

She shook her head. 'I mean why do you want custody of the girls?'

He looked at her, then at the saddle sitting beside him, before glancing back at her. 'I don't need the money, if that's what you're wondering. I have plenty. I'm doing it because they are my nieces. I promised Rowland that I would take care of them, and I will.'

He certainly sounded trustworthy, but she didn't have anything to compare him with. Not really. Other than that he seemed more like the old Duke than the new one. And the old Duke must have thought he was trustworthy to have named him guardian in his will. The old Duke and Duchess had loved the girls dearly, and if he was the person they wanted to take care of them... Her nerves were making her stomach churn. 'They won't like it, me being there,' she said. 'The Duke and Duchess. They ordered me off the property.'

He chuckled. 'Trust me, that won't be the only thing they won't like. Havenbrook is as much my home as it is theirs. Moreover, it's Fern and Ivy's home. You let me worry about Percy and Hazel. All you need to worry about is the twins, seeing that they get the best care possible, just like they have for the last four years.'

Her reservations about his suggestion were gradually being overridden by her love for the girls, and what their parents had wanted for them. Being there to keep Fern and Ivy safe, from Caldwell, his tutor, and the Duke and Duchess, was worth any wrath that might be cast down upon her.

He was looking at her expectantly. Aislinn didn't know if he was expecting her to agree with the arrangement he suggested, her helping him, or to only worry about Fern and Ivy. The girls would always be her first concern, but to not worry about other things would be impossible. Including him. He hadn't been at Havenbrook for eight years, whereas she'd lived with the new Duke and Duchess, and it wasn't pleasant. They had made it feel like she didn't belong there, and was sure to do the same to him.

She let her breath out slowly. 'I truly don't know how much help I can be to you.'

He tipped the brim of his hat back a bit and looked up at the sky. 'The challenge of the unknown is what makes it an adventure.'

He was saying that to the most unadventurous person in the world, but she couldn't say no to a chance to be the one to see to Fern and Ivy's care.

'What do you say, partner?' he said, holding out a hand.

'Partner?' she asked.

'Yes, that's what we are. Partners.' His grin increased. 'I've had partners in several adventures. Raf—he's minding the ranch back in Montana—and I have been partners for the past five years. Just like you and that other nanny were partners when Fern and Ivy were babies. This time, it's me and you.'

She wouldn't compare him to Claire, not in any way, but took a hold of his hand. The moment her palm met his, a warmth raced up her arm, making her insides tingle. There was a connection there, a trust, that she might have to think about later. Right now, he was using their connected hands to pull her up to her feet.

'Time to get this adventure started.' He released her hand. 'I'll throw the saddle on old lazy bones, and we'll be on our way.'

Aislinn curled her hand into a fist and waited for the tingling to end before she gathered up the empty cloth and tucked it back in her bag, along with the empty jar.

He'd carried the saddle, blanket, saddlebag, and bridle over to the horse all at once. She walked over to see if she could be of some help, although that was highly unlikely. She'd rarely stepped foot in the stable.

After the saddle was secure, and the bag tied behind it, he said, 'I had to take the reins off the bridle so I had a way to tie him up. Then tie the two together so it was long enough that he could eat, drink, and move about some. It'll just take a minute to put it back together and get it on him. You can climb up.'

She glanced between him and the tall, very tall, horse. The idea of riding a horse, with him, made her knees tremble.

'Don't worry,' he said, while untying the long leather straps. 'Old Bones here is as gentle as they come. Truth be, if I'd made him walk another four miles last night, it might have been the last of him. He was plumb tuckered out. When I told the man at the livery that I wasn't sure how long I'd need a horse for, he narrowed my options down to Old Bones here, said he was the only horse available for sale. So, I bought him and the tack.'

With the leather reins now attached to it, he slid the

bridle on the horse's face and fastened the buckle, before flipping the reins over the horse's neck.

She didn't move, even though he was expecting her to.

'I'll help you up,' he said, holding out a hand towards her.

'No, thank you.' She had a hard time not saying 'my lord', or 'sir'. He was her employer, so it would be proper, but he said he didn't like it and to call him Luke. That seemed far too personal. As personal as riding the same horse.

'All right, I'll hold him steady while you climb on. You can sit in the saddle. I'll ride behind it.'

She didn't want to be rude, but fear of the unknown was gurgling in her stomach. 'I'll walk.'

He tipped back the brim of his hat and levelled a steady stare at her. 'You've never been on a horse, have you?'

She let out a sigh, but was unable to lie. 'No, I have not.' Feeling a need to defend herself, she added, 'There weren't any horses at the orphanage, and Fern and Ivy are too young to ride.'

He shook his head, but his permanent grin had become a full-blown smile. 'No one is ever too young to ride, and today is your lucky day, because I'm an excellent teacher.'

Before she had time to protest, he grasped her by the waist with both hands and plopped her on the horse.

'Now, here in England, women ride side-saddle, with both legs on one side of the horse, like you're sitting now. In America, they ride astride. Like men.'

He swung up on the horse behind her so quickly, she let out a tiny squeal at the fear of falling.

'You're fine,' he said, reaching around both sides of her and grasping hold of the reins.

She held on tighter to the handle of the bag on her lap. 'I know that much. How men and women ride.'

'All right then, just relax, sink your rump into the saddle and find your balance.'

'My balance?'

'Yes, your balance. Like when you're walking on something slippery and you have to shift your weight until you know you're stable, that you aren't going to fall?'

That made some sense, perhaps.

'Do that,' he said. 'Find your balance.'

Taking a deep breath, she told herself to relax, and settled her bottom more firmly into the saddle, shifting her spine until she felt stable.

'Good. We're going to take a couple steps. I won't let you fall, so just go with the movement until you feel balanced.'

The horse moved and every muscle in her body stiffened.

'Relax,' he said softly. 'Just relax. Close your eyes, it'll help. Imagine you're sitting in a rocking chair.'

She wasn't about to close her eyes, and this was nothing like a rocking chair, but as the horse began to slowly walk forward, the movement was close enough that she could relate. Within a short time, a sense of calm allowed her to grow more relaxed. Riding a horse wasn't nearly as frightening as she'd thought.

'Beats walking,' he said, as if he knew her exact thoughts. 'I know, I've been left afoot a time or two.'

'How far did you have to walk?' she asked, hoping he wasn't able to read her mind. The horse wasn't as frightening as she'd thought, but having his arms around her, his thigh touching hers and her shoulder rubbing against his chest, was making her entire body tingle in odd ways.

'Which time?' He laughed. 'A few years ago, I was in Colorado. It's a beautiful place. Not as beautiful as Montana, but close. Both have mountains so tall that even in the middle of the summer, when I'm dripping with sweat, I can look up and see snow on the mountaintops. Anyway, there I was, in Colorado, riding along, minding my own business, when a mountain lion thought I should be his dinner. He landed on my back, knocked me off my horse. We tussled before he took off, figuring something else might be easier pickings.'

Aislinn's breath was caught in her throat. She'd heard of mountain lions, and of Colorado, Montana and the Rocky Mountains. The old Duke had books about America, and she'd read every one of them, fascinated by the places Luke had written about. The horse below her, even the tingling in her body, suddenly didn't matter. 'Tussled? Were you hurt?'

That might not have been the best story to tell her, but Luke had wanted her to forget her qualms about being on a horse for the first time. The story was true. He and the lion had tussled, and the cat had taken off. He'd looked over his shoulder for the next three days, all on foot and nursing a slash in one arm from his shoulder to his elbow and two puncture wounds from the cat's teeth in the back of his neck. His hat had saved him from losing his head that day. 'Just a couple of scratches, but it took me three days to walk back to the mining camp.'

'The Duke, the old Duke, read your letter about mining for gold.'

'I wrote him about that.'

'Did you find a lot?'

'Miners call it seeing colour, because of the way a nugget can cause a rainbow to form in the water, and I saw colour. Enough for me to put a grubstake in on another venture.'

'What was that?'

'Cattle.'

'Your ranch in Montana?'

The story was a lot longer than that, but simple was easier. 'Yes.' He could tell her more about the ranch, the Montana Territory, or a hundred other things, but now that she was comfortable, there was information he needed to know. 'Tell me about the manor house. Who is currently living there?'

She started naming staff, many he recognised from before he'd left, some he didn't.

He'd never considered himself one to get easily distracted, but dang if her voice wasn't lovely to listen to. It was soft, like a melody of words that didn't need music, and she smelled like a rose garden.

Before he knew it, the peaks of the house were in view, and he had to clear his mind of Aislinn, then ask her to repeat a few things, just to make sure he'd have the upper hand the moment he climbed off the tired old horse. If his brother thought that having the Dukedom behind him was all he needed to win this battle, and Percy *would* think that way, then he was sorely wrong.

Being six years older than him, there were many years when Percy was bigger, taller, stronger than him, and Percy had taken advantage of that on a regular basis. That's how Percy had always been. Never facing an adversary that was equal to him in size or stamina, he chose to pick on the smallest and weakest, believing he was guaranteed a win. There was no reason for Luke to believe Percy had changed. No reason to believe his brother would ever change.

In fact, Aislinn was proof of that. Picking on a woman, that's what Percy had done. He'd used her most vulnerable aspect—her love of Fern and Ivy—to get what he wanted.

It was time to show him that he hadn't won, and that he wasn't *going* to win.

Luke dang near pulled up a grin, knowing that he was showing up at Havenbrook dressed and acting like the outrageously unrefined Americans that the aristocrats took delight in gossiping about behind their backs and turning their noses up at when they walked past. Those very behaviours had been his incentive to set sail for the States when he left.

The house, the entire place, didn't look any different from what he remembered. Three stories tall, the rooftop rivalled the height of the trees surrounding it, and the various other buildings on the property were still standing proudly. He was glad it had been kept up over the years. Rowland would have seen to that, and a small part of him—a part he almost hated to admit—knew that Percy would, too. They didn't see eye to eye on everything, but Percy took pride in the family name and holdings.

Would take even more now that he was the Duke of Havenbrook.

Their arrival wasn't going unnoticed. Not only were Percy and Hazel standing at the top of the wide front steps of the manor house, but curtains in nearly every window were drawn back, and heads were peeking out from around the hedge and the stable doors.

Hazel, who was exactly as full of herself as Luke remembered, was the first to react. As soon as they were within shouting distance, she let out a screech that sent birds aflight and damned near pierced his eardrums.

'You will regret this!' she shouted. 'You were ordered off this property!'

Feeling Aislinn's shiver, Luke whispered, 'She can't hurt you. I won't let her.' Tipping the brim of his hat down, so it hid a good portion of his face, he continued to steer the horse straight to the front door.

'You! Man!' Hazel shouted. 'She's not allowed on this property. Take her away! Neither of you are welcome here!'

If he'd been on Buck, the horse he'd had for five years—the one he got after the last one deserted him in the mountains—he would have urged the horse up the steps and onto the porch. Buck was as sure-footed as a mountain goat.

As it was, he settled for reaching the bottom step, and pulled up on the reins to stop the horse he'd named Old Bones.

'See here, now, Miss Blaydon,' Percy said, his voice full of self-imposed authority as he moved to the edge of the top step. 'What is the meaning of this?'

Aislinn hadn't said a word, and Luke was proud of her for not giving away his identity. Then again, as a servant, she would know it was not her place to speak. Once again, his ire ticked up a notch.

He swung out of the saddle and lifted her down. The apprehension in her eyes fuelled two things—a bout of empathy for her, and a fiery flare of wrath towards his brother. She was afraid. Downright afraid.

Fear could strike anyone now and again, but no one should have to live their life afraid.

'I suggest you get back on that horse—' Percy was saying as Luke reached up and tipped back the brim of his hat.

His brother went silent, other than a hiss filled with a bit of spittle.

Hazel, however, hissed like the snake he knew her to be. 'You!' she shouted.

With his hand on Aislinn's back, he escorted her up the steps, stopping on the top one. 'I'm home,' he belted out with exaggerated cheerfulness.

No one laughed. He hadn't expected them to.

'This is not your home,' Hazel hissed.

Some things would never change. Hazel's muddy brown hair was still ratted and piled high on her head, in hopes of making her look taller, he assumed, and her eyes were still as beady as a crow's. With a slight nod, he said dryly, 'Hello, Hazel. I see you're as welcoming as ever.'

Then he turned to his brother, with half a mind to shake his hand, just so things wouldn't get off to a bad start. But Percy's nostrils were flared, his eyes narrowed.

That's all it took. Suddenly, Luke saw the brother who held his head down in horse muck when he was five, who locked him in the attic when he was seven, and who was the villain in a number of other unpleasant childhood memories. But he also saw a man who's only reaction to his son pushing an innocent little girl towards the stairs was to fire an innocent bystander.

Luke balled his hand into a fist, but, at the last moment, common sense won over the desire to smack his brother square in the nose. It wouldn't have been a hard punch, he justified in his own mind. Wouldn't even have stung his knuckles, because he would have pulled back as soon as he'd made contact.

As if reading his mind, or just plain scared because he was no longer the bigger or stronger of the two of them, Percy stumbled backwards, managing to trip over his own feet and end up on the porch floor.

Seeing that was even more satisfying than a knuckle to nose punch would have been.

Hazel screeched. Screamed. 'You are an animal! A wild animal!'

Luke rolled his eyes. 'I didn't touch him. He tripped over his own feet.'

'You're still a beast,' she screeched. 'Always have been!'

'And you've always been irritating.' Luke narrowed his stare on Percy, who was still sitting on the porch floor. 'Tell me, whose idea was it not to write to me about Rowland's death? Yours or hers?'

Before Percy could open his mouth, Hazel was running hers again. Though she had switched gears, and was now shouting at Aislinn, something about being in cahoots with him, about bringing him here.

Aislinn was on the step behind him, and he didn't need to turn to know that she was bowing her head. Damn, it was hard to keep his temper in check. Especially with the way Percy and Hazel kept making themselves perfect targets for his wrath.

He took a sliding sidestep, so he was face to face

with his sister-in-law. 'Miss Blaydon is under my employment.'

Hazel let out an indignant hiss. 'Employment for what?'

He clamped his back teeth together while pulling out the papers in his pocket. Waving the papers before Hazel's face, he said, 'As governess to the two children, Fern and Ivy Carlisle, who are under my guardianship.'

Hazel backed up, and he reached behind him, taking hold of Aislinn's elbow and leading her up onto the porch landing, past both Hazel and Percy, and into the house.

The smile that Christopher, the old goat that he was, was freely displaying gave Luke a solid bout of happiness. The butler no longer had a single black hair. They were all grey now, and there were a few more wrinkles on his face. Otherwise, he looked as fit as ever. 'Hello, Christopher.'

'Hello, Master Luke,' the butler replied. 'It's good to see you.'

'It's good to be home,' he lied, only because it was necessary. There were people here, things here, that he did like and would enjoy seeing. 'Will you have someone see to my horse, please?'

'Right away, sir.' Christopher waved a hand towards a young man standing in the hallway, then nodded at Aislinn. 'It's good to see you, too, Miss Blaydon. The girls will be overjoyed.'

She didn't reply, other than a slight nod.

'Go see them,' Luke told her.

She gave him a nod, but it was the happiness on her face that made his heart screw up, missing a beat or two. At some point, he would have to consider all the consequences of his promise to Rowland, but right now, he was happy for her.

Bag in one hand, and skirt hitched up above her ankles by the other, she darted left towards the staircase and nearly flew up the steps.

'We ran into each other along the road,' Luke told Christopher. 'Good thing we did.'

'Good thing, indeed, sir,' Christopher said.

'Got room for me for a few weeks?' he asked.

'Of course. Your old room?'

Knowing that Percy would have taken over the rooms that once housed their parents, Luke shook his head. 'The other side of the house.' There were suites on that side reserved for guests. Luke didn't mind being housed as a guest rather than family. It would give him space, which he needed, because he already had that old feeling of being smothered.

'Very well, sir,' Christopher said. 'I'll have it prepared immediately.'

'Thanks, and you might need to scrounge me up some clothes.' Luke gestured to himself. 'Besides a few like items in my saddlebag, what you see is what you get.'

'Very well, sir.'

Christopher left and Luke pivoted about on one heel to face his brother. Percy was there, chest puffed out like a pigeon.

Luke's anger had dissolved into disgust. 'Not writing to me was wrong. You know that.'

Percy didn't speak, but his neck turned red.

Luke pointed to the hall, the one that led to the study, and headed in that direction.

Chapter Three

Aislinn wanted to hold on to both Fern and Ivy and never let go, yet understood that they had no idea what had transpired while they'd been asleep. All they knew was that she hadn't been there when they'd awoken.

Fern was mad about that, and wanted to know where Aislinn had been, whereas Ivy simply wanted her to fix the bow in her hair because Mrs Taylor had tied it too tight.

While quickly fixing Ivy's bow, Aislinn answered Fern's questions by simply saying she'd been busy and was sorry, but that she was here now. Satisfied that life was in order, Fern asked if they could have a tea party, which was one of her favourite activities. They had received the tiny blue and white tea set for their fourth birthday, and a day didn't go by when they didn't play with it.

As she had every day since their parents died, Aislinn tried to make their lives as normal as possible. She got the tea set down off the shelf, then removed each delicate piece from the soft cotton cloths she kept them wrapped with when not in use.

Once the girls were fully engaged in play, she picked

up the bag she'd dropped near the door and carried it into the small window alcove that housed her bed and the chest where she kept her clothing.

Upon emptying the tapestry bag, Aislinn considered putting on one of her light blue governess dresses, but decided not to, because last night the Duke and Duchess had informed her that the dresses belonged to them, not her. She would have to ask Luke about that, so she could return the skirts and blouses that Mrs Taylor had given her. It was getting easier to use Luke's name in thought, but she doubted she would ever get used to saying it aloud.

It was true that, in private, staff referred to members of the family by their first names, but never in their presence, and most certainly not directly to them.

She should have asked Luke questions pertaining to being employed by him, but the idea of returning to Fern and Ivy had been her only thought. Other than ones about him. She'd never met a man like him and, truthfully, had found it difficult to think straight in his presence. Memories of the many tales Rowland had shared from Luke's letters kept filtering into her mind. Even though she'd read the books in the library about America already, she now wanted to read them again.

However, if she did take one from the library, it might attract attention to the books. That could lead to them being ordered to be destroyed by Percy and Hazel, just as they had done with several mementoes that Luke had sent to the old Duke over the years.

The door to the nursery opened, and for a moment, Aislinn's heart leaped into her throat, until she realised it was Victoria.

Slipping into the room, Victoria, wearing a kitchen

apron over her grey dress, quickly closed the door behind her. With her green eyes as round as saucers, she
whispered, 'You must tell me everything! How did you
come upon Mr Carlisle?'

Aislinn stepped closer, so they could talk quietly
without disturbing the girls. She also kept one eye on
the door, afraid someone else might barge in and find
them. Percy and Hazel were not glad she had returned.
'He was at the edge of the property, near the main road.
He'd spent the night there. The new Duke never wrote to
him about the old Duke's and Duchess's passing.' Giving them distinction by new and old is how all of the
staff referred to the recent changes in the household,
but Aislinn realised that, privately, she was starting to
think of them as Rowland and Percy. It was uncanny
how being in Luke's presence for such a short amount
of time had influenced her thoughts.

'He didn't know?' Victoria asked, pressing four fingers against her lips, her expression sympathetic.

Like her, the entire household had been deeply saddened by their deaths, and still missed Rowland and
Leslie greatly. 'He knew, because the old Duke's solicitor wrote to him,' Aislinn said.

A flash of anger crossed Victoria's face as she shook
her head. 'Christopher said this morning that he'd been
certain the youngest brother would come home once he
heard about the deaths.'

'This morning?' Aislinn's pulse quickened. 'Did he
know that Luke—Mr Carlisle—was expected to arrive?' She'd told Luke that she hadn't known, and had
assumed that no one in the household had been aware
of his impending arrival.

'No, I don't think he knew. Everyone was frustrated

about them ordering you off the property, and wondering what we could do. After what they did to you, none of us feel secure in our positions. Christopher said our only hope would be for the youngest brother to come home, but he was growing fearful that he wouldn't, because it had already been so long.'

'He would have been here earlier,' Aislinn said, with true conviction, 'had he known.'

'The household is full of whispers about his arrival.' Victoria pressed a hand to her breastbone. 'How he strode straight up the steps and popped the Duke square in the nose!'

'He didn't punch Percy.' Aislinn shook her head to get her thoughts straight. 'The Duke stumbled all on his own and fell.'

'Oh, well, I guess people were wishing that was what happened,' Victoria said.

Aislinn attempted to hide the way her pulse increased by glancing to where the girls sat in tiny chairs, drinking imaginary tea. 'You didn't see him?'

'No, I was in the kitchen. Tell me. Is he as devilishly handsome as others are saying?'

Aislinn couldn't lie. 'Yes.'

'Tell me more,' Victoria insisted, the excitement evident in her voice. 'Does he dress like an American?'

'It sounds like you already know.'

'I only know what I've been told. You've seen him! Rode on a horse with him! You must tell me more. Is he like the old Duke said? An adventurer?'

Aislinn mentally cautioned herself not to say too much, but did admit, 'Yes, he's much like the old Duke described.'

'In what ways?' Victoria wanted to know.

'He's audacious,' Aislinn answered, and then realised something she hadn't thought of until now. His voice. It hadn't sounded British, in speech or accent. 'He has adopted many of the American ways.'

'Such as?' Victoria sighed. 'I'm so anxious to catch a glimpse of him. How long will he be here?'

'I don't know,' Aislinn replied to the last question. 'He is here to secure his guardianship of Fern and Ivy.'

Victoria gasped. 'Guardianship? Is he going to take them back to America with him? Oh, Aislinn, what will you do then?'

A chill encompassed her entire being. Never once since meeting him had that thought crossed her mind. She desperately tried to recall if he had indicated that was his design. Maybe she hadn't heard because her mind had been too befuddled by him, by his good looks and his offer for her to stay with the girls.

What had he said?

She recalled him saying that he'd need a governess while he fought for guardianship, and beyond, because he *would* win. Did beyond mean that he would be taking the girls back to America?

Catching Victoria's eyes, the empathy in them, Aislinn twisted, staring at the girls still engrossed in their tea party. Had she made a dreadful mistake? Had she come back just to lose them all over again?

Luke sat in a wooden armed chair, with one ankle resting on the opposite knee, and nursed a brandy as he watched his brother pour a second glass for himself. He'd downed the first in practically one swallow. He hadn't expected Percy to follow him immediately, because Percy had to show him who was the boss. He had followed, though, and was taking his time with his second drink, making a point of Luke waiting on him.

Luke didn't mind. It felt good to sit in a comfortable chair and sip on a drink after weeks of travelling. He was also glad that he hadn't punched Percy in the nose, because he was hoping they could come to an agreement about what was best for Rowland's daughters. Civilly. Although Percy should be grateful that he'd learned to control his temper.

Nose in the air, Percy crossed the room. He'd changed some in the last eight years. Had grown rounder in the belly, added a chin, and lost a fair amount of hair.

Percy set himself down on the chair opposite Luke, which also had carved wooden arms and legs, but hosted a padded seat and back, both covered in thick leather. It had been their father's favourite chair, the Duke's chair, and the sole reason Luke hadn't sat in it. He did have some respect for family tradition.

Perched there, like a king overseeing his kingdom of royal servants, whose only purpose was to react to his beck and call, Percy lifted a single finger. Pointed it like it was some sort of weapon. 'Let's get one thing straight. Hazel is the Duchess of Havenbrook, and you will respect that.'

Luke wouldn't deny any man the right to defend his wife. Defend any woman. They deserved a man's protection. He took a sip of brandy, then set his glass down on the table beside his chair. 'Getting things straight is a good place to start. I have always respected your wife, just as I do all women, and men. However, I will not condone her behaviour today.' He wanted to point out that what they'd done to Aislinn had been completely disrespectful, but chose to keep to the topic at hand.

Hazel. 'Taking over the title of duchess does not provide one with integrity, nor wisdom or scruples, which are all respectful traits that were decidedly lacking in your wife's behaviour upon my arrival.' Hazel had to have been ecstatic over her new title. Having been a not-so-respectable baron's daughter, she'd had her eyes set on more for years.

'So,' Luke continued, 'while we are getting things straight, Hazel will not oversee, nor have anything to do with, Miss Blaydon and her care of Fern and Ivy. That's my job.'

Turning red in the face, Percy said, 'This is my house, and when I dismiss someone, they remain dismissed.'

Like it or not, Luke had to admit that the Dukedom did give his brother an unending list of irrevocable rights. None of which were going to stop him from fulfilling his promise to Rowland. 'Why did you *dismiss* Miss Blaydon?'

Percy lifted his chin arrogantly. 'Her care was not up to our standards.'

Luke had only known Miss Blaydon for a few hours, yet knew instinctively that was not the case. 'Your standards?' He shook his head. 'I believe you did so because you knew I'd return and you wanted to make it as difficult as possible for me to oversee the girls' inheritance.'

'Inheritance?' Percy huffed out a breath and shook his head. 'You have nothing to do with that. I am the rightful heir.'

Luke's gut churned, and he struggled to maintain his anger. He had to hold that for when it was truly needed. 'I can imagine how you and Hazel danced in your night-clothes when that happened.'

Percy's face turned redder, and Luke's jaw tightened

at knowing just how close to the mark his words had hit. Hazel wasn't the first woman to marry a man for money. It happened all the time.

'You're still an insufferable—'

'That's all you have?' Luke asked. 'Name calling?'

Lips drawn tight, Percy sat still for several seconds, nostrils flaring. 'You shouldn't even be here.'

Luke laughed, an act he knew wouldn't be appreciated. 'You, dear brother, sat in this very room when our father was ailing, dying from a heart that had been weakened by fever, while our mother willed her very life in hopes that he would be spared.' That is exactly what happened. A mere month after their father had died, their mother passed in her sleep. Weakened first by desperation, then by grief, her heart simply stopped beating.

'Our father's wish,' Luke continued to make his point, 'was not only that the family wealth and title were passed down to the next generation, but he wanted prosperity for *each* of us. Each of his sons. Rowland, with you and I at his sides, promised our father that he would take on the obligations bestowed upon him when the time came, and that he would assure that we, you and I, were given the opportunities to pursue our own ambitions.' Luke would never forget that day, because he'd felt as if his father had given him permission to deviate from the life he'd always known. 'Rowland fulfilled that promise, and I ask you, do you believe that he would do no different when it came to his own children?'

Percy twisted his shoulders as if an itch was tickling his spine and he couldn't scratch it. 'We were men when our father died,' he said. 'At least two of us were.

You were still filled with childish tendencies that you obviously have yet to outgrow.'

Luke understood that Percy was referring to the life he'd lived since leaving home. The only adventure Percy had ever wanted was the one he now had, being the duke.

'Rowland's daughters are children,' Percy continued. 'Girls who need a stable upbringing, so they can grow into women of refinement in order to someday assume their positions in society.'

Luke knew the positions in society that the girls had to look forward to under Percy's care. Married off to men more for what the marriage would bring to the family than for their own happiness. He had no doubt that Percy had already thought of that, had likely created a list of sons from families that would suit his desire for more money and power.

'You can't possibly be under the belief that you could provide those children with what they need,' Percy said. 'You don't even live in this country. Don't want to live here. You've spent the last eight years chasing whims. Gambling, digging for gold, farming, and—'

'It's a ranch, not a farm, and I sluiced for gold, I didn't dig for it.' The gambling every so often was true, so he skipped over that. They weren't whims, either, but he was choosing his battles. 'But none of that makes a difference, because Rowland chose me to be the guardian of his children. I have the papers to prove it.' He dropped the foot on his knee to the floor, and leaned forward in his chair. 'We can make this easy, or we can make this hard. You can withdraw your petition, or you can continue to challenge the rights granted to me upon Rowland's will.'

Percy's nostrils were flaring again. 'For goodness' sake, will you stop acting as if the only way to settle disagreements is by throwing fists at each other! Think like a man. Think about what those girls need. You can't provide it, and I can.'

'You have no idea what I can and can't provide.'

'Yes, I do. The duchy letters patent clearly defines the inheritance orders. Those girls—'

'Rowland's daughters are not part of the duchy,' Luke interrupted. 'That is all you care about, isn't it? What you can inherit and what others can't.' Anger shot him to his feet. 'Don't tell me to act like a man, when you're the one acting like a child. A greedy child who isn't willing to share. Your choice is obvious. The hard way it is.' He strode to the doorway, before he turned to give the only warning he would give when it came to the safety of his nieces. 'Fern and Ivy are under my care, and anyone who hurts them will answer to me.'

Without waiting for a response, he strode into the hallway, but only took a step before he turned about and stuck his head back in the doorway. He knew his brother's ways, how he'd use all means to an end. 'Add Miss Blaydon to that list.'

Percy sneered, but kept his mouth shut.

Fully disgusted, Luke shook his head. 'I can only imagine how disappointed our mother and father would be in you right now.'

Aislinn was again startled by the opening of the nursery door. Victoria had left a short time ago, and her heart jolted, fearing her friend had been reprimanded, or worse, for being absent from her kitchen duties for too long. Then it fully leaped into her throat at the sight of Luke standing in the doorway.

The permanent grin on his face was absent.

'What are you doing here?' he asked, stepping into the room and giving it a scrutinising stare.

The room was small, crowded with the girls' bed and their playthings. Nothing like their old, spacious nursery, with brightly painted walls, frilly curtains on the windows, and colourful rugs on the floor.

Ivy was instantly behind one of Aislinn's knees, while Fern remained standing on the other side of the small table that no longer held their tea set. Their imaginary party had ended, and several blocks had been set on the table for a game of counting.

'This is the nursery,' Aislinn stated, keeping her voice calm and steady, as to not frighten the girls any more than his unexpected arrival had.

His frown increased. 'This room is on the third floor.'

'Yes, it is.' She bit her bottom lip to keep from addressing him formally by adding my lord, and kept biting it to keep from explaining that this hadn't always been the nursery. That room, near the Duke and Duchess's, was now occupied by Caldwell and Mr Horton. It was only natural that they would want their son near their room; she fully understood that.

Luke looked at her for a long moment, before glancing down towards Ivy, and then to Fern, who still stood near the table. His grin returned as he bent down on one knee. 'Hello, Ivy.'

Aislinn nodded at the quick glance he shot up towards her, silently questioning whether he'd correctly guessed Ivy was the one hiding behind her skirt. She also allowed herself to release the air she'd been holding.

'I'm your uncle,' he said. 'Uncle Luke.'

'I've heard of you,' Fern said, making her way around the table. 'You send letters that Papa reads.'

Aislinn momentarily closed her eyes. Though she had tried to explain to the girls that their parents would not be returning, they still talked as if they were alive and would someday come home.

'I do, Fern,' Luke replied.

'You have cows at your house,' Fern said.

He nodded. 'I do.'

'Papa says too many to count,' Fern said.

'There are a lot of them,' he said.

'Did you bring one here?' Ivy asked.

Aislinn patted Ivy's back, letting the child know she was still safe as Ivy took a step out from behind her.

'No, I didn't,' Luke said. 'I had to ride on a ship, an ocean liner, to get here, and cows don't much like riding on boats.'

'We have cows,' Fern said quite proudly. 'That's where milk comes from.'

His smile grew wide. 'It is. Do you milk them?'

'No,' Fern replied, as if that was a disappointment to her. 'I'm too small.'

'There's nothing wrong with being small.' Then, with an exaggerated frown, he looked around the room. 'Are your cows in here? I don't see them.'

Both girls giggled. A sound that lifted Aislinn's spirits greatly. The old Duke spent time with his daughters daily, as had their mum. But since their deaths, she was the only one to interact with them on a regular basis.

'They're outside!' the girls exclaimed in unison.

'I miss my cows.' Luke rubbed his chin as if thinking. 'Would you show me yours?'

He and both girls looked up at her. She nodded. They often spent time outside, but not knowing what commotion might have been ensuing downstairs, she'd chosen to keep the girls safely tucked away in their room since arriving.

With the same enduring charm that he'd used on her this morning, he had the girls chatting non-stop as they walked from the third floor all the way down to the first, and out through the back door. Aislinn couldn't help but remember walking down the stairs this morning, with Christopher at her side. She'd believed she would never see the girls again, and would forever be grateful for whatever additional time she had with them. Any amount of time was more than she'd been able to hope for this morning.

Yet, she couldn't deny an inner fear that had crept in at the thought of him taking the girls to America. Dare she ask him about that? It certainly wouldn't be her place, but neither was calling him by his first name. He was so different from any man she'd ever met, and deep down, that scared her, too.

Once they stepped outside, Luke took hold of each girl's hand and jogged between them as they ran towards the barn that housed the animals, other than the horses, which were kept in the stable near the front of the house.

Glancing about, Aislinn hurried to keep up. She wasn't concerned that he would allow the girls to get hurt in any way. Her worries lay in who might be watching them.

There was a lot she didn't know about him, for they'd only met a few hours ago. She truly wanted to believe that he was honourable and trustworthy, much like his oldest brother. Rowland would have been overjoyed that his daughters had easily taken to Luke. There had been a love between those two brothers. That had been clear from the way the old Duke had spoken so fondly about his youngest brother. That—a love, or even liking—was genuinely lacking between the new Duke and Luke.

The old Duke had never spoken despairingly about any of his family members, nor had he displayed the animosity that the other two brothers did towards each other. Older staff members had suggested that Rowland was often the peacekeeper between his siblings, and Aislinn was concerned that there was no one who could fulfil that role now. She'd always been diligent about the girls not being exposed to ill-mannered behaviours, and had become even more protective after the death of their parents.

The next half hour or more was filled with giggles, teasing questions from Luke, and righteous answers, mainly from Fern, but Ivy was putting in her thoughts, as well. Both of their blue eyes were lit up with merriment as Luke led the way through the barn, pens, and even the chicken coop, which had hens leaving feathers in their wakes at the disruption.

He collected two brown feathers and stuck one in each of the girls' hair, secured back by the yellow ribbons that matched their dresses. After leaving the coop, he showed them how to pluck the white dandelion clocks from the grass and blow on them to make the tiny seeds scatter in the air.

While the girls were running, looking for the next clock, he said, 'The nursery will be moved from the third floor.'

It wasn't her place to disagree, yet she feared repercussions. 'We have become comfortable where we are.'

'I'm sure you have. You'd make them comfortable living in a cave. I, on the other hand, will not see my nieces sleeping in the servants' quarters. Nor their governess.'

She withheld from pointing out that she, too, was a servant, and instead asked a direct question, one that she should have asked before, but had been working up the nerve. 'How long will you be here?'

'As long as it takes,' he answered.

She didn't doubt that his actions were what he felt was best for the girls, but the changes he made could cause trouble once he left. Which prompted her to ask about the one thing she truly wanted to know. 'Are you planning on taking the girls back to America with you?'

He frowned, deeply, and turned his gaze towards the girls. He was silent for so long her heart was once again residing in her throat.

'No, that is not my plan.' He removed his hat and ran a hand through his hair before replacing it. 'This is their home. Once I've secured guardianship, I will make arrangements that will be best for everyone.'

'Arrangements?'

'I can't tell you what those will be, not yet, but I will make them.' He grinned at her. 'We're partners. I'll keep you updated and let you know what to expect. You just have to trust me.'

Her ability to trust him wasn't what scared her.

His grin grew and he winked at her, in such a way that her heart fluttered slightly. Not in fear. That was for sure. His handsomeness affected her in ways that were quite confusing. Standing this close to him made it difficult to think straight.

'I can't tell you because I don't know yet,' he said. 'I have some things to figure out, some things to do, some things to get in order, but it will all happen. I guarantee it.'

'Uncle Luke! Look!' Fern yelled, holding up a large dandelion clock.

'I'd say that is the granddaddy of dandelions.' He jogged towards the girls. 'Wait for me!'

Aislinn watched half in fascination, and half in dread, as the three of them blew on the seed pod. For now that he was no longer standing at her side, her mind began to work again, and one thing was for sure. When he left, it was going to be another devastating blow to the girls. They would be waiting on three people to return to their lives.

Unless, of course, he took them with him to America. Then she'd be the one waiting on people who would never return.

Chapter Four

True to his word, for that was something he never went back on, Luke had the nursery moved off the third floor and into one of the rooms in the north wing of the house. Near his room. Just like he didn't want to be sleeping near Percy, he didn't want the girls sleeping on that side of the house, either.

Nor Aislinn.

That had been the only positive thing about them being up on the third floor—that Aislinn was with the girls. She was as protective as a mother hen, and he appreciated that.

He still believed that he was the reason Percy had fired her. First, they'd tried to make her life so miserable that she'd leave on her own, and when that hadn't worked, they'd taken another route.

Aislinn's care was more than up to anyone's standards. Beyond anyone's standards. Percy and Hazel had wanted her gone, before he ever arrived. Moving her and the girls to the third floor had been an attempt to make her leave.

Though the tiny space up there had been neat and clean, moving them into that room had been to prove one thing. That Percy had control over everyone and everything in the house.

Or so he thought.

His brother had inherited the Dukedom, as was his right as the second brother, the next male in succession. It could only be taken away by an Act of Parliament or Royal prerogative, which rarely, if ever, happened, and in this case wouldn't, because Percy wasn't committing treason or some other vital disrespect of the crown. If Rowland had left behind a son, instead of daughters, things would be different. The son would have inherited the title and consequential holdings.

Now, according to all rights and passages, the next in line was Caldwell—the young lad Luke had yet to meet.

That would happen in time, but it wasn't the issue at hand. Luke wasn't interested in having the Dukedom removed from his brother or his brother's son. He had never wanted the title, nor the life that went along with it, and never would. However, in opposition to what others may think, he did want his family's name to remain in good grace. He also wanted Fern and Ivy to receive what was rightfully theirs.

Where Percy was overstepping was in the fact that he was pretending to have inherited *everything*, which he had not. The title did come with holdings, including an estate, but that estate wasn't this manor house. The ruins of what had been a castle, six miles to the north, that had been abandoned by the Duke four generations before them, was the home that went with the title. Their great-grandfather had married a neighbour and, subsequently, moved into her home—the manor house. The manor had become their family home, but was not part of the entitled holdings of the Duke of Havenbrook.

Luke knew the story well. As a child, he'd often pretended to be a knight, fighting off foot soldiers with branches broken off the trees that had grown up around the broken-down stone wall surrounding the ruins.

He grinned at the memory. Not only because he'd always had fun exploring the old ruins, but because he remembered when Aislinn had asked him how far he'd had to walk, and he'd asked her which time.

There, at those ruins, had been the first time he'd been left afoot. His horse had become spooked by a flock of birds that had been roosting in the trees and, unprepared, he'd lost his seat in the saddle. He'd walked the full six miles. Upon arriving home after dark, by which time his mother had been near the peak of hysterics, fearing something dreadful had happened to him, his father had told him all about their ancestor. The first Duke of Havenbrook had been a commoner, but the monarch had bestowed the title upon him for his bravery and skill on the battlefield.

It was after hearing that story that his own wanderlust had fully taken root. Dreams of travelling to foreign lands, of battling unknown adversaries and taking on new challenges, consumed his young mind. He'd known then that he could never stay here. Knew deep in his very soul that he needed to leave, to find the place where he could create a life, build a legacy that would make him happy.

He'd found that life in America, but he still had duties that he needed to fulfil from his old life, because that, too, was a part of who he was.

The manor had housed the family for generations and would continue to do so. But it was a Carlisle family holding, not a Duke of Havenbrook holding. Upon the death of their father, ownership had been divided equally between him, Percy, and Rowland. Now, since Rowland's death, the house belonged to him, Percy, and Fern and Ivy. With him being the twins' guardian, that meant he owned two-thirds to Percy's one-third.

Letting out a sigh of longing, Luke looked at the pair of boots he'd taken off a short time ago, which were now sitting next to the wardrobe in the suite he'd be calling his room for the time being. He and those boots had put in a lot of miles together. The leather had formed to his feet long ago, making them comfortable and familiar.

The ones he'd just pulled on came up to his knees, and had his toes bunched up together like five puppies vying for the same teat.

He didn't know where Christopher had come up with the clothes filling the wardrobe, but they would do while he was here. They wouldn't be as comfortable as he was used to, because they were far more formal. The ruffles on the white shirt were already tickling his neck, and not in a way that made him want to laugh.

Pushing himself off the chair, he had a quick glance in the mirror and let out a chuckle. If he were back in Montana, Raf would have several choice words for his attire. He'd claim the ruffles alone would spook the cattle.

The high-waisted, grey and black plaid wool pants were snug. The suspenders were more for looks than actually needed to hold up the pants. The white shirt had ruffles down the front and around the neck and wrists, and the vest was made of silk, both the gold printed front and black back. So was the ascot around his neck.

He'd put these clothes on after his bath because he was

respectful of customs. His family had always dressed for dinner, and he was certain that hadn't changed.

The clothes might have been Rowland's, and considering he no longer needed them, Luke was certain his brother wouldn't mind him wearing them. Truth was, if Rowland was here, he would have given him the shirt off his back if needed. That's the kind of man, and brother, Rowland had been.

The house, the whole place, felt different, empty and sad, without Rowland here, and Luke had to admit that he felt that way, too.

Maybe the clothes would make him feel like a part of Rowland was with him. He wouldn't mind that even one little iota.

He'd thanked Christopher for the clothes, and for Benjamin, the young man he'd sent to see to his needs, whose parents worked the estate. Up until today, he'd been a stable boy. Having someone to run errands and make requests on his behalf would be just fine, and he'd informed the young Benjamin, who was clearly still wet behind the ears, that he'd welcome his help, other than with getting dressed. He'd do that all on his own, and had sent him away as soon as his bath was ready.

Forgoing a hat, despite how naked he felt without it, Luke grabbed the frock coat from where it had been laid out on the bed. Hooking it over his shoulder with one thumb, he left the bedroom and crossed the sitting room to exit the suite.

A short distance down the hall, he knocked on a door.

The door opened, and he gave Aislinn a nod. 'Are the three of you all settled in the new rooms?'

'Yes, thank you.' She stepped back so he could see into the room.

The sitting room furniture had been rearranged to make room for a child-sized table and chairs, shelves holding books and toys, and several other items. 'You each have a bed?' he asked. The girls had shared one bed in the room on the third floor, and from what he'd seen, Aislinn's bed had been nothing but a narrow cot.

'Yes, thank you.'

He'd instructed Christopher that the new nursery should have two bedrooms, and had examined this suite of rooms himself to make sure it would be suitable before he'd ordered the move to take place.

Fern and Ivy had noticed it was him at the door and left their small table. In the past, he'd never taken a lot of notice of children, leastwise not since he'd been one, but had to say that these two girls were as cute as they came. They'd inherited the Carlisle hair, black and thick. He had to have his cut regularly or he ended up looking like a sheep needing to be sheared.

On his nieces, the hair was adorable. Long, with sections tied on their crowns with ribbons, it was a thick mass of soft waves that reached well past their shoulders. Their deep blue eyes stood out on their round little faces, where button noses and rosy cheeks added to their cherub appearances. While outside earlier, he'd noticed the tiny mole on Ivy's nose that Aislinn had mentioned, and he'd also observed that she'd been correct in saying Fern was more outgoing, while Ivy waited to see how things were playing out before joining the foray.

Even now, Ivy stood a step behind her sister.

'Would you like to have a tea party with us?' Fern asked.

He could guarantee he'd never tried a cup of invisible tea in his life, yet it sounded far more inviting than what was waiting downstairs for him. His mother had been a stickler for the entire family being present for pre-dinner drinks at least half an hour prior to dinner being served.

'Your uncle is due downstairs for dinner,' Aislinn said softly.

Fern accepted the answer with a nod, though Luke saw the disappointment on her face, and on Ivy's. While they'd been outside, blowing the heads off dandelions, Aislinn had mentioned how Rowland had spent time with the twins regularly, and how much they'd missed that.

He was no replacement for their father. Never would be, but he was their uncle and that was a role he could create to be the next best thing.

'I am due downstairs,' he said, mind made up. 'But I have time for a cup of tea.'

Fern took one hand and, in order for Ivy to take the other, he handed Aislinn his frock coat. The girls led him to the table, where, afraid of breaking the legs off the small chair, he chose to sit on the floor.

As well as invisible tea, he was given a plate holding invisible biscuits with sweet icing. He could imagine them. They had been a favourite of his. That was one of the things American's got wrong. A biscuit is a cookie, not a bread roll.

'Did you have a biscuit after your dinner?' he asked, knowing they, along with Aislinn, had already eaten their dinner in this room. That's where he'd eaten his meals too, in the nursery with whatever household staff had been assigned to watch over him. He was sure he'd had a governess as an infant, even a small child, just couldn't completely recall any one in particular. At age ten, he was sent to boarding school, and during his time at home from then on he was allowed to eat with the adults, unless there was a specific event that he was still considered too young to attend.

'No,' Fern replied with a sigh. 'We haven't had biscuits in ages.'

'Ages, is it?' he asked, holding in a chuckle at her embellished grievance.

'The Duchess says they aren't good for little girls,' Fern said.

Ivy nodded. 'Only boys.'

Luke set down the tiny teacup, afraid the ire creeping in might make his fingers tighten so hard the tiny handle would snap. 'Well, now, I must say, I've never heard that before. But these biscuits that you just gave me were the best I've ever eaten.' He gave them each a tiny flick on the ends of their noses, then stood up. 'I must be going, but will see you both tomorrow.'

He'd have biscuits for them, too, but would keep that as a surprise.

They bid him goodbye, and Aislinn handed him his coat.

She also walked him to the door, where she quietly said, 'Forgive me, but considering that I now work for you, there is something I'd like to know before morning.'

'All right. What's that?' She hadn't dipped into a curtsey, and he appreciated that. Putting aside mannerisms that she'd been required to use for years would take time, and he'd have to give her that. He did wish that she didn't appear to be ready to take flight anytime he stepped close. Then again, he could understand her wariness, for she had been mistreated. She and the twins had all been mistreated, and he didn't like that. Not at all.

'I was wondering what you would like me to wear.'

Her head was dipped down, but he noticed the flush of her cheeks. He scratched the side of his face, wondering when and if he'd said something about her dress. Something unflattering? He was certain he hadn't, but might have inadvertently. He was known to speak before he thought at times. 'Wear?'

'Yes.' She swallowed visibly and turned redder.

He glanced down at her white blouse and black skirt. They covered everything from her neck to her wrists and ankles. 'What's wrong with what you have on?'

'They—' She took a deep breath and lifted her face to look at him. 'They aren't mine. When I was dismissed, I was told that, although the governess uniforms had been purchased on my behalf, they were property of the Duke.'

He'd thought he had enough fodder against Percy, but it just kept coming. At every corner... It. Just. Kept. Coming. 'Is that what you're wearing now? A governess's uniform?'

'No. Mrs Taylor gave me this skirt and blouse so I'd have something to wear when I left.'

He had to take a deep breath and hold it until it burned his lungs, to keep from saying the curses that were in his mind. The silent words he was calling Percy and Hazel were as unpleasant as words could get. If anyone deserved them, though, it was those two. They would have sent her away naked and not given it a second thought.

While letting the air out slowly through his nose, he ran his tongue over his upper front teeth, just to make sure he had full control over it. 'Do you have the uniforms?'

She nodded.

'Wear them.'

The way she blinked and leaned back told him that his tone was harsher than it should have been. He hadn't meant to scare her. Without her, he'd be up a creek without a paddle. Reaching out, he touched her arm, softly and quietly cleared his throat. 'You can wear anything you want.'

She nodded, and did her best to give him a ghost of a smile.

It wasn't like him to be unsure of himself, yet he was with her. There was something about her that made him genuinely want to comfort her, to wrap his arms around her and give her a solid hug. Tell her that he was here now, that things were going to work out just fine.

He'd never thought twice about protecting a woman in danger. Hell, he'd saved two women from drowning in a river once, at the same time. He'd dragged them both up onto the bank before Raf had pulled his boots off. In Raf's defence, they had been new boots and his horse wasn't as fast as Buck, which meant Raf had only just arrived at the riverbank when he was already pulling the women onto dry ground.

This was different, though. She was different—and not just because she wasn't a dance hall gal like those women had been.

She was different from all other women he'd met, in a way that he couldn't quite put his finger on, but she sure did tug at his insides. There was something really compelling about her. More than compelling, she was captivating, and he couldn't claim that it was just because of her caring nature towards Fern and Ivy.

At the same time, the idea of him finding any woman

captivating was as out of character for him as the ruffles on the shirt he wore.

Stepping backwards, he grabbed the doorknob and pulled the door open behind him. 'Good night, Aislinn.'

'Good night,' she said.

He walked into the hall, pulling the door closed behind him. There, while drawing in a well needed breath of air, he realised she hadn't said his name. Not once since he met her.

Why should that matter to him? He had far bigger fish to fry.

Just the same, he'd like to hear her say it.

The air escaping Aislinn felt as shaky as her hands, which were indeed trembling. Her intention had been to not offend anyone by wearing the wrong thing, but it appeared as if she'd made a catastrophe out of something as silly as a uniform. She could have simply asked Mrs Taylor if she could keep the skirt and blouse for now.

Instead, she'd vexed Luke. The anger in his eyes had been startling, as had the harshness of his tone.

She took a hesitant step forward and grasped the knob to check that the door was shut securely. Unaccustomed to the trials, tribulations, and chaos of the day, she leaned her head against the door and closed her eyes.

The quiet solace she sought wasn't there. Instead, her usually steadfast mind, filled with a common sense that she often prided herself on, told her to get used to it. Because as long as Luke was in this house, there would be chaos.

His letters had been full of chaos. Luke, and the old Duke, had referred to them as adventures. But tussling with a mountain lion was *not* a grand adventure. It was dangerous. Maddeningly dangerous.

So was fighting with the new duke.

Luke shouldn't have been worried about being blind-sided, he should have feared entering the lion's den. That's what he'd done, and she wasn't the kind of part-ner he needed to help him.

She was a governess, for goodness' sake.

A lowly servant. All she knew how to do was care for children.

An involuntary stiffness entered her spine, and she turned, looking at where Fern and Ivy were busy play-ing with their dolls. Now that they'd been moved into a larger room, there was space for their doll beds and other toys that had been boxed up and stored on the third floor. Much like they themselves had been boxed up and stored there.

That's what it had felt like, and she should have protested. This was Fern and Ivy's home. They should never have been moved to the third floor. It's just that she'd never been one to protest or cause problems. It scared her to be in the middle of all that was going on, but that was exactly where she was.

Yet, she knew that wasn't the only thing unsettling her. Luke himself, his handsomeness, his overall cha-risma, did strange things to her insides. He was quite extraordinary—in many ways—which would explain why she found it difficult to draw a steady breath in his presence.

If he was successful in keeping guardianship, some-thing she sincerely hoped would happen, and then re-turned to America, he would need someone who knew more than simply how to care for children to remain with the girls. He would need someone who could stand up for Fern and Ivy, someone who would fight future injustices on their behalf during his absence. One who wouldn't sit back and allow them to happen.

Someone more like him.

If she had any hope of remaining with the girls, she needed to become that person, rather than acting like a ninny who had never seen a handsome man before.

She stiffened her spine even more, squared her shoulders. What happened this morning would not happen again. She would not be separated from Fern and Ivy until her job was done. Until the day arrived when they were mature enough to not need her any longer.

For that to happen, for them to grow into women who would one day assume their positions in the ranks of society, their birthrights as daughters of a duke, they would need more than a governess. Without their mother, who had not only been loving and kind, but steadfast and confident, the girls only had one woman to look up to. To count on. To emulate. That was her.

A splattering of shame washed over Aislinn. The old Duchess would have been sorely disappointed to know that she hadn't fought against being moved to the third floor. Fought against abandoning the girls.

Leslie would have been more than sorely disappointed, she would have been outraged over the treatment of her children.

Just like Luke had been. Just like she should have been.

She'd told herself that she was simply a governess and couldn't do anything to oppose the new Duke and Duchess. That was an excuse. She wasn't simply a governess. She was *the* governess.

The one who had been put in charge of the Duke and Duchess's most prized possessions.

The one who was now Luke's partner. He needed someone he could count on. She trusted him, but she needed to become someone he could trust in return. He'd said he needed her help, and so far, she hadn't offered any.

She'd been granted four years of watching and admiring the old Duchess; it was time she used what she'd learned.

'Is something wrong, Aislinn?' Fern asked, staring at her from across the room.

'No,' Aislinn assured her. From the moment she'd become their governess, these girls became her family. The family she'd never had. She moved, crossing the room towards them. 'But it is time to put your dolls to bed and for the two of you to put on your nightclothes.'

'You won't be gone when we wake up again, will you?' Ivy asked.

Aislinn's heart nearly broke in two, yet at the same time, her determination to make the needed changes inside herself was doubly reinforced. Dropping to her knees, she pulled Ivy into a hug. 'No, poppet. I won't be gone. I'll be right here when you wake up, I promise.'

Holding out a single arm, she invited Fern to join in on the hug.

They were so precious, and they needed her, loved her, as much as she did them. She couldn't fail them again. Wouldn't fail them again. This time, she did have a saving grace. He went by the name of Luke Carlisle.

She wouldn't fail him, either. There was too much at stake.

'I like our new room,' Fern said, wiggling out of the hug.

Aislinn released Ivy and planted a quick kiss on each of their foreheads. 'I do, too.'

'I like Uncle Luke,' Ivy said.

'I do, too,' Aislinn agreed. Her heart had beat frantically earlier, when she opened the door and saw him standing there, dressed in his finery. He was handsome no matter what he wore. He was also confident. His stature alone said he was a man to be reckoned with. She couldn't let that scare her—for that had to be the cause of her racing pulse. He was exactly what the girls needed.

'Come,' she said, rising to her feet. 'Let's put on your nightclothes and then you can each pick out a book for me to read to you before bedtime.'

The girls readily agreed, and soon all three of them were snuggled on the sofa, reading two of their favourite books. The stories were long and both girls were asleep before she was halfway through the second story.

One at a time, she carried them to their beds, and after tucking the covers around each twin, she stood between the beds for several still moments, simply watching them sleep, much like she'd stood in the doorway this morning.

That had been mere hours ago, yet it felt like a lifetime. So much had happened since then. She truly had been given a second chance, and would not squander it.

As if he stood behind her, rather than in her mind, Aislinn heard the words that Luke had spoken that morning.

'The challenge of the unknown is what makes it an adventure.'

She had to become adventurous, and strong, and steadfast, and confident, and a number of other things. For the girls and for him.

The idea scared her. She'd never been adventurous, but it was also thrilling to think of all the things he'd seen and done. He was all that she'd imagined he'd be, and more.

Brushing her hair as she prepared for bed, her thoughts remained on Luke, and something else he'd said. About wagon trains. She'd read about them, but the conviction in his voice when he talked about them is what struck a chord in her. How he'd said that those people were armed with little more than determination. How that took courage, bravery.

What she remembered most, though, about what he'd said, was how he respected those people.

She was a servant, nothing would ever change that, but what he'd said defined the difference between being submissive and being respectful in a way she'd never considered.

Setting the brush on the dresser, she concluded that she had a lot to learn.

Later, after putting on her nightgown and lying in her bed, which was much more comfortable than the one she'd had the last few months, Aislinn closed her eyes and willed her mind to go back in time. To remember everything that she could about the old Duchess. The things she'd said, the way she'd carried herself, the way she'd interacted with others.

Leslie Carlisle had been a beautiful woman, slender, elegant in structure, with golden hair and blue eyes. She never appeared alarmed or overly excited. She'd been poised at all times, regal in how she ran the household, and loving towards her husband and children.

That was the kind of woman Luke needed as a partner. Aislinn knew she could never become the person

Leslie had been, but she couldn't imagine a better example from whom to learn all she needed to know. Except the old Duchess was no longer alive. Memories were all she had, so when faced with a challenge, she would need to ask herself—how would the old Duchess have responded? And hope to heaven she remembered correctly.

Or at least remembered enough.

It wasn't going to be easy, but at least she had a starting point.

Chapter Five

From where he sat at the table laden with more food than three people could ever eat, Luke allowed his gaze to wander from Percy to Hazel and back again. The two barely looked up from their plates, and most certainly never met his gaze. Nor had they spoken a single word to him.

They hadn't been in the sitting room prior to dinner, either, which had been smart on Percy's part. Luke had been angry upon leaving Aislinn, and he had several choice words for the way his brother was treating her. He was still mad, but his temper had cooled to a more controllable temperature. She was an asset, and he was very glad that she was on his side. He wouldn't let the fact that they'd denied her clothing upon her dismissal go unchecked.

Among other things.

As the meal ended, he politely requested his brother's presence in the study. He hadn't included his sister-in-law in the invitation, but wouldn't object to her hearing what he had to say. He'd stopped in the kitchen earlier, before going to the sitting room, and had requested that the biscuits the girls hadn't had in *ages* be prepared. The downright meanness that had been portrayed was ridiculous, and not something he was willing to ignore. Nor would he tolerate it continuing.

Without a word, which was clearly a snub, but didn't faze Luke in the least, Hazel parted ways with him and Percy in the hallway. Upon entering the study, Percy closed the door behind them.

Luke proceeded to the credenza and poured two glasses of brandy, then carried one to Percy.

While his brother took a seat in the Duke's chair, Luke sat in the one opposite and took a sip of his drink. He had plenty to say, but after the silent dinner, figured he'd let his brother be the first to speak. Whether that took a minute, or an hour, he truly didn't care. The game he and Hazel were playing was intended to provoke him. They'd already done that.

'This is all for naught,' Percy finally said.

Since it had taken his brother so long to find his tongue, Luke had finished his drink and twisted the empty glass on the table beside his chair. 'What is it you feel is for naught?'

'Everything. I've already submitted my petition to the Lord Chancellor of the Court of Chancery.'

Luke nodded. 'I know you have.'

'I expect their decision to arrive any day now, so you're too late.'

'No, dear brother, I'm not.' Luke leaned back in his chair and levelled an uncompromising stare. 'The messenger you sent to London shortly after my arrival this morning will not be returning with a decision in your favour. Rowland's solicitor heard of your petition and, knowing my whereabouts, as you all did, he submitted an affidavit that I was being informed of Rowland's death, since no one in my family had chosen to do that.

He also submitted my petition to accept the guardianship granted to me in Rowland's will.'

The grin on Percy's face was unexpected, but not the narrowing of his eyes, which turned them into little more than slits. 'You've been gone a long time, little brother. I, on the other hand, have been here, maintaining friendships. I know what was submitted, and when it was submitted, and can confidently assure you that it will make no difference.'

'I beg to differ,' Luke said, even though his brother was right in that he'd been here the entire time, maintaining friendships with clearly unsavoury characters, somehow connected to the courts. 'I was named in Rowland's will, and his choice of guardian holds precedence.'

Percy stood and walked to the credenza to refill his glass. After replacing the top of the decanter, he took a drink, before turning about. 'Not when there is proof that the appointed guardian is only interested in that role in order to gain access to the wards' property and money.'

Someone was seeking to gain assets, but it wasn't him. 'Lies are not proof.'

With one of his signature smug smirks in place, Percy elongated the time it took him to take a drink of his brandy. 'I always knew your letters were full of fabrication, but they're going to prove rather useful now.' Percy had a distinct hint of amusement in his eyes as he set his glass down.

Luke's spine stiffened. He wasn't amused whatsoever. 'You've taken up forgery, have you? We both know I never wrote to you.'

'Of course, you didn't.' Percy returned to his chair, sat and folded his hands on his stomach. 'You wrote to

Rowland. Continuously. Sharing all your adventures. Tell me, do you believe the courts will grant guardianship, will or no will, to a man who spent the last eight years gambling on riverboats and in saloons? Spent months searching for gold? Befriended train robbers, swam in rivers with dance hall gals? Oh, and let's not forget, rustled cattle and then bought the ranch from the widow whose husband *died* fending off rustlers!'

'Congratulations, you have misconstrued every event I wrote about.' Luke was fighting to control his breathing, and anger. Percy had twisted everything. However, the letters he'd written to Rowland were long, and Percy clearly had them in his possession. If he chose to only turn over small snippets, and not the entire letters, readers could get the wrong impression. 'Even with your misinterpretations, none of that is proof that I'm looking to gain access to anything.'

Percy shrugged. 'What other reason could there be? You haven't lived here for eight years, have no permanent residence in which to raise the girls. Or did you plan to take them to America? To a home where the previous owner left because it was too dangerous? I don't believe the courts would favour that. Their father was a duke. An English duke. This is where the girls need to live. In a country where they'll receive all the benefits of being a duke's daughter, not in some godforsaken country not fit for wild animals.'

Luke's back teeth clenched together so tightly his jaw stung. Unfortunately, his brother's assumption of the court's possible favour was too accurate. This fight had just started and he had to pace himself. He had an ace in the hole, and was going to keep it there. He had some cleaning up to do before it came time to show his full hand.

'Reason?' he asked. 'Because I care what happens to my nieces. And you're wrong, I do have a permanent residence. Right here.' He stood. 'You didn't inherit this house with the duchy. It was split three ways when our father died, and remains that way. Fern and Ivy have a third, I have a third and you have a third.'

Percy lifted his chin, as if unaffected. But the way he wrung his hands together said differently.

'I was wrong earlier, when I said our parents would be disappointed to see how you're behaving. They would have been ashamed. Completely ashamed of you. You were always selfish, but the way you've treated Rowland's daughters and Miss Blaydon goes beyond that. It's malicious, and I don't know how you can live with yourself.' Without waiting for a response, Luke rose and left the room knowing one thing. He had to get to London.

Normally, with a need so urgent, he'd have saddled up and ridden all night. He'd done that before, but he couldn't do so right now. Not without telling Aislinn.

Scanning each and every shadowed corner, for he wouldn't put it past Percy to have staff assigned to watch his every move, Luke made his way straight to the nursery.

The room was silent. There wasn't even the tick of a clock hand. Heavy curtains covered whatever moonlight might have assisted him in making his way through the sitting area to the smaller of the two bedrooms.

Moonlight filtered into that room due to the curtains being left open, and he imagined that had been done on purpose, so the rising sun would wake her.

As he paused in the doorway, he felt a softening inside him. With the day she'd had, she'd probably fallen asleep the minute her head had hit the pillow. He could wait until morning to tell her, probably should, but wanted to be on his way to London before sunup.

She was sleeping on her side, with her hands tucked up beneath the pillow, and her long, dark hair, plaited in a single braid, was curled around her neck, disappearing beneath the covers. His breath momentarily caught in his throat at the thought that she was as lovely asleep as she was awake.

A pit formed deep in his stomach. He'd just called Percy selfish, yet wasn't he also being selfish by pulling her so deep into this mess? By playing on the love she had for Fern and Ivy?

He knew he was, and that flustered him. He'd always fought his own battles, but he needed her for this one. He knew nothing about taking care of children. Granted, he could hire another governess, but she had history with Fern and Ivy, and the girls loved her as much as she loved them. He could see why.

She was very likeable. He'd discovered that within minutes this morning. Around the same time he'd figured out that she could be a great help to him. Would he have been so quick to come to that conclusion if she'd been someone else? Someone older, not as attractive?

Of course, he would have. He was doing all of this for the girls, not for himself. Anything he did for himself was back in Montana, not here. This was all just a damn mess, that's what it was.

He'd been truthful when he told her that he didn't know what the plan was, still didn't, but would make sure that she was compensated for all her help and for all she'd been through with Percy.

Luke moved closer to the side of the bed and quietly cleared his throat, hoping that would wake her.

She didn't so much as twitch.

'Aislinn,' he said quietly.

Still no movement.

'Aislinn,' he repeated, this time while softly touching her shoulder.

She jolted upright so fast he stepped backwards, half expecting her to leap off the bed.

'What? The girls?' she asked, throwing the blankets off her legs.

'The girls are fine,' he said, holding both hands upright, as if she was pointing a gun at him. 'It's just me, Luke.' He then lowered his hands and stepped forward, pulling the blankets back over her lower legs, which were bare because her gown was bunched up around her thighs. The sight of her silky, bare skin was too enjoyable. And something he shouldn't be looking at. 'I—I need to talk to you.'

She blinked quickly, as if getting rid of the haze of sleep. Her eyes widened as full recognition hit, and she quickly grabbed the blankets, pulling them upwards.

Nodding, her fingers curled tighter around the covers, as she tugged them all the way up over the nightdress that was buttoned to her chin.

She looked bewildered and utterly frightened. Rightfully so. She'd probably never had a man standing beside her bed before.

He wasn't in the habit of being in a woman's bedroom, and the reality of that sent a shiver up his spine. If he could enter her room this easily, anyone could. Which meant he couldn't just leave them here. Not without him. Not without his protection.

She was still staring at him wide-eyed.

He attempted to pull his thoughts back in line. 'I need to go to London,' he said. 'Cut them off at the pass.'

'Cut who, where?'

He shook his head, not meaning to say his thoughts aloud. 'Sorry. It appears that Percy has someone inside the court, trying to influence the decision on guardianship. I need to rectify that immediately.'

She sat up straighter. 'How?'

'I'm not sure, but I need to go to London to do it. I know that much.'

'When?'

'Right away.' It rankled him clear to his core to know that Percy was using the letters he'd sent to Rowland against him, even though he knew his brother. Percy would use any tactics to get his way. He always had. 'I'm not sure what information they have, but I'm convinced Percy is using everything that I mailed to Rowland over the years, using bits and pieces of the letters to make it sound like I'm interested in gaining access to the untitled assets Rowland willed to the girls.'

'He destroyed everything that you sent.' She shook her head. 'He had staff remove it all from the shelves in the study.'

The items he'd sent over the years hadn't been of great value, just things he'd thought Rowland would like to see. At the moment, he couldn't remember all that he'd sent, nor what he'd said in his letters, but knew full well that Percy would use anything he could against him. 'I'm sure he has the letters.'

'He might,' she said quietly. 'I honestly don't know

where Rowland kept your letters, but I do know that he cherished them.'

The pain that struck was sharp enough to take his breath away. He'd cherished the letters Rowland had sent to him, too. As much as he hadn't wanted to be here, he'd looked forward to hearing from Rowland about his life at Havenbrook. 'It shouldn't be this way,' he said. 'Rowland—' He shook his head, unable to say more.

She released the blanket and softly touched his arm. 'I know,' she said.

He shouldn't be able to feel the warmth of her fingers through the sleeves of his coat and shirt, but he did. The sensation spread up his arm. The sort of comforting warmth that he hadn't felt in a long time. 'I'm not saying it should have been Percy instead. I wouldn't wish that on either of my brothers.' He wouldn't admit that to just anyone, but it was the honest truth.

'I know,' she said. 'It just seems unfair.'

'Yes, it does.' He huffed out a breath. 'Everything about this is wrong. Percy knows what Rowland wanted, but he can't stomach the idea of me besting him in any way. Never could. Even though I was never competing with him. I knew my place. There *wasn't* a competition.'

'Yes, there was,' she whispered.

'No, there wasn't. That's why I wanted something different. something that fit me. I found that.'

'In America?'

'Yup. I have everything I need there. Everything I'll ever need.' He shook his head, questioning why he was doing telling her all of this. In her bedroom in the middle of the night. As his sense returned, he said, 'Anyway, I can't leave you and the girls here alone. I'll need you to come to London with me.'

'All right. When do we leave?'

Should he be surprised that she agreed so quickly? Or just be thankful? He went with the latter, because he'd already done enough overthinking. 'First thing in the morning.'

'We'll be ready.'

Even though she'd had a terrible time falling back to sleep after Luke left her room, Aislinn kept her promise. By the time the sun was rising, she ushered the girls downstairs, fed, dressed, and toting items to keep them occupied during the long journey. Of course, there had been a ruckus concerning their leaving, but Luke had been there, and planted himself in front of the Duke. Today, he was dressed in his American clothes and looked more formidable than ever.

She had a hard time meeting his gaze, because even with all the uproar caused by their leaving, her mind kept going back to him in her bedroom last night. The impropriety would increase the already out of control friction between him and Percy, if his brother knew.

Someone in the household had alerted Percy and Hazel of their leaving, because both of them had arrived downstairs hastily dressed. The Duchess hadn't even taken the time to have her hair pinned up.

The Duchess had tried to block Aislinn's way to the door, but Luke had put an arm out, stopping Hazel from getting too close. Aislinn's first instinct had been to bow her head and curtsey, but knowing she had to become more assertive, she'd kept her chin up, her knees stiff and her spine straight.

Hazel had turned beet red, and Aislinn probably should have considered what might have happened if

Luke hadn't been there. Instead, at his nod, she merely ushered the girls out the door, as Percy stepped in front of Hazel, so he and Luke were standing nose to nose. Actually, it was toe-to-toe, because the Duke's nose only came up to Luke's chin. He was taller and broader than his brother by a long way.

Yesterday, he'd been standing on the top step, rather than the porch, when the two brothers had faced each other. Heavens, that seemed like eons ago, but truly less than twenty-four hours had passed.

With her heart racing as fast as it had been last night, when she'd woken to see him standing at the side of her bed, she helped Fern and Ivy into the waiting carriage.

She'd seen Luke's eyes a moment ago. They'd been as cold as ice, as sharp as shards of glass. The harshness in them made her shiver, and the severe set of his lips had been completely void of his usually permanent grin. She certainly didn't want the girls exposed to whatever might be happening inside the house.

If the row ensuing between the brothers came to fisticuffs, she was sure of who would win, and just as sure that there would be repercussions.

There were sure to be consequences for how she'd disrespected the Duchess, too, so she was glad they were leaving. Though she knew that wouldn't solve the issues. Percy and Hazel were sure to be even madder when they returned with Luke having secured guardianship of the girls. He was set on that happening, and from what she knew of him, he didn't quit until he achieved whatever goal he'd set.

Not wanting the girls to be alarmed, Aislinn leaned across the open space to where they both sat, pulling the hems of their dresses down and settling the bag of toys between them. 'There, now you'll have plenty of room to read your books and—'

Startled by Luke's voice telling the driver to leave, she leaned back in her seat and scooted over as he climbed in and shut the door.

'You will be riding with us in here?' she asked, before taking the time to think about it. If she'd thought about that possibility, she'd have seated herself between the girls.

Sitting down next to her, he winked at the girls. 'I don't plan on walking.'

Normally when they travelled to London, the old Duke had ridden his horse, and she and the girls had ridden in the carriage with the Duchess. On the rare occasion when the old Duke rode with the Duchess in the carriage, Aislinn had travelled in a second coach with the other servants. The girls had ridden with their parents, but she'd seen to her charges upon every stop.

'Old Bones would never make this trip,' he said.

Nodding, she tucked the material of her skirt behind her knees, giving him more room. Riding with him in a carriage had to be improper, even with the girls and the driver. Yet, there were no other options. Furthermore, it probably wasn't as improper as him being in her bedroom in the middle of the night. She'd been mortified upon seeing him, wearing nothing but her nightgown, but that had all disappeared when she'd seen the pain on his face as he spoke of Rowland. Then, her heart had ached for him.

He patted her arm. 'I've plenty of room.' Then, addressing the girls, he asked, 'Who wants to guess what I have?'

'Me!' Fern exclaimed.

'Me, too!' Ivy followed.

'Well, then, I will give each of you a clue.' He looked at Ivy first. 'They are not invisible.' Shifting to Fern, he said, 'You haven't had them in ages.'

'Biscuits!' Fern shouted.

'With sweet icing!' Ivy added.

He produced a basket, as if out of thin air. Aislinn certainly hadn't seen it in the carriage when they'd climbed in, nor in his hand when he'd entered. Then again, she hadn't been of a mind to be looking for a basket, either.

Upon pulling back the cloth covering the basket, revealing it was full of biscuits, he looked at her, one brow raised in silent question.

She nodded, for if she didn't, there could have been a mutiny and she'd be walking, like she had been at this time yesterday. The idea of that, a mutiny, or maybe the delighted squeals coming from Fern and Ivy, made her smile.

Once the girls had each taken a biscuit, he held the basket out to her. It was such a treat for the girls, she should decline, but the basket was filled to the top, so she indulged and took one. She too had missed the desserts and sweets that used to be provided with each meal.

He took two from the basket, and bit into one. 'Mmm… Mmm… I sure have missed these.'

'Me, too,' Fern said.

'And me,' came from Ivy.

'Do they not have biscuits in America?' Aislinn asked, in an attempt to keep her mind from focusing on how sitting next to him was making butterflies flutter in her stomach.

'Yes and no.'

He held the basket out for the girls to each take another one, which they did, after her silent approval.

'What we refer to as biscuits here, they call cookies.' He took another one from the basket. 'What they declare biscuits are like our crumpets, but lighter and fluffier. They are quite delicious.'

He held the basket in her direction.

She shook her head. 'No, thank you.'

He set the basket down on the seat between them. The girls, very satisfied with the treat they'd received, turned their attention to their canvas bags filled with books and toys.

Looking at the twins with a gentle grin on his face, he asked, 'Do you ever wonder what they think when they look at each other and see the exact thing that they see when looking in the mirror?'

'No,' she replied. 'Because I see them so differently and believe they see the differences, too.'

He nodded. 'They are different. I'm sure I'll see more differences in time. I was in Colorado when I got Rowland's letter announcing their birth. He said Leslie knew the differences between them right away, but that it had taken him a few days, because he'd still been getting over the shock of having two babies.' He glanced at her. 'I suppose you know that Fern was our mother's name, and Ivy was Leslie's mother's name.'

'I do,' she said.

'It's sad that all four of them, our parents and Leslie's, died before meeting them.'

'It is,' she replied. Then, because it had been on her mind since last night, she asked, 'What from your letters do you think they could use to jeopardise your claim for guardianship?'

'Did you read them?' he asked.

'No. I was present when the old Duke read them to the girls.' Others had been present when they'd been read, too. If not in the room, they'd stood outside the doorway, listening, for all of the staff had loved his letters. He had a way with words and had written the letters in such a way that they sounded like stories from a book that kept her holding her breath until the very end.

'Rowland,' he said quietly. 'When it's just me and you, let's forget all titles.'

He was doing so much to help the girls, and her, that she easily agreed, 'All right.'

'You might recall that my letters were long, and cheeky in nature,' he said. 'For instance, I remember one where I wrote *"your youngest brother has become a cattle rustler".*'

She nodded, clearly recalling how that first line had held everyone's attention, and it hadn't been until later in the letter that they'd learned more details. 'That was the same letter where you wrote about buying your ranch.'

'Yes. But I didn't rustle any cattle. I explained later in the letter how Raf and I had come upon cattle rustlers and steered clear, until a few miles later, when we came upon a woman burying her husband, who the rustlers had just killed. We helped her, then we went and got the cattle back for her and turned the rustlers in to the law. She had two children. Small children. A boy and a girl. We stayed on, helped her for a time, but she was set on moving back to Missouri, where she had family. I bought the ranch and cattle from her, at a fair price. More than what she was asking, and more than she would have got from anyone else, because I wanted it to be fair, and to make sure that she and the children had enough to start over. All of that was on another page. If someone doesn't see the whole letter, they'll think I confessed to being a cattle rustler. End of story.'

'But that's not the end of the story,' she whispered, fully understanding how someone only reading the first page could think poorly of him.

'Precisely why I need to get to London and find out who inside the courts Percy has on his side.'

'What else is he saying?'

'I don't know, but I'm guessing that he's turned around every event I wrote about, and to be honest, I don't even remember everything I wrote in the past eight years.'

She wanted to say that she did, but that wouldn't be true, because he'd been gone for four years before she'd been employed by the Duke and Duchess. What she did remember, did know, was that those letters should prove what a good man he was, not the opposite. His bravery had been apparent in his letters. At one time, she had assumed that some tales had been exaggerated, but no longer believed that. The same was true of his handsomeness. 'How are you going to find out who is spreading the rumours?'

'I'm going to start with Mr Watson, Rowland's solicitor, and now mine. I trust him. I doubt that he knows what's happening, but hopefully he can find out if there is an infiltrator in the courts.'

'Will we be staying at the London home?' That was what she'd assumed, but perhaps shouldn't have, because Percy may have said they couldn't stay there.

'Yes. That was Rowland's house, and now it's theirs.' He nodded to the girls. 'My father was still alive when Percy and Hazel got married, and he let them live in the town house that belonged to the duchy. Rowland bought his own house, knowing he'd need a place to live when the time came for him to sit in the House of Lords, and that Leslie wouldn't want to live with Hazel.'

'She wouldn't?' The old Duchess had never said an unkind word about Hazel. She'd always been welcoming when her husband's family had come to stay at Havenbrook.

He shook his head. 'No one blamed her, either. Percy and Hazel have always been...well, Percy and Hazel. But I don't remember them being this nasty.'

He looked at her, and she shrugged, shaking her head. 'I only saw them a few times prior to Rowland and Leslie's deaths.'

Letting out a sigh, he shrugged. 'Even though he tried to stop us this morning, stop me from taking you and the girls to London, Percy knows I'm in the right. Rowland's will appointed me guardian, and he has to abide by that until—*if*—the courts say differently. Which they won't. I'll make sure of that.'

Thinking of the plan she'd set for herself, of what she had to do in order to help him, and knowing she had much to learn, she asked, 'Did you know the old—Leslie well?'

He nodded. 'I don't remember not knowing her. Her father and mine were good friends. It wasn't an official arrangement, but everyone knew that Rowland and Leslie would get married one day. He was eight years older than me, and my best friend. I waited for him to come home during school breaks. I remember one time, when I was seven or so, Leslie was at Havenbrook, waiting for him to come home, too. I was mad, because I thought Rowland would spend all of his time with her. I was wrong. She was the one to make sure to include me, even when I'm sure they'd rather not have had me tag along.'

Aislinn believed that. It sounded like the old Duchess—she'd always spoken very highly of Luke.

'Percy tried to nose his way in between them for years,' Luke said. 'When he couldn't do it, he paired up with Hazel, and the two of them made sure they got married before Rowland and Leslie.' Luke shook his head. 'He'd been boastfully proud of being the first one married, and our mother said that we needed to let him have his time, because as the middle son, he rarely got that. Rowland was the oldest, and I'm the youngest, and that made Percy feel left out.'

In Aislinn's mind, feeling left out was no reason to behave the way she'd seen Percy behave. It still shamed her that she hadn't done more to protect her charges. That would never happen again.

'Do you remember much about the letters Rowland read?' Luke asked.

'Yes, they were very interesting,' she replied.

He was frowning slightly, as if contemplating something thoroughly. 'You said Claire, I believe was her name, the other nanny at one time, is still living at the London house?'

'Yes, she is.'

He was rubbing his chin and nodding. 'Good, then she will be able to take care of Fern and Ivy while you go with me.'

Her nerves tingled. 'Go where?'

'To see the solicitor.' He leaned sideways, closer to her, until his upper arm bumped her shoulder gently. 'We're partners, remember?'

Chapter Six

Despite stopping at roadside inns to eat and stretch their legs, Luke was stiff and his rump numb by the time they finally arrived in London. He hadn't ridden that long in a carriage since he was a youngster. However, other than the stiffness, he had to admit it hadn't been all that bad. He could now tell Fern and Ivy apart without even looking for the little mole on Ivy's face, and Aislinn, well… He knew one thing. If he'd had a governess like her, he might have been better behaved. The feeling of being rewarded with one of her smiles was beyond comprehension. Even at his current age.

Night had fallen some time ago. The streets were quiet, the houses dark. He hadn't sent a messenger ahead for the house to be prepared for them. Hadn't even thought about it, until Aislinn had questioned if he had done so a short time ago.

He'd been on his own for so long, that simply showing up and leaving whenever he chose had become a habit. One he might have to break.

Strike that.

It's one he *would* have to break.

He'd never been responsible for anyone other than himself, but he was now, and that was not something he would fail at, in any way.

There were probably several other habits that he'd need to break. He just wasn't sure what they were right now. Looking at Aislinn, who was sitting across from him, with a sleeping child on each side using her lap as a pillow, he said, 'I'm going to need your help.'

She nodded, waited for him to say more. So far, she was turning out to be a good partner. The best looking one he'd ever had, that was for sure, and she sure knew how to take care of children. He'd never seen more well-behaved youngsters than Fern and Ivy. All Aislinn had to do was smile and nod, or shake her head, still always with a smile, and they complied. Maybe that's how it was with girls, because he knew for certain he hadn't been that well behaved as a boy.

'I haven't been here in eight years,' he said, 'have lived a very different life. You'll need to remind me—tell me—things I need to do at times. Like send a messenger ahead so the servants are prepared for our arrival.'

The moonlight shining in through the open windows gave her face a golden glow as she smiled. 'I can do that.'

He gave her a grin. 'Up for the challenge, are you?'

'Yes, I am.'

There was that smile again, and it sent his heart careening sideways a bit. She was different today, more confident. Then again, being away from Havenbrook was sure to make her feel better. He was glad about that. 'Good. I will remember—strike that—I will *try* to remember some things.'

Tilting her head slightly to one side, she asked, 'I've heard you say strike that before. Why?'

'It comes from a tutor I had years ago. He'd make me read what I'd written aloud, and when there was something wrong, or that he didn't like, he'd say strike that. Then make me write something in its place. It just stuck with me.' Mr Westerly had always reminded him of a wise old owl, with his glasses perched low on his nose and his forehead lined with wrinkles. His 'strike that' remarks had often referred to things that might have been false. He'd say, if it can't be proven, don't write it.

Luke grinned. That had stuck with him, too, and he was glad, because he'd used that advice when writing to Rowland. Everything in his letters had been true.

The coach rolled to a stop, and he leaned over and opened the door. 'Wait here. I'll go to the house, announce our arrival. You said the butler's name is Gabriel Houghton?'

'Yes. His wife works here, too. Her name is Mary Ann. Besides Claire, and her husband, John, there are also a couple of maids and a cook.'

'Thanks. I'll be back shortly. The driver will remain with the coach, so don't fear.'

'We'll be fine,' she said.

With a nod, he climbed out and, after speaking with Benjamin, his personal attendant, now driver, because Percy had insisted that the staff at Havenbrook were all under his employ, and that was a battle he'd chosen to let his brother think he'd won, Luke made his way to the front door. It was opened on the second knock, by a man wearing a floor-length nightshirt, pointed sleeping hat, and holding a lighted lamp before his face.

'I apologise for the lateness of the hour,' Luke said, while avoiding the blaze of the flame blinding him. 'I presume you are Gabriel Houghton.'

Frowning, the man gave a nod. 'I am.'

'I'm the late Duke of Havenbrook's younger brother, Luke Carlisle.'

The man's eyes nearly popped out of his head, and he lowered the lamp. 'Oh—' With a slight bow, he said, 'Welcome, my lord, welcome. I do notice a strong resemblance. Forgive me, sir, my apologies.'

'Nothing to forgive on your part,' Luke said. 'I have Aislinn—Miss Blaydon, and Fern and Ivy in the carriage. We'll be staying here for a time.'

'Oh, that is wonderful, my lord,' Gabriel said, genuinely enthusiastic. 'Truly wonderful. The entire house will be very happy to have them here, and yourself. I'll alert the staff immediately, and your rooms will be ready promptly. Will you be requiring a meal be served before retiring?'

'No, thank you, we ate along the way,' Luke replied.

'Did you cook it over a campfire?' a voice asked.

Luke turned towards a darkened hallway, watching as a somewhat burly man with a mass of blond hair stepped into the foyer.

'This is—' the butler started, but the other man cut him off.

'I know who it is, and I know he's been cooking over a campfire since he was about five.' The man, with a face that looked boyish in comparison to his size, walked closer. 'I know, because I was with him most of the time.'

Recognition hit full force and Luke threw his head back with laughter. 'Doolittle Dobbs! What are you doing here?' Doo, as he'd been known back then, had been his first playmate. He'd lived on one of the farms with his grandparents and mother, who had provided extra help at the house when needed. Luke had been sorely disappointed when, upon a break from boarding school one year, he'd learned Doo's mother had remarried and they'd moved to London.

'I am—was—your brother, the Duke's, chef.' Doo gave his hand a hard shake. 'So sorry about that. We all miss the Duke and Duchess.'

'Thank you,' Luke said, giving Doo a slap of friendship on the shoulder. 'It was a great loss.'

Doo nodded, then glanced at the door. 'I'll go warm up some milk for the little misses. It'll help them fall back to sleep after being roused.'

'Thanks,' Luke said. 'I'll go get them, and Doo, it's great seeing you.' He wondered why Rowland hadn't told him about Doo working here. Then again, he might have mentioned it in a letter, and he'd forgotten. His brother had mentioned people he'd known regularly.

Not wanting to leave Aislinn waiting too long, he hurried back outside.

He told Benjamin to see that the luggage was carried inside, and then take the carriage around to the carriage house and see that the horses were taken care of.

The girls were awake and wearing cute little capes over their dresses as they climbed out of the carriage. Both yawned and rubbed at their eyes. He picked Ivy up first, settling her in one arm, then lifted Fern with the other. 'Mr Dobbs is making you some warm milk.'

They each nodded, but leaned their heads on his shoulders as if too tired to do more. They were. It had been a long day. 'The rooms are being prepared,' he told Aislinn. 'It shouldn't take long.'

With Aislinn directing, because he'd only been to the house a handful of times, he carried Fern and Ivy into the kitchen, where Doo already had a fire going in the cook stove.

'Hello, Miss Blaydon,' Doo greeted cheerily.

'Hello, Mr Dobbs,' she replied. 'I hope all is well here.'

It was no surprise for the two to know each other, but an odd sensation tickled Luke's spine at the way Doo looked at Aislinn. Should Luke be wondering if there was something between her and the cook? He wasn't one to jump to conclusions, nor was he one to have a jealous streak. Still, something wasn't settling well within him. Aislinn was a very pretty woman, and the first nanny had fallen in love with the stableman here. He didn't want to believe he was jealous of anyone, but that's how it felt.

'We've all been missing the Duke and Duchess.' Doo set a pot on the stove. 'More and more.'

The large wooden worktable stood between Doo and Aislinn, and Luke glanced back and forth between them. The hairs on the back of his neck were popping up into standing positions. He had the distinct impression that something was being left unsaid.

'It's certainly been an adjustment,' Aislinn said.

'That it has, miss,' Doo replied.

A brown-haired woman, with a beaming smile on her face, hurried into the room. 'For a moment I thought I was dreaming!' she exclaimed, hurrying towards Aislinn. Stopping suddenly when she saw him holding the girls, she bowed her head. 'Forgive me, my lord.'

He met Aislinn's gaze, which silently told him not to worry about the curtsey or the address. She was right, and he knew who the newcomer must be. 'Hello, Mrs Moore,' he said. 'Aislinn's told me about you.'

Claire's cheeks pinkened as she nodded, then glanced at Aislinn and quietly said, 'The nursery is ready.'

Aislinn stepped forward, holding out her arms. 'We will take the girls upstairs.'

'I'll have the milk brought up as soon as it's warm,' Doo said.

Luke handed Fern to Aislinn, and Ivy to Claire, then waited until they were gone from the room and the door was closed before he asked Doo, 'What wasn't being said between you and Aislinn?' He'd never been one to beat around the bush, and wasn't going to start now. If the two of them were in love, he needed to know.

Doo remained silent the entire time he poured milk into the pot and put the jar back in the icebox. Then he took a wooden spoon out of a drawer and walked back to the stove. 'Do you want me to answer that as a friend, or as an employee?'

Luke was about to say that he wasn't Doo's employer, but realised that he was, for now anyway, and would continue to be once the guardianship was settled. His life had changed and he would have to get used to that. In some ways. 'As a friend,' he replied.

Doo nodded. 'As your friend, I'll first say, I have no intentions towards Aislinn, other than being worried about her and those little girls. As her friend, I'll say, you better be good to her.'

He wasn't sure if he should be relieved or worried. 'I have every intention of being good to her.'

Doo nodded in acceptance and continued to stir the milk. 'Your brother has left this place in dire straits.'

Luke didn't believe that. 'Rowland would never—'

'Not that brother,' Doo said. 'The late Duke was an

excellent employer. It's the other one who has left us paying for everything out of our wages.'

Luke didn't hold back the curse that struck. 'Your wages,' he said, not in question, just in disgust.

'Yes, which he also cut in half,' Doo said. 'In my opinion, he was hoping we'd abandon the place before you showed up.'

Percy had struck again. Luke was really getting tired of being ambushed. He ran a hand through his hair. 'I need to know everything.'

'And I don't mind being the one to tell you.' Doo pointed towards a chair. 'You want warm milk or something stronger?'

'Stronger,' Luke replied.

'I truly thought I was dreaming when John said you and the girls were here.' Claire rubbed Ivy's back and planted a kiss upon her head. 'I'm so happy to see all of you. It is like a dream come true. We've all been so worried about you and the girls being at Havenbrook with Hazel.'

'Things have been different,' Aislinn admitted as they started walking up the stairway to the second floor, 'but we are all fine. We are happy to be here, too.'

'Doo was certain that Mr Carlisle would come home,' Claire said. 'They were friends as young children.'

'I wasn't aware of that,' Aislinn said.

'He is just as I imagined,' Claire whispered. 'Just as others described in looks. Very handsome.'

Aislinn took a deep breath in an attempt to keep her heart in check. It had been out of control all day, even after she'd switched seats, so she sat across from him instead of beside him. Life was a bit out of control right now, with all the changes and worries about how things would eventually turn out, but that wasn't the only reason she felt so out of sorts. It was him. You would think she would be getting used to him. Yet, the more she got to know him, the more time she spent in his company, the more the butterflies in her stomach increased and her pulse thudded harder beneath her skin.

Claire was looking at her with more than curiosity. It was not only logical to agree, it was the truth. Aislinn nodded. 'He is.'

'Did he return because of the letter Doo wrote to him?' Claire asked, as she opened the door to the nursery.

Lamps had been lit and Aislinn was grateful that the room looked just as it had the last time they'd been here. Carrying Fern to one of the two beds, she said, 'Luke didn't mention a letter from Doo. Rowland's solicitor wrote to him. His family had not informed him of what had happened.'

'By family, you mean Percy. That's exactly what Doo assumed, and why he sent a letter off last month. He said Luke would come home as soon as he heard about his brother.' Claire set Ivy on the bed and began to undress her. 'When did he arrive?'

'Yesterday morning.' Setting aside Fern's dress, Aislinn reached for the nightdress that had been laid out on the bed. The girls were both so drowsy, they wouldn't need any warm milk to aid them in falling back to sleep.

'I can imagine that Percy wasn't happy to see him,' Clair said while putting on Ivy's night dress.

'No, he was not. He and Hazel are fighting Luke for guardianship.'

'I'm not surprised.' Claire said. 'Considering everything else they've done. It appears as if their only goal is to make everyone's life miserable.'

'They are certainly doing that.' Aislinn pulled back the covers, laid Fern down on the bed and pulled the blankets over her, before giving her cheek a soft kiss.

Claire did the same with Ivy, then they switched places to repeat the process, much like they had done when the girls were infants.

They each collected the discarded clothing, and as they stepped away from the beds, Claire shook her head. 'Poor little poppets. It still just breaks my heart that they lost both their mama and papa.'

'I know.' Aislinn stared at the girls, who had each turned onto their sides and were already slumbering. 'I've tried to explain, but it's so difficult. They just don't understand, and talk as if their parents will return someday.'

'It's hard for all of us to understand,' Claire said, walking towards the wardrobe. 'And it's inconceivable that their very own uncle is making everything so much worse.'

Aislinn inspected Fern's dress as she crossed the room, checking for smears or marks that would become stains if she didn't see to them immediately. 'I'm glad to see that things here are normal.'

'They might look normal, but they aren't.' Claire hung up Ivy's dress and cape and then walked back towards the beds to collect the socks and shoes. 'Staff from Percy's other home were here, trying to take things, furniture and such, but Doo and Gabe wouldn't let them. Doo insisted that everything here stayed until Luke arrived. He knew that Rowland had willed everything outside of the duchy to Luke.'

'He could have been fired,' Aislinn said, worried for Doo. The cook had been here before she arrived four years ago, and though his size could be intimidating, he'd always been very kind. She'd sensed something different about him when he'd greeted her downstairs, and now understood why. Things here were as bad as they'd been at Havenbrook.

'Doo said that Percy couldn't fire any of us,' Claire said. 'That only Luke could do that, and he told the man who was here this morning that Luke was also the only person who could close this house down. That none of us would leave until we heard directly from him.'

Aislinn frowned, taking in what Claire had said. 'This morning? What man?'

'He said he was from the courts, and would return tomorrow with an official order from a judge for us to shut the house down and vacate the property.'

Aislinn had several questions, but was prevented from asking any of them by a knock on the door. Being closer to the door, she crossed the room and pulled it open.

'I thought I'd bring this up myself, tell the girls good night,' Luke said, carrying a tray that held two small glasses of milk as he stepped into the room.

Rather than going crazy, this time Aislinn's heart melted a bit. He was so caring towards the girls. Throughout the day, he'd read to them, told them stories, and even played a game of tag when they'd stopped to stretch their legs. Had they been awake, they would have loved the opportunity to say good night to him. 'They are already asleep,' she said, feeling his disappointment. 'I don't believe they fully awakened upon arrival.'

'I'm sure they didn't,' he answered. 'It was a long day for them. A long ride.' He glanced towards Claire and gave her a nod, before turning back to her. 'In that case, could we talk for a moment?'

'Of course.' She wanted to tell him what Claire had just told her.

'Excuse me, my lord,' Claire said, approaching with her hands held out. 'I will return that to the kitchen.'

Luke handed her the tray. 'Thank you, Claire.'

Claire left and Luke closed the door behind her. 'I'm sorry. I know it's late, but this won't take long.'

'It's perfectly fine.' Aislinn wasn't sure where to start with all she'd learned.

'Did Percy cut your wage in half?'

Unprepared for this question, because her mind had been so full of things to tell him, she nodded.

'By God!' he hissed quietly. 'He's going to ruin our family's name with his greed and manipulations.' Pacing the floor in front of her, he asked, 'Have you been paid any wages in the past three months?'

A fleeting thought of justifying herself for not objecting to the lack of pay formed, but she chose to simply answer, 'No.'

'Did everyone at Havenbrook have their wages cut?' he asked. 'Have they not been paid?'

'I don't know. I was told if I discussed it with anyone, told anyone, I would be fired. I can only assume it was the same for others. But I need to tell you that a man came here this morning, to this house, ordering that the place be closed down and that everyone vacate the property. He's to return tomorrow morning.'

'I know. Doo told me. Told me a whole lot more than that. No one will need to vacate.' He shook his head.

'No one has been paid their wages since Rowland died. The staff here are paying for everything, food, lamp oil, feed for the horses, with their own money. Percy wanted them all to quit, to be gone by the time I arrived, including you, so I would have to start from scratch in taking care of the girls.'

She covered her mouth to hold in a gasp, because it made perfect sense. Percy and Hazel knew she would never leave the girls willingly. Not for lack of payment or anything else. The girls were the only family she'd truly known, and she wouldn't give that up. Not again.

This was all so wrong. The old Duke and Duchess would have been appalled to know what was happening.

'We have a lot to do tomorrow,' Luke said. 'We'll need to get started early. Can you be ready by eight?'

Forcing herself not to tremble was practically impossible, because she was sure she couldn't be of any help to him. She was simply the governess, and he needed far more than she could give. Fear of failing him and the girls made her eyes burn. Holding her breath, she nodded. 'Of course.'

His smile was tender, as was the way he took a hold of her hand, squeezing it. 'I know I'm asking a lot of you.'

She squeezed her eyes closed to hold the stinging from turning into tears. If only there was something, something real and tangible, that she could do to really help him.

Before she realised what was happening, Luke wrapped his arm around her, holding her in a tight hug. On their own, her arms wrapped around his waist, as if hugging him was completely natural. It felt that way, too. His strong hold, his firm, solid body pressed up against hers, felt right and eased the fear that had been threatening to consume her.

'We can do this,' he whispered.

She nodded, not because she was convinced, but because he gave her hope.

It wasn't until he released her that it dawned on her just how inappropriate it was for her to hug him. Or him her. That was also when she realised the chaos happening inside her. Not only was her heart thudding erratically, other parts of her were tingling and swirling with warmth. Private parts.

She stepped backwards and did her best not to meet his gaze, without it looking like she was avoiding his eyes.

He touched her arm, gave it a slight pat. 'Get some rest, Aislinn. I'll see you in the morning.'

'Good night.'

He closed the door and her knees gave out. She sank down on the closest chair. What was happening to her? She was woefully unsophisticated and had no experience with men, especially not one so strong and formidable. Yet, she knew her body's reaction right now had nothing to do with the girls. If he was someone different, would she be so willing to help? So committed to helping him, even though she had no idea what the final outcome would be? She could do all of this and never see the girls again if he chose to take them to America.

All in all, she could be working towards the one thing she didn't want to happen—to have the girls taken away from her.

Was she merely fooling herself? She was from a very different class of life than him, and the girls, and nothing would ever change that. Nothing would ever make them a true family.

Chapter Seven

The girls were still sleeping in the room connected to hers when Aislinn, fully dressed in one of her governess dresses, put the final pin in her hair, securing it into a tight bun at the back of her head. There were so many thoughts in her mind, she didn't know which one to focus on. But she did know that none of them would ease the nervousness encompassing her.

Thinking about Luke reminded her that she should never have hugged him. No matter how much she liked him, she knew her position in life and needed that role to remain unblemished for the sake of the girls.

Thoughts of Fern and Ivy increased her nerves, too. If Luke failed to secure guardianship, life would be so very difficult for them.

Percy's exceeding enmity, as well as Hazel's, not only irritated her nerves, it made her blood boil. His narcissistic behaviour was hurting so many people.

It rankled her to think about all of the good, kind people who worked here and at Havenbrook. People who had been devoted to the old Duke and Duchess, had enjoyed working for them.

It was all so unjust, so unfair, to all of them, including Luke. He'd found a life in America that he loved, and then all of this had been thrust upon him.

A knock on the door stifled her wandering thoughts, and she lifted her chin, hoping to ease her qualms as she crossed the room to open the door.

'Just as I suspected,' Claire said, entering the room and carrying a tray from the kitchen. She was followed by Millie, the upstairs maid with red-brown hair and big brown eyes, who also had her hands full, mainly with a frilly dress.

Aislinn closed the door. 'Suspected what?'

'That you needed something suitable to wear,' Claire said, setting the tray on the table. 'You can't go about town dressed as a governess.'

'I am a governess,' Aislinn needlessly reminded her.

'You are, but right now, you are also our only hope.' Claire said, gesturing to the bed where Millie laid a lovely bright yellow and white lace dress. 'Mr Carlisle needs the courts to know that he is the right guardian for the girls, and there is no one better to help him than you. Once his guardianship is fully confirmed, we can all start living normally again.'

Whilst speaking, Claire had gestured as if telling Aislinn to take off her dress. She hadn't, because she recognised the yellow dress. 'I can't wear that. It belonged to the Duchess.'

'One of the few that Hazel didn't confiscate. She took any that she thought she could have altered to fit her.' Claire had her hands on her hips. 'I'm sure the Duchess would rather see you wear her clothing than her sister-in-law, especially when you are the one working to secure the future of her daughters.'

'But I can't—'

'It's not a ball gown,' Claire interrupted. 'It's a simple day dress, which is another reason Hazel didn't take it. Now, take off your dress. Millie will fix your hair as soon as we get this on you. You can eat your breakfast while she's doing that.'

Aislinn was still unsure.

'Think of Mr Carlisle,' Claire said. 'He's wearing a suit today. Don't you think he'd prefer you be dressed well also?'

She was unsure of many things, but there was one thing she knew. If she kept telling herself that she couldn't do this, then she wouldn't be able to. Huffing out a sigh, Aislinn unbuttoned the front of her dress.

Within moments, she was wearing the yellow dress, adorned with several layers of white lace around the full skirt and the detailed, fitted bodice. Unlike the drab, shapeless dress she'd removed, this one hugged her in places that enhanced her feminine curves. 'Perhaps this is too much,' she said, seeing her reflection in the mirror.

'Nonsense,' Claire said. 'It fits you like a glove, even without a corset.'

Between the square, lace-trimmed neckline and the short sleeves, her shoulders were barely covered, let alone her upper chest, neck and arms. She tugged at the front, hoping to pull it up a smidgen.

'There's a matching yellow cape, so don't worry about being covered,' Claire said, pulling her towards a chair. 'Millie is ready to fashion your hair and pin on the hat.'

Aislinn's back was to the mirror, so it wasn't until after Millie had removed the pins from her hair, brushed it, braided it, pinned it back up, and added the hat, that she got a glimpse of herself.

She barely recognised the image staring back at her. Millie had fashioned her hair into a bun, but had added a braid on each side of her face that looped down over her ears, before being pinned up with the rest of her hair. The small yellow hat sat jauntily at an angle on one side of her head, and made her look so different. She felt different, too. The dress was lovely, and the soft leather shoes that Claire had also provided were as comfortable as slippers.

'You look so beautiful,' Claire said, looking in the mirror over one of Aislinn's shoulders.

'Like a true lady,' Millie said, gazing into the mirror over Aislinn's other shoulder.

Aislinn had never considered herself vain, but at this moment, wondered if Luke would think she was pretty. Her heartbeat increased and, drawing in a deep breath, she gave her head a clearing shake. This wasn't about whether she was pretty or not, nor what Luke thought of her. It was about the guardianship of Fern and Ivy.

She had to remember that, because too often, her thoughts were centred around Luke, and not the girls.

The one thing she didn't need to worry about was if the girls would be well cared for in her absence, yet she asked, 'You will assure the girls that I'll be back later? I don't want them worrying.'

'Yes, I will,' Claire said, hooking arms with Aislinn. 'Time to go. Mr Carlisle is waiting in the study, and dare I say, he looks very handsome in his finery.'

The air Aislinn attempted to draw in caught in her throat, and she questioned if she should have eaten the toast and egg, for it wasn't settling well.

* * *

Luke had made a mental list of places he needed to stop by today, starting with Mr Watson's office. As expected, a man had arrived early this morning, hoping to catch the household still sleeping, with what looked like official paperwork for the property to be closed. But it held no court order, was nothing more than a request from a solicitor. Percy's solicitor no doubt.

With a few choice words, Luke had sent the man away. He was convinced of his rights when it came to this house and the other things that Rowland had specified in his will, but would give the paperwork to Mr Watson to make sure.

The list of things he needed to discuss with the solicitor was growing by the minute, when the rustling of skirts and soft footfalls sounded in the hallway. He collected his morning jacket, that had once belonged to Rowland, from the back of the chair and shrugged it on as he walked across the room.

The mantel clock in the study, where he'd been waiting, said it wasn't yet eight, and he grinned. Aislinn was true to her word again.

His feet danged near tripped over each other at the sight of her standing in the doorway, and his heart started thudding as hard as it had the first time he'd found a gold nugget. That's what she reminded him of, a sparkling yellow gold nugget.

Except when he'd found that nugget, he'd whooped so loud it echoed off the mountains. This time, his tongue was tied tighter than a mast knot.

'Good morning,' she said.

Her head was tilted slightly to the left, as he noticed she did often, and that little hat perched upon her head looked as if it could topple off. She was a fine-looking woman. Finer than any other he'd ever seen. He gave his throat a quick clearing. 'Morning.' Not able to think of anything more to say, he settled for, 'I'll have Benjamin bring around the carriage. He already hitched up the horses.'

She stepped aside and he nearly bolted past her, knowing he needed a minute or two—or five—to get his mind back in order. He didn't believe clothes made a person, but damn, she looked amazing in that dress. It fit her to perfection, and was filling his mind with thoughts and images of her that he shouldn't be having. Not because she was his nieces' governess, but because she was his partner. They had a lot they needed to accomplish, and he needed all his wits about him.

He'd never had that problem before, but then again, he'd never become so enamoured with a woman. He didn't want to admit that was the case, but it sure seemed to be. She was on his mind non-stop. Which was understandable, given their situation, except for the fact that the thoughts he kept having had nothing to do with the issues at hand.

Gabe was in the hallway, and with a slight bow, stated, 'The carriage is being brought around, sir.'

Luke sucked in a breath. So much for a minute to get his thoughts in order. 'Thanks, Gabe. We'll be right there.' Spinning on his heel, he studied Aislinn for a long moment. Pretty women had never left him tongue-tied, nor scared him. She *didn't* scare him. He'd just been caught off guard. Like last night, when he'd seen unshed tears in her eyes. He'd acted on impulse then and had given her a hug. That had proven to be a bad idea. The feel of holding her in his arms had stuck with him all night.

She was doing him a mighty favour. He knew it was because of the girls—she loved them as if they were her very own. He appreciated that, too. Appreciated everything she was doing, and he sure as hell didn't need to complicate things with foolish thoughts.

'Shall we?' he asked, crooking his elbow for her to take a hold of.

'Where is Mr Watson's office?' she asked, as her hand hooked the inside of his elbow.

'Other side of town, but we have plenty of time.' Then, a normal thought occurred, and he asked, 'Have you eaten breakfast?'

'Yes.'

He had to get all his thoughts in order. It couldn't be that hard. Not even with her at his side. He'd recognised her beauty before now, and her kindness and dedication. She was caring, too, and likeable. An all-around good person. The kind he liked. That's all there was to it. Getting his thoughts in order wouldn't be hard at all.

Ironically, that was completely true. As soon as they entered the coach, she began asking questions about things they would discuss with the solicitor, and lo and behold, his mind was back. Although he continued to admire her. He'd lucked out when it came to Aislinn. Not only for meeting her along the road, or the way she cared for the girls, or her willingness to help him, or numerous other things, but for her beauty. A pretty woman had a way of making everything look bright and hopeful.

It was good to know that lady luck hadn't completely abandoned him.

That held true when they arrived across town. Ethan Watson was in his office and turned out to be an affable man, short and stocky, with a head full of silver-white hair. Luke made introductions and waited for Aislinn to sit on a chair before he lowered onto the one beside her.

Across the desk, in a small office that smelled of pipe smoke, Mr Watson sat and lifted a pair of wire-framed glasses off a stack of papers. Hooking the wires behind his ears, one at a time, he said, 'Thank you for coming to see me. Although I didn't expect it this quickly. I didn't think my message would have got to you, yet.'

'It was waiting for me when I got off the boat,' Luke said.

'I was referring to the one I sent yesterday, to Havenbrook,' Mr Watson said.

'I didn't see that one,' Luke said, irritated that Percy would now have that message. 'We left Havenbrook at daybreak yesterday.'

'I informed the messenger to deliver it only to you, so I'm sure he'll return with it sometime today.' Mr Watson placed his elbows on his desk. 'It appears we've had a few more developments in this case since our last messages.'

Luke nodded and started rattling off a list of grievances that Percy had created, including the lack of wages paid to the employees and the attempted closing of the London home, amongst other things more directly related to Percy's character—or lack thereof—and the guardianship.

Mr Watson listened without interruption, taking notes and adjusting his glasses every now and again, especially while looking over the notice to vacate the property that had been delivered that morning.

Luke was sure there was more he should mention, but at the moment, couldn't think of what else to add. He looked over at Aislinn, who shrugged slightly and shook her head. He wasn't completely sure she would have voiced them even if she had other grievances. She wasn't one to complain—he already knew that. He also knew that she still looked awfully fetching in that dress.

'Well, then,' Mr Watson said, with a glance towards Aislinn, 'I shall start with the payment of wages. There is no law against a man setting a price that he'll pay for wages, and as long as the employees have agreed, either verbally or in writing, there is nothing to be done about it.'

Luke's jaw tightened. He'd figured as much, but it was wrong the way Percy went about it. So wrong.

'I agree it's not a fair way to treat loyal employees, but it's not illegal,' Mr Watson said, while he made a mark on his list. 'As far as the London home, Rowland clearly willed it to you. Now that you are here and, for the time being, have guardianship of your nieces, the house and employees are under your charge.'

Luke reached into his breast pocket and pulled out a leather wallet. One by one, he took out pieces of papers and handed them across the desk. 'This is a line of credit from the bank in Bozeman, Montana Territory, secured by my deposits. This one is from Denver, Colorado, also secured by my deposits, as is this last one from New Orleans. I plan on going to the bank and having funds transferred to an account here in London, so the staff and household bills can be paid post-haste. And I will continue to pay all expenses acquired by the London house, including Miss Blaydon's wages.'

He would see that the dedicated servants at Havenbrook were paid, as well, but would discuss that with Aislinn privately, because he'd seen a few people there whom he didn't know, but were clearly dedicated to Percy. His brother could pay their wages, and Aislinn could give him a list of the original staff, whom he'd see were paid in full.

Mr Watson was examining each piece of paper he'd given him with interest.

'I guarantee they're good,' Luke said.

'I don't doubt that, Mr Carlisle. You have acquired a great deal of wealth in America.'

'I've been lucky in some instances,' Luke said. This was an ace up his sleeve. 'I'd prefer that my brother not learn about my assets quite yet.'

'There is no need for him to know,' Mr Watson said, as he slid a sheet of paper from one of his piles across the desk. 'Nor is there a need to transfer money. You have substantial holdings here.'

Luke picked up the paper. The top number was recognisable—it had been the monies he'd inherited from his father. 'I gave this to Rowland,' he said. 'I sent him back the amount that I'd taken with me when I left for America, and when I decided that I probably wouldn't live here again, I told him to add my share to his.' That galled him now, thinking that Percy could very well end up with it.

'I am aware of what you requested,' Mr Watson said, 'but your brother chose instead to keep it in your name and to manage it along with the property you had inherited. The reimbursement you sent him, along with your yearly gains, are listed. The bottom total is what is currently on account in your name. As you can see, it's quite substantial.'

It was at that. Yet, he'd given his funds to Rowland in good faith, and would honour that. Becoming independent had been his goal, and upon doing so, he'd taken pride in the ability to cut ties to the life that had never been the one he wanted. 'I will use some of this to pay the household expenses, including wages, until a transfer can arrive. Then I'll repay it and, once the guardianship is secured, I will request these funds be put on account for Fern and Ivy.'

'As you wish.' Mr Watson made more notes. 'Your financial state may assist in our defence that you are not interested in the guardianship for the monies and holdings your nieces have inherited.'

'Good, because I'm not. No money or holdings will replace their parents.'

'I agree. The children have suffered a great loss that nothing will ever replace. However, your brother, Rowland, left his daughters a great deal of wealth in monies and holdings that are separate from his title. The courts are taking the guardianship of Miss Fern and Miss Ivy very seriously and scrutinising every detail.'

Luke fully understood what the man was saying. 'What do you know about the accusations against my character brought forth by my brother? Do you know whose feeding them to the court?'

Mr Watson leaned back in his chair. 'I have my suspicions, but knowing who it is isn't as important as proving them wrong.'

Aislinn saw the way Luke's jaw tightened as he sat back in his chair. Much like she would do when one of the girls was growing agitated, she reached over and laid a hand atop his. 'I can vouch for what had been written in many of those letters,' she told Mr Watson, who seemed truly genuine in wanting to help. 'I was present when the Duke read them aloud.'

'I'm assuming you are referring to Mr Carlisle's oldest brother, Rowland,' Mr Watson said.

'Yes, sir, I am. The arrival of Luke—Mr Carlisle's letters always brought excitement. He has a way with words that had everyone wanting to listen when his letters were read.'

'You're saying that others were present when they were read, besides yourself?' Mr Watson asked.

'Yes, sir.'

'Do you believe they would be willing to offer testimony?'

She started to say yes, but the truth was, they might not. 'I believe some would, but they may have been told they will lose their employment if they do.'

'I see,' he said, jotting down something on the paper. 'Do you know where these letters are located?'

Frustrated, she shook her head. 'No, sir. The Duke, Mr Carlisle's brother Percy, took possession of everything that Mr Carlisle had mailed to his oldest brother.' Not willing to leave it at that, she continued, 'If I may, sir, in one of his letters, Luke started out by saying that he could now be referred to as a cattle rustler, that he'd acquired a fine herd of cattle.'

After Luke had talked about that letter, she remembered more about it and some others. 'He then wrote about the breeds of cattle, their hardiness, then the land, the people, the weather. It wasn't until much later in the letter that he explained he hadn't actually rustled the cattle, but that other men had, and Luke had helped return the stolen cattle to their rightful owner.'

Mr Watson glanced between her and Luke. When his gaze landed on her hand, still resting atop Luke's, she removed it and folded both hands in her lap, cheeks burning.

'Is that a correct summary?' he asked Luke.

'Yes, it is.' Luke leaned forward, hands planted on his knees. 'It was that way with all the letters—they were easy to misconstrue. I gambled some on river-boats, but the boat I wrote about, I bought off a guy in Tennessee who was about to lose it in a game. I fixed it up, hired some new people, and sailed it down to New Orleans, where I sold it. I also spent time in the gold fields, found some colour, but I discovered that also wasn't what I wanted to do for the rest of my life, so I bought a smelter to process other people's finds. I ended up selling that, too. As far as the dance hall gals, they'd managed to fall in the river. I simply came upon them and fished them out, then found their horse and buggy, and sent them on their way.'

Aislinn didn't remember a letter concerning a riv-erboat or dance hall gals, and was listening as intently as Mr Watson.

'Did he mention this?' Luke asked, as he untied his ascot and unbuttoned his shirt, then pulled out a leather strap. 'The bear claw that a little boy's grandfather gave me for rescuing his grandson?'

Aislinn didn't recall that story, either, but believed every word. It also endeared him to her even more. Anyone who knew him would find it impossible to be-lieve that he had anything in mind except the very best interests for Fern and Ivy.

'The courts need to see the whole letters,' Luke said, while retying his ascot, after tucking the leather necklace back beneath his clothing and buttoning his shirt. 'Not just the sections that Percy is secretly serving them.'

Mr Watson nodded. 'I'll include that in my petition to the courts.' He leaned back and rubbed his chin. 'There is still, possibly, the most important aspect. The current Duke and Duchess, Percy and Hazel, are just that. A Duke and Duchess. A married couple, with a child of their own, who live here, in England. You, even without a blemish on your character, are a single man, who does not reside in this country. You just admitted to me that you gave the assets you have here to your oldest brother, because you never planned on living here again.'

Aislinn's heart sank clear to her toes. There was nothing she could say about that, it was true. There was nothing she could do about it, either. Luke was verbally attempting to justify his status to Mr Watson, but nothing he was saying would help. Percy and Hazel sounded like better guardians than him. But they weren't.

Her stomach was burning, her heart aching. All of this was for naught.

'I am well aware that Rowland appointed you guardian,' Mr Watson was saying in response to Luke's justifications. 'Great consideration is given to that, but there have been instances when the Court of Chancery has thought it necessary to override the father's nomination.'

'This is not one of them,' Luke stated angrily. 'The courts would be failing those girls by giving them to Percy and Hazel!'

Aislinn couldn't agree more and could fully understand Luke's anger. Her own emotions and thoughts were raging out of control. Fear for Fern and Ivy was creating chaos inside her. They'd already lost so much, and this was truly devasting. Percy and Hazel would find another way to get rid of her, and the girls would be left completely vulnerable to the Duke and Duchess.

'Those two will strip Fern and Ivy of all Rowland left them,' Luke declared as he leaped to his feet and slapped the top of the desk. 'They are probably scheming about marrying the girls off as we speak! To some filthy old goats for God only knows what favours!'

A chill sliced through Aislinn, right through her heart. She'd heard of such things. Arranged marriage happened all the time. She couldn't allow such a wicked life to be imposed upon Fern and Ivy. Would not.

The mayhem inside her hit a boiling point. Her charges would *not* be forced to marry—

Her thoughts paused, and everything around her seemed to go quiet, even though they weren't. Luke was still shouting, and Mr Watson was attempting to calm him down. She could see all that, hear all that, even as her own thoughts drowned it all out as they battled against each other in her mind.

One side of her was telling her she couldn't. The other side was saying it was their only chance. Their only hope.

His only hope. Luke had travelled halfway around the world to fulfil a promise to his brother. He'd left behind a ranch, a life full of adventures, a life that he loved. But he loved his brother more. Loved him so much he was here, fighting, doing everything he could for Rowland's final wish to be granted.

Before the other side of her could challenge her desperate idea any further, she stood. 'Luke and I are getting married as soon as possible.'

It had just so happened that silence had fallen be-

tween the men a split second before she'd spoken, and
now it grew even deeper.

A silence so deep, the only thing she could hear was
her own heart echoing in her ears.

She'd never known a person could be sweating and
have the chills at the same time, unless of course they'd
come down with a terrible fever. Maybe she had. Maybe
she'd come down with a fever so high she'd completely
lost her mind.

At least the part that was normally sensible.

Marriage had never crossed her mind. Not until a
moment ago, when it seemed like a solution. The only
solution.

Mr Watson's gaze was bouncing between her and
Luke, and Luke's gaze was fixed on her. She could feel
it burning the side of her face. Her nerves were completely frazzled, and she would bet that the permanent
grin was not on his face just then. It hadn't been moments ago, either, while he'd been so upset over the
guardianship battle. Now she was quite sure that he was
looking at her with undisguised repulsion.

She was a governess. He was a man of the ton.
Whether he wanted it that way or not, that was the
truth. His family was a member of the high society,
therefore, no matter where he chose to live, he was too.
It was a birthright.

Men of his station in life did not marry the likes of
her. A woman who had no claim to status even in the
most meagre way.

Her only hope, her greatest hope, was that he loved
his nieces as much as she did. Which was completely
unfair of her, but what else were they do to?

She bit down on the tip of her tongue. Clearly, she

shouldn't have blurted out that they were getting married. Discussing that as a possible option would have been far more prudent. But time was of the essence. Perhaps later, once his temper had cooled, she could make her point, explain in earnest that they truly had very few options. And the risks...the risks were so very high for Fern and Ivy.

Slowly, cautiously, she prepared to face him. To break the still silence that was filling the room, making her heartbeat echo in her ears. She had decided that she needed to become stronger, bolder, more assertive. Well, she had certainly mastered that. With only one sentence.

Holding her breath, and with her teeth still embedded in her tongue, she twisted her neck and lifted her eyes to meet Luke's.

Chapter Eight

Coward. Luke wasn't referring to Aislinn, who was looking up at him with her chin up, determination in her eyes, and all the courage of a badger facing off a bear. He was the coward. Marriage? Few things scared the hell out of him, but that word did. He was committed to himself. Committed to a life of adventure and excitement. Of going where he wanted, when he wanted. That need had been within him for as long as he could remember, and he hadn't known happiness, true happiness, until he'd followed that longing.

He'd said he was willing to do whatever it took for Fern and Ivy, and had truly believed that. Until a moment ago, when she'd announced they would wed as soon as possible. A commitment like that was not within him. Never had been. He didn't want anyone to depend on him to that level.

There had to be another way. A simpler, far less complicated option than marriage. Although it could solve the issues he was facing. Possibly. Nothing was guaranteed in this situation.

Furthermore, marriage was certain to introduce other

problems, in too many ways to count. He had a ranch to return to and couldn't do that with a wife here in England. A wife! What the hell was he thinking? He'd sworn off marriage years ago, when he'd learned that a woman would take the wanderlust out of him. His father had told him that, as had Rowland. Hell, even Percy had changed when he married Hazel. He'd always been selfish, but had turned even more so, claiming that whatever Hazel wanted, Hazel got.

No, marriage was off the table.

'Well, now,' Mr Watson said, 'that is an interesting addition, and brings up another topic that has been brought to my attention.'

Luke pulled his eyes off Aislinn to look at the solicitor. For a moment, he'd forgotten the man was in the room with them. Now, that was ironic, considering they were in his office. Letting the air out of his lungs slowly, Luke asked, 'What topic would that be?'

What else could there be? Percy had already thwarted him at every corner, and Luke was more than tired of having to deal with his brother's vast collection of attacks.

'It concerns Miss Blaydon,' Mr Watson said.

The man was still seated, and Luke reached over to touch Aislinn's arm, encouraging her to sit. Once she had, he returned to his seat, as well. 'What concerns Miss Blaydon?' he asked.

'Your brother is not the only one who has informants inside the courts,' Mr Watson said.

Luke wasn't surprised that the solicitor would have insiders, nor overly interested at that specific moment. His concerns were heavily leaning towards Aislinn and whatever she had to do with a topic that had been brought to the solicitor's attention.

'Along with the petitions the Duke of Havenbrook submitted to obtain guardianship of Fern and Ivy,' Mr Watson said, 'was a petition for him to become Miss Blaydon's guardian, as well.'

'My guardian?' Aislinn questioned.

At the same time, Luke said, 'She doesn't need a guardian.'

Mr Watson nodded at her, before stating, 'No, she doesn't, because she already has one assigned to her until the age of twenty-one. The Duke is looking to have guardianship transferred to him.'

'How can I have a guardian?' she questioned, glancing between him and the solicitor. 'I've never been informed of such a person.'

Luke took a hold of her hand, squeezed it. 'Assigned by whom? For what purpose?'

'You were raised in an orphanage, were you not?' Mr Watson asked her.

'Yes.'

'All orphans, as well as others who are incapable of taking care of themselves and without direct family to oversee their care, are considered to be under the Monarch's care by law,' Mr Watson explained. 'The Monarch has delegated the care of such charges to the Lord Chancellor of the Court of Chancery. Due to the large number of orphans and those in need of oversight, their guardianships are assigned to a number of solicitors who work with the court.'

'She's assigned to you?' Luke asked.

'No, but to a close acquaintance of mine, Mr Gaines. He became aware of the Duke's desire to obtain guardianship of your nieces and contacted me yesterday about the unusual request that he'd received concerning Miss Blaydon.' Mr Watson shifted his gaze to her again. 'It is my understanding that you lived at the orphanage until the age of sixteen.'

'Yes, that's when I went to work for the Duke and Duchess,' she replied, 'and have remained there for over four years.'

'So you are not yet twenty-one?'

'No,' she replied. 'I will be this fall.'

Luke held on tighter to her hand at the way it trembled. 'There is no reason for Percy to have guardianship over her.'

Mr Watson took off his glasses. 'Until she is twenty-one, a guardian is the only person who can grant permission for her to marry.'

Luke's mind suddenly raced in several directions, all leading to one end. The same end as always. Percy. Was this one more way he was trying to thwart him? Making every aspect of this harder than it needed to be?

'I've never been interested in marriage,' she told Mr Watson. 'Not until…' She swallowed visibly and her cheeks flushed red. 'I met Luke.'

Damn it. That comment just caused his heart to lose its foothold inside his chest. It felt as if it was tumbling over a cliff, head over heels, and there was nothing he could do to stop it. Hell. He wanted to fulfil Rowland's wishes, wanted to be the guardian of his nieces, and was willing to do whatever it took. But marriage? To Aislinn? He was already having a hard time controlling his thoughts. Thoughts that would go as wild as his heart if they were married.

He'd just determined that was not going to happen,

therefore, gathering the few bits of common sense that he could, he asked, Mr Watson, 'Has the change in her guardianship been granted?'

'No,' the man answered.

Luke nodded, processing all he could, while trying to figure out what to do. 'At the present moment, the only person who can grant permission for Aislinn to marry is this solicitor friend of yours?'

'Yes.' Mr Watson looked at him over the rim of his glasses. 'Would you like me to contact him? Meet with him?'

What he wanted was more time to think about this, to process things. To talk to Aislinn. Yes, that's what he needed to do. Talk to her about this. In private. There had to be a reason that Percy wanted guardianship over her. Control, no doubt, but if that was the case, why had he fired her?

'Yes, please contact him,' Luke said. Maybe her guardian could shed some light on the situation. He stood. 'We will return in a few hours to meet with both of you.'

Mr Watson stated a time, and Luke agreed. Then he stepped back, waiting for Aislinn to rise, and gently took a hold of her elbow to escort her to the door.

Luke had been scared a time or two, confused as to which trail to take, but had ultimately got over his fear and chosen a path. That's what he needed to do right now.

Trouble was, it wasn't just about him this time. Aislinn was innocent in all of this. He'd pulled her into it and made her vulnerable, someone who needed him as badly as the girls.

While travelling to England, he'd figured that all

he'd need to do was confirm the wants of Rowland's will, put a few things in place to make sure the girls were safe and secure, and then he'd be able to return to America. Of course, he'd planned that he'd need to make regular trips to England yearly, to see for himself that all was well.

That had been his plan. That he'd find someone to see to the actual raising of Fern and Ivy. It may not have been the best plan, but it had been the one he'd come up with, and meeting her on the road had suggested it could work out. She certainly loved the girls and would do a fine job raising them. However, he'd come up with that plan before witnessing just how adamant Percy was about not honouring Rowland's wishes.

Everything was up in the air now, and he hated that.

'I'm sorry,' she whispered as they walked out of the building. 'I shouldn't have said that.'

'Hold that thought,' he said, and gestured for her to climb into the carriage. Once she had, he told Benjamin to take them to the bank that held his assets.

As soon as he climbed in, she said, 'I am truly sorry.'

He took a seat on the padded bench across from her. 'Why did you say that?'

'I don't know. The thought just popped into my head while you were talking about Percy marrying the girls off. I couldn't stand the thought of that, and—' She shook her head. 'I should have kept my mouth shut.'

'Well, let's just think about this for a minute,' he said, needing to do just that.

She pinched her lips together and turned her gaze to the window as the carriage began to roll.

A sigh built up at how sorrowful and timid she looked. 'It's not a bad idea, it just took me by surprise.'

He had to let the air out of his lungs and did so as quietly as possible. 'And it won't work.'

Without looking his way, she nodded. 'I understand that someone of your stature would never marry the likes of me.'

Ire flared inside him. 'The likes of you? There is nothing wrong with you. Any man would be honoured to marry you.'

She sighed and turned from the window. 'I've never thought of marriage before today. Honestly.' The sorrow in her eyes increased as she added, 'I only said that I'd thought about it after meeting you to make Mr Watson believe that we were getting married. I—I didn't want him to think I was lying, or scheming, or...' She huffed out a breath. 'I don't know. It's just that it seemed like a good plan in my head. If you were married, there would be no reason for you to not get guardianship. Mr Watson said that—'

'I know what he said,' Luke interrupted. He didn't want to be convinced that this plan might be a good one. 'You don't want to be married to me.'

'This isn't about what I want—it's about Fern and Ivy. I can't bear the idea of them being married off—'

'I know,' he interrupted again, not wanting to think about Percy arranging marriages for them. That idea nearly gutted him. Flipping the subject back to her, he asked, 'Why haven't you thought of marriage before? Every woman wants to get married.'

'Perhaps they do, just not me. Fern and Ivy are... well, I love them. Love them dearly, and I can't imagine living without them. I want to be with them until they no longer need me.'

'What happens then? Once they are grown?'

She shrugged. 'I've never thought that far ahead, because it doesn't matter. What matters is the here and now.'

Right now, that was true. He shook his head. 'Marriage is for ever.'

'I understand why it won't work for you,' she said.

'No, it's not me that I'm thinking about.' That wasn't completely true. 'Strike that. It's not *just* me that I'm thinking about. If we were to get married, it would be for ever. Is that something we could *both* live with?'

'We wouldn't really have to be married,' she said.

'I don't believe there is a way to get married, without being married.' Other than an annulment, and he really didn't want to have to explain what that meant to her. She might know. He wasn't sure either way, but just the thought of that discussion made his throat lock up. It affected other parts of him, too. This whole conversation needed to end. They couldn't get married, that's all there was to it.

'There is,' she said. 'Once you've obtained guardianship, you could return to America, and I would remain here with the girls, at the London home. Plenty of women have husbands who are sea captains, or men who work away from home for extended lengths of time. We'll have the servants to help us.'

'What if you find someone that you want to be married to?' he asked. 'Someone you love?'

'That won't happen,' she said immediately. 'I love the girls too much for that to ever happen.' She grimaced. 'But I suppose that won't work for you, if you find someone you want to marry.'

'No,' he said, thinking that the plan she'd just come up with was a close match for the one he'd planned while travelling to England. 'I mean, yes, that would work for me, because I also have no interest in a real marriage.' In fact, what she said would stop him from ever having to worry about getting married again. He could travel back here once a year or so, and with Doo at the house, she and the girls would be protected.

'You don't?'

'No, never have.'

'So this could work for us?' she asked. 'To be married, but not really married?'

He heard the hope in her voice, but was still questioning if it was something he could live with when a knock sounded on the carriage door. He wasn't sure how long they had been sitting still.

Opening the door, he nodded at Benjamin. 'Thank you. We won't be long.'

Luke exited the carriage and held out a hand to assist Aislinn in stepping out.

He had to admit that the idea was growing on him, but there was one thing he needed to know before making up his mind. Why Percy had wanted to become her guardian. There had to be a reason, and he was beginning to wonder if it was because Percy had already thought of this plan. The two of them marrying. It would solve things. And it was devious enough to be something that Percy would have thought of and attempted to prevent from happening. For the very reason that Mr Watson had pointed out. As an unmarried man, he was not a suitable candidate to be a guardian. Leastwise, not as suitable as the married brother.

Percy, once again, was not taking into consideration that he was willing to do whatever it took to fulfil his promise to Rowland. It was the least he could do for a brother who had loved him unconditionally.

Taking hold of her elbow, he escorted Aislinn inside the bank, the idea growing on him.

Seriously growing on him.

After taking care of his banking needs, he escorted her inside the tailor's shop, since it was right across the street. He needed a pair of boots that didn't hurt his feet. They wouldn't compare to his old ones, but those were too scruffy to wear around town. The tailor referred him to a boot maker up the street, but while he was there, he ordered shirts, pants, coats, and other items that wouldn't be so tight that he was afraid of ripping out seams at every step.

The tailor, a balding man with a flat nose, also referred him next door, to his wife's dress shop. Actually, the man had suggested that Aislinn might be more comfortable waiting next door while he was measured for the new clothes.

Luke answered for her. Said she'd wait for him.

She didn't utter a word in agreement nor disagreement. He didn't know where the yellow dress she was wearing had come from, but he knew the small bag she'd brought from Havenbrook for herself hadn't held much.

As they left the tailor's shop, with his destination clear, she stopped walking. 'There is no need to stop at the dressmakers.'

'Yes, there is,' he said, slightly tugging her towards the shop door. 'The wife of a Carlisle can't walk around dressed like a servant.'

She gasped slightly, and her eyes grew as round as gold coins.

Though his heart hammered in his chest at the idea of marriage, he shrugged. 'It's a viable plan. Right now, we have a lot of errands to see to.'

She nodded, but as soon as they entered the store, she quietly said, 'I don't need much.'

'Consider it part of the job,' he replied, then grinned at the shop owner and told her that Aislinn would need several dresses and whatever else went with them.

Like her husband, the shop owner referred him next door, to wait while Aislinn was measured and items were chosen. He said he'd wait right there.

Tall, with reddish brown hair, the woman offered him a newspaper, before leading Aislinn into a back room.

He glanced at the paper, but didn't read the words. Truth was, he didn't mind the silence. It was giving his anger time to fully solidify. An anger that would remain with him for eternity. He was no one's fool, and once again, fury at Percy for attempting to make him look like one took hold.

It could be quite humiliating, being forced into the one thing he'd never wanted. Marriage. But he wouldn't let it bruise his pride, nor would he let it break him. Instead, he would use it to his full advantage. He would step back into his role as a Carlisle, as a man who took advantage of his family's social status, and show Percy how powerful he could be, without needing to inherit a title.

What felt like hours later, they left the dress shop, then visited the boot maker. After that, he directed Benjamin to take them to the nearest stable. He needed a horse. A decent one, so he could travel at will.

He made his choice—a sound thoroughbred gelding, brown, with four white socks—and requested it be delivered to the London home. Then they set about visiting various stores and vendors to set up accounts for the necessary supplies for the house. As Doo had told him, all of the accounts had been closed by Percy.

The shop owners and venders were all friendly and glad he'd brought the household's business back to them, having feared they'd done something wrong.

Aislinn remained quiet, answering only when questioned directly.

By the time all that was done, it was well into the afternoon. 'I'm sorry, there's not enough time to eat at a restaurant before we are due back at Mr Watson's office, but we could find a street vendor if you'd like.'

'No,' she replied. 'I'm not hungry.'

She'd grown pale. Her face nearly as white as the lace on her dress, and that concerned him. Made him wonder if she was regretting coming up with this plan. 'Are you sure?'

'Yes, I'm sure.'

He wasn't hungry, either. 'Well, then, let's go see what they have to say.'

Luke wasn't overly sure what he hoped to hear. That he and Aislinn could, or couldn't, get married. There was a chance that her guardian would say no if he felt it was a sham. It wasn't a sham, as much as a plan. A plan that could work, for both of them. That's where his fear came in. Could he be married to her, but not *really* be married to her? He wasn't made of stone, and she was an incredibly attractive woman. His mind and body had recognised that from the moment he'd met her.

Standing at the elaborate altar in one of the finest churches in all of London, Aislinn desperately fought back a bout of tears. She wasn't afraid, nor sad, she was just very nervous about what she was embarking upon. Marriage was not something she'd ever thought about for herself. There had been no reason. While growing up in the orphanage, she'd wanted a family, but had never connected that to marriage. She'd thought about parents and siblings, not a husband. That was for women, and she'd just been a girl.

Upon accepting her position with the Duke and Duchess, she'd felt as if she'd found the family she'd sought. In Fern and Ivy. That was probably hard for others to understand, but it wasn't for her. They'd filled her heart with a love that she'd never known. Or at least couldn't remember.

Maybe she should have thought about it, because she was worried about what this marriage would do to Luke. She had come to care for him, and that's what made her so very nervous. What if he did find someone he wanted to marry? In America? Was it fair of her to take away his future happiness?

Perhaps she should have put more thought into the future, rather than just thinking about the present. But all she'd thought about was Fern and Ivy.

She still couldn't figure out why Percy had wanted to obtain guardianship over her. That made no logical sense. Mr Gaines was a tall man, who blinked his eyes excessively, but seemed kind. Although he hadn't been able to provide any insight into why Percy had wanted guardianship over her.

Not that they'd had much of a chance to discuss the topic. The meeting had focused on their wedding.

It had all happened so quickly, she still felt as if her head was spinning.

Mr Gaines had explained that he'd secured the special licence, after he'd questioned if either of them were being coerced into the union unwillingly. The licence would be null and void if that were the case.

Luke had said no, and she'd agreed with his answer. Immediately following that, they'd travelled here, to the church, for the marriage to take place.

Both solicitors were in attendance for the service, as two witnesses were required by law.

Luke had been unusually quiet during the trip to the church and since arriving. That made her nervous, too, wondering if he already regretted agreeing to her plan. She had been the one to come up with it, blurt it out in front of Mr Watson. Luke had agreed, but that didn't mean he wanted it.

She wasn't convinced that she wanted it, either. Being married to him would change her position, and that was a role she had not been trained for. Anxiety over what might be expected of her had every ounce of her being trembling.

The first words spoken by the clergyman startled her. The church was empty, and the man's words echoed off the walls and ceiling. Luke stood across from her. The permanent grin was on his face, but it looked strained.

She had a difficult time meeting his gaze, yet forced herself to do so as the ceremony commenced. It was short. Lasted no longer than it took for each of them to repeat their vows and the clergyman to pronounce them man and wife.

Luke kissed her cheek, an action that made her stomach bubble, before they walked down the aisle much as they'd walked up it. With a deep silence echoing around them. Aislinn had never dreamed of a fairy-tale wedding. In fact, her thoughts about weddings had been similar to those about marriage. Nil.

However, she had attended a wedding or two, and this one held no comparison to the joviality and fanfare of those events.

Near the door of the church, they paused long enough to sign their names, at which point Mr Watson had to remind her to write Carlisle instead of Blaydon. Then both solicitors wished them well, and Mr Watson explained that he would have an official notice of their wedding published in the papers the following morning.

Aislinn tried her best to act natural, grateful for their help, but it was growing harder and harder.

Upon climbing in the carriage, she leaned against the padded backrest and closed her eyes. Between the extraordinarily unusual events of the day, her nerves, and not eating, her head was pounding. The carriage wheels rolling over the cobblestones sounded extra loud, adding to the pain, and the thought of returning to the house, where everyone would learn that they were married, made her empty stomach churn.

It didn't take long before that happened—the arrival at the house.

'I'll let the staff know what happened today,' Luke said, as he opened the carriage door.

She nodded, even though her head was still aching. A moment later, the joyous greeting she was provided from Fern and Ivy made her briefly forget her headache.

Their giggles and hugs affected Luke, too. His eyes shone as both Fern and Ivy declared that they'd missed him.

'I was just taking them up to the nursery,' Claire

said, from where they all stood in the foyer. 'For the evening meal.'

'I will take them up,' Aislinn said, not ready to answer the questions she was sure everyone would soon have.

Luke gave her a slight nod, before he said to Claire, 'Mrs Moore, I would like to speak with you for a moment.' He then looked at the butler. 'You, too, Mr Houghton.'

It wasn't lost on Aislinn that he'd hadn't used their first names as usual, nor was it lost on the servants.

Gabe and Claire agreed, and as Luke walked down the hallway, Claire took a hold of Aislinn's hand.

'What happened?' Claire asked quietly. 'With all the supplies that arrived, we thought everything would be fine.'

'Everything is fine,' Aislinn said, hoping it wasn't a lie. 'We'll talk later.' She pulled up a smile for Fern and Ivy and, taking their hands, listened as they excitedly told her about their day while climbing the steps to the second floor.

Lamps had been lit in the nursery, for the sun had slipped towards the horizon, leaving a slow-growing dusk in its wake. Aislinn directed the girls to the washstand, and while they were cleaning their hands, she removed the hat from her head and carried it through the connecting door to her room.

There, she quickly drank a glass of water poured from the pitcher on the stand, hoping that would help ease her headache, and then returned to the nursery. There wasn't time to change her dress, though that may have helped, too. She wished things could return to normal, but that could never happen now.

How could it? She was married.

Married.

That was surreal.

She didn't feel married, but she wasn't supposed to. That is what they'd agreed upon. Being married, but not being married. She'd suggested that, but had no idea what it meant.

A knock on the door sounded when the girls' evening meal arrived, and she was glad to see the pot of tea. She could use the fortification.

Once the girls were settled at the table, eating, she poured herself a cup. But she was only halfway through drinking the warm brew when the door opened.

Claire walked in, shaking her head and hosting a befuddled expression. She closed the door and leaned against it. 'Mr Carlisle would like to see you in the study. What in the world happened?'

The cup clattered as Aislinn set it on the saucer, wondering exactly what Luke had said. Drawing in a breath of air, she stood. 'Too much to explain right now.'

'It's true?' Claire asked. 'The two of you are married?'

'Yes, that is true,' Aislinn admitted, walking towards the door.

Claire shifted uneasily. 'Gabe is sharing the news with the others.' Her gaze went to the girls. 'Mr Carlisle informed me that I'll be Fern and Ivy's governess for the time being.'

Air rushed into her lungs so fast, Aislinn coughed to the point she couldn't speak.

'I agreed, of course, but Aislinn…' Claire shook her head and shrugged.

A flash of anger erupted inside Aislinn. She had not

married him to give up her post. Staying with the girls was the very reason she had married him. Stepping forward, she gave Claire a quick embrace. 'All will be fine. I promise.'

As she left the room, she wished someone would tell her that, but there was no one. She was not only on her own, there were others she needed to protect. Claire had duties here, and her husband. More importantly, the girls were her responsibility, and the very essence of the marriage.

She forced herself to take a deep breath, before she worked herself into a frenzy of nerves all over again. He'd understood her reasons earlier today, so why not now?

Luke wasn't waiting for her in the study, he was in the hallway. 'Dinner is being served,' he said, with a nod towards the dining room. 'I know you haven't eaten since breakfast.'

He hadn't eaten all day, either, and she now understood why there hadn't been a plate for her on the tray delivered to the nursery. Maybe food would put them both in a better mood. Furthermore, she wasn't going to have a discussion with him in the hallway.

She gave a slight nod, then walked beside him to the dining room.

They were served and ate, with Gabe standing near the door that led to the kitchen, ready to respond if anything was needed. The food was plentiful, and she was sure it was delicious, Doo's meals always were, but she had too many other things on her mind to pay a lot of attention to the meal. She ate enough to ease the emptiness in her stomach, feeling guilty at the waste, but she was still queasy. That could very well increase when she and Luke began talking.

She rehearsed things she wanted to say during the silence and kept needing to push down the sense of panic that wanted to overtake her. Being bold or vocal wasn't comfortable for her, but she had to make her point.

As Gabe set a piece of lemon cake before her, she smiled at him. 'Please tell Mr Dobbs the meal was delicious.'

'I shall, my lady.'

The address made her spine stiffen. Her role had changed, and with that came responsibilities that she'd have to fulfil and a lot of learning to do. She ate a couple bites of the cake, just to be polite, then set down her fork and looked at Luke.

He set down his fork, too. 'Let's take a walk outside.'

'Outside?' she asked, surprised at the suggestion.

He stood and walked around the corner of the table to her chair. 'Yes, outside.' He leaned closer as she rose from her chair. 'At the moment, there is not a room in this house that wouldn't have an ear pressed against the door.'

She couldn't deny that possibility.

They exited the house through the back door, into the garden that smelled of flowers in bloom. Rosebushes lined the back of the house below the private balcony of the family bedrooms. It was that time of night when dusk had given way completely, but the stars and moon weren't at their brightest, leaving things just dark enough to be blurry.

Halfway across the backyard there was a bench that she often sat upon while the girls played, and that is where she and Luke stopped. Neither took a seat, just stood, side by side, silent for a moment.

She used that time to build up her courage, then said,

'I did not suggest marriage as a solution only to lose my post as governess.'

'I know.' He let out a long sigh. 'I'm afraid that there are several things we didn't think about while discussing this plan today.'

The courage she had managed to find began to wane. She walked over to the bench, rested her hands on the back of it for support. 'What things?'

He walked to the front of the bench and faced her. 'I apologise. I should have thought things through more thoroughly, but I didn't. Not until the ceremony, after Mr Gaines mentioned either of us being coerced into the marriage.'

Confused, she shook her head. 'We weren't coerced.'

'Not by each other, but the idea was formed because we were both worried about what Percy might do if he obtained guardianship.'

She nodded.

'In a sense, that is coercion, and if Percy can make a claim that that's the reason we got married, he could petition for our marriage to be dissolved.'

She knew little of the legalities involved. 'How can we make sure that doesn't happen?'

'By making sure everyone believes our marriage was because we...' He shook his head and then nodded. 'That we got married because we wanted to wed for ourselves, not for the girls. And most certainly not because Percy and Hazel are married, and I was not. Percy would take that straight to the courts.'

'How would anyone know that, unless we told them?'

He shrugged. 'It doesn't take much to get gossip started, and once ignited, it spreads like wildfire. People soon believe things whether they are true or not. We have to make sure there are no rumours.'

'How do we do that?'

'Between us, in private, we will keep the marriage in name only. However, no one but you and I can know that. Around others, we must appear to be a happily married couple. All others. Including here, at the house.'

A chill rippled down her spine and she tightened her hold on the bench. It was hard to believe that he thought someone here would tell Percy anything, but that was clearly what he thought.

'I know you trust everyone here, and I have no reason not to, either. But if they even accidently made a comment about us having separate bedrooms, it could get back to Percy, and we both know he'll use anything and everything against me in the fight for guardianship.'

She did know that, but couldn't get past what he'd said concerning bedrooms.

'I'm sorry,' he continued, 'I know this upsets you, but as my wife, the wife of a Carlisle, you can no longer be Fern and Ivy's governess. Claire has agreed to take over that role.'

What had she done? Continuing to be Fern and Ivy's governess was the reason she'd agreed to marry him. She had to point out, 'Claire has other duties.'

'She felt that wouldn't be an issue.' He laid a hand over one of hers, still clutching the back of the bench seat. 'You will still be here, be with Fern and Ivy every day. It's just their dressing, bathing, feeding and other duties that Claire will see to.'

Her heart was pounding, her throat burning. She was devastated, but couldn't be mad at him, because she did understand that his wife couldn't be a governess. She hadn't thought any of this through before she impulsively blurted out that they were getting married. It was not only unlikely that he'd ever marry someone like her, but she was also completely unqualified to be his wife. Others would see that as clearly as she did. She couldn't let that happen. 'I never thought about any of this,' she whispered.

'I didn't, either, not completely, and I'm sorry about that. But the deed is done, and now we have to make it work.' His hand gently caressed the back of hers. 'Millie, I believe her name is, will move into your room, to be near the girls at night, and will assist with any other general care needs. I will open an account in your name and deposit monies for you to use as needed.'

His hand, the way it was touching hers, was making her skin tingle, her entire arm warming, and that was making it hard to think. 'What will I do?'

'You will take over the running of the house,' he said, 'and any other duties required of my wife.'

Her head was swirling. She didn't know how to be anyone's wife; her training was that of a governess. Her entire life had been dedicated to that, and nothing more. Yet, she knew enough to know what husbands and wives did together, behind closed doors. He couldn't possibly mean that! She pulled her hand out from beneath his. 'What other duties?'

'I can't say for sure, but I suspect there will be some.'

'Oh.' She didn't know what else to say. What to think. This was all more than she'd bargained for. Her hand was still tingling and she rubbed it with her other one.

'This won't be for ever,' he said. 'Just until the guardianship is resolved, then we'll decide on our next steps.'

Her mind was too jumbled to think about next steps,

and even if she could, she wouldn't voice them. She'd learned her lesson.

'We'll get through this, Aislinn,' he said softly. 'We're partners.'

She nodded, but wasn't nearly as convinced as he sounded.

He gestured to the house. 'Shall we retire for the evening then?'

That is what she needed. To crawl into bed and think this whole thing through. She'd never imagined being in such a predicament. How could she have? It was like a nightmare that kept getting worse, and she couldn't wake up from it.

Well, not a complete nightmare. He was being very kind and understanding, it was just that none of this was as she'd expected. Then again, she hadn't known what to expect.

He walked around the bench and stopped, waiting for her.

She turned, took a step, but a heart-stopping thought occurred. 'If Millie is sleeping in my bed, where am I supposed to sleep?'

The grin that appeared on his face wasn't his permanent one. It was more like a grimace. 'In my room. Where else?'

Chapter Nine

For all his adventures, all his experiences of places, people, all of the situations and circumstances that he'd found himself in, Luke knew this was his greatest challenge of all. He wasn't upset with Aislinn, but he was borderline furious with himself. Why the hell hadn't he thought this through today? All the details that had eluded him were ones that should have been front and centre. He'd been too focused on stopping Percy to think about the situation he was putting himself in.

Married. He had no one to blame but himself.

He liked Aislinn, and she was a beautiful woman. But therein lay the issue. Acting as if they were a happily married couple, but not actually being one, could damn well be the death of him.

Keeping his mind off Aislinn and focused on the reason for the marriage was what he needed to do. He needed to become a damn good actor, too. There was no way in hell that he could let Percy find out that he and Aislinn were not… He shook his head to block out the thought that was forming.

There had never been an unwilling woman in his

bed, and there never would be. Married or not. Entering the study, alone, for he'd instructed Aislinn to go up to bed upon entering the house, he walked straight to the side cabinet and pulled the topper off the decanter of whiskey. He reached for a glass, but then merely lifted the bottle to his lips. It was probably one of the most uncouth things a man of his social status could do, drinking straight from the bottle, but right now, he didn't care. He'd swigged from a bottle many times over the last eight years and would never promise that it wouldn't happen again.

There were too many issues up in the air. Things he hadn't thought of until it was too late.

He had no idea how long it would take for the guardianship to become settled, and even if—strike that—*when* guardianship was granted to him, he couldn't be sure if stipulations would be put in place. Percy spouted that the girls needed to live here, where they would receive all the benefits of being a duke's daughter, and as much as it goaded him to agree with his brother on anything, Percy was right.

He'd already known that. That's why his original plan had been to find someone to raise the girls here.

Montana wasn't a godforsaken land. It was a glorious place, but it was rough country. That's what had drawn him to it. What he loved about it.

But that was him.

He was a man. Not a woman or a child.

Mrs Brings, whom he had bought the ranch from, had left because it was too rough, too challenging for her and her children.

Sucking in air as the whiskey burned his throat on its way down, he carried the bottle to a chair. Set it on the table beside him. There was no one better to raise Fern and Ivy than Aislinn, and that's where he worried this plan might implode.

He wasn't sure that he would be able to leave her here alone for months on end, when the time came. She'd been right when she said others did that, but he suspected his conscience wouldn't allow it. That's why he'd left here years ago. To avoid being committed to anyone but himself, because when you commit yourself to someone, they come first.

He'd wished many times that Rowland was still alive, for many reasons. Right now, it was because he needed someone to talk to, to consult with, confide in. Hells bells, there wasn't anyone he could talk to, anyone he could trust. He thought about Doo, but a man in his station couldn't consult with a servant, which only caused more irritation.

Other than Aislinn. He trusted her. But he'd already shot enough holes in her plan and didn't want to disappoint her further.

There was Mr Watson. He'd pay another visit to the solicitor tomorrow. Have him dig deeper, check to see if there might be any conditions placed on guardianship.

A noise somewhere in the house had him looking towards the door. The staff here were sure to wonder why he was sitting in the study, drinking straight out of the bottle, while his lovely bride was upstairs in his bedroom.

So much for lady luck. Why couldn't Aislinn have the face of an old maid and be three times his age? That would have been luck.

Strike that. No one would ever have believed he'd marry a woman like that.

Marrying Aislinn was far more believable, and it

was time for him to start playing the part of the happy bridegroom.

He stood, carried the bottle back to the side cabinet, replaced the stopper, and left the room.

Upstairs, he entered his bedroom. It was a fair-sized room. Besides hosting the large, four-poster bed and a sitting area near the fireplace, there was a separate bathing room, and a dressing room. The room seemed significantly smaller when his gaze settled on the bed. Every lamp had been turned down, leaving only faint glimmers to lighten the darkness.

She was huddled beneath the blankets, close to the edge of the bed. Any closer and she'd be on the floor. Her eyes were closed, and she didn't move as he closed the door, but he doubted she was sleeping. Like him, she was probably distraught over questions about what the day's events meant for the rest of her life.

Her life had changed as drastically as his.

Deep in his heart, he wanted to comfort her, tell her everything was going to be fine. But in his mind, where common sense thankfully prevailed, he knew he couldn't do that, because if he gave himself an inch when it came to her, he'd end up taking a mile. He was attracted to her. Overly attracted, even though he damn well knew this marriage was in name only.

Ignoring her, as she was him, he proceeded to the changing chamber. After removing his coat, vest, and ascot, he sat down and used the bootjack to remove his boots. His toes appreciated that, and he was grateful that the new pair he'd purchased, along with some of the clothes, his and hers, had been delivered earlier in the day.

They'd already been put away in the room.

For the first time in his life, there were women's garments hanging close to his, women's shoes sitting on the floor near his well-worn boots, and he imagined the drawers of the bureau had been rearranged to accommodate her other necessities.

After pulling off his socks, he rose, pulled down the unnecessary suspenders, and unbuttoned his shirt. He'd slept in his clothes more often than not some years, and could do so again, but not this shirt. It was too tight. The pants were snug, too, but he was sure to be uncomfortable simply sharing his bed, so could live with tight pants.

He returned to the main room and extinguished the lamps, before making his way to the bed. Without folding back the covers, he lay down

Aislinn didn't move, but her breathing was not slow and even, it was quick and short.

He considered rolling onto his side so they were back to back, but instead, knowing he wouldn't fall asleep easily no matter what position he was in, he lifted his arms and threaded his fingers together, then slid his hands between the back of his head and the pillow.

The silence in the room was only interrupted by her quick breathing, and his own deep sighs. Though there was plenty of room between them, he could feel that her body was tense, stiff. The tension between them hung heavily in the air.

'Go to sleep, Aislinn,' he whispered, hoping his own mind would obey.

She still didn't move, didn't acknowledge his statement, and it was a long time before her breathing evened out. Only then did he, too, relax enough to follow his own advice.

* * *

Hours later, he wasn't sure what roused him from sleep. It may have been the sun peeking in through the window, or it could have been an inner instinct that told him he wasn't alone. Having slept alone his entire life, less a few nights now and again, the instinct was too strong to ignore and he opened his eyes.

He was on his side, as was she. They were facing each other. The fog of sleep was clouding his mind, and he stared at the sleeping beauty lying next to him. The covers were over her shoulders, leaving only her face exposed. Her delicate features were fully tranquil.

Her hands were folded beneath her chin and one cheek was buried deep in the soft pillow.

An unfathomable warmth spread throughout his body, and he had no control over the smile that tugged on his lips as her long lashes fluttered softly.

He waited, holding his breath, as they fluttered again before opening. She blinked, as if needing to focus, then her lips turned up in a soft smile as she looked directly at him.

It was a moment or two until the cogs in his brain rolled into sync, giving him full use of his cognitive abilities. Memories, the reason as to why they were in bed together, struck with full force.

Evidently, the same happened to her.

Despite all he knew, he had to admit that it was somewhat comical the way they both jolted, then flipped over and climbed off the bed simultaneously.

Not attempting to hold back the humour that was making him grin from seeping into his tone, he said, 'Good morning.' Heading straight to the dressing room, he asked, 'Sleep well?'

'Fine, thank you, and you?' she replied.

He was already in the dressing room, looking for a set of britches that might hide his morning condition. 'Very well.' He grabbed a new set of trousers and quickly switched them out for the too tight pair he'd slept in.

Rustling sounds came from the other room as he shrugged on a new shirt while walking to the door. She had covered her nightgown with a wrapper and was making the bed. Her half of it. His only needed a little straightening. 'There are others who do that,' he said.

Without looking his way, she said, 'Others have enough to do.'

He turned around and re-entered the dressing room to complete his day's attire. 'I suppose we'll need to hire a few more people.'

'What for?'

Sitting down, he pulled on one sock while asking, 'Didn't staff travel with Rowland and Leslie from Havenbrook during their visits to London?'

'Yes.'

'Who?' He pulled on his other sock and then stuck a foot in the new boots.

'The Duchess's ladies' maid, the Duke's personal attendant, and a footman, amongst others.'

'Others meaning you,' he questioned, testing out the new boots and finding their fit as satisfactory as he had when he'd tried them on yesterday.

'Yes.'

He buttoned his shirt and carried the vest and jacket to the doorway. 'Well, then, I guess the least we should do is hire you a ladies' maid.'

She was seated on a small bench, brushing her hair before a mirror on a dressing table that must have been carried in at some point last evening. A chestnut shade, her hair was long, past her shoulders, and thick.

Her eyes caught his reflection in the mirror. 'What about a personal attendant for you? Or a footman?'

He leaned a hand on the door jam. 'Don't need them. I have Benjamin and Gabe.'

She set the brush down, and swiftly braided her hair, almost as if she had eyes in the back of her head. Or simply didn't need them to see what she was doing. 'And I have Claire and Millie.'

'They have other duties.' He knew the reassignments he'd requested had greatly irritated her.

After pining up the braid, she stood, pivoted, and met his gaze as she walked towards him. 'There is also Mary Ann, as well as Penny.'

'And John and Doo,' he said.

'I believe that's enough.' She stopped before him, nodding towards the dressing room behind him. 'Are you finished?'

He stepped forward and gestured towards the room. 'It's all yours.'

'Thank you.' She entered the room and closed the door.

Though their conversation had been amicable, there had been an icy tone to it on both of their parts, telling him what he already knew. None of this was any easier for her than it was for him. Tossing his vest and jacket on the bed, he walked into the water closet and used the tepid water in the pitcher to give himself a quick shave.

He exited moments before the dressing room door opened and she appeared, wearing a light green dress with a row of lace-covered buttons down the front, well past her waistline. The sleeves came down to her elbows, and exposed a layer of lace beneath the green material. There was lace around her neck, too, and like the yellow one yesterday, the dress fit her like a glove.

Rubbing his tongue on the roof of his mouth to work up enough salvia to swallow, so he could speak, he gave a nod towards the door. 'Shall we?'

She crossed the room. 'I will be stopping at the nursery before going downstairs.'

He opened the door. 'I will join you.'

Attempting to act normal, to sound normal, when everything was utterly *ab*normal, was difficult. But worse than that was the awkwardness that overcame Aislinn at times. She'd always been exceedingly comfortable both here and at Havenbrook, prior to Percy and Hazel moving in, that is, but today, that comfort was escaping her. In part due to the attitude of the other staff.

They were still the kind, efficient, even gracious people she'd always known. It was just that she felt a barrier between them and herself. Even Claire.

It had been clear that new roles had been established as soon as she'd entered the nursery. Claire had faded into the woodwork, just like she used to do when the Duke and Duchess would enter the room to visit with Fern and Ivy.

Both of the girls had already been dressed and were ready for the day, simply waiting on their breakfast to be brought up to them. She and Luke stayed until that happened and then proceeded downstairs to the dining room, where they were served a variety of meats and vegetables, along with the eggs and toast that she normally ate for breakfast.

Other than their exchange about additional staff in

the bedroom, few words had passed between her and Luke. The meal was reminiscent of last night, with little more than the clink of silverware touching plates.

'Dash it to hell.' Luke's muttered words broke the heavy silence.

'Excuse me?' she asked. 'Is something wrong with your meal?'

'No, it's not that.' He waved a hand, letting Gabe, who was standing near the door, know that his assistance wasn't needed, then leaned back in his chair. 'We are going to be here, in this house, in London, for as long as it takes to get things worked out.'

She nodded, already fully aware of that, but so very unsure about so many things.

'What do you say we make things a little less formal?' he asked.

She wasn't sure how to answer, because she didn't know the extent of his question, and merely waited for him to say more.

'In America, even the littlest tykes sit at the table, eating together. I know it's the English way for children to eat in the nursery. I did until I was ten or so. But what purpose does it serve? I'd understand if they were sick, naughty, or if they ate with their hands.'

Aislinn took a drink of water to wash down the bite of toast that became stuck in her throat. 'Fern and Ivy know how to use utensils.'

'Exactly. So why can't they eat down here with us? Unless there is some kind of formal meal, in which case they wouldn't want to be down here—I sure hadn't wanted to be— then I think we should allow them to eat with us.'

A wave of happiness washed over her. That would

certainly make meal times more tolerable, and it would give her more of an opportunity to oversee the care of Fern and Ivy. She trusted Claire, but giving up her old duties was filling her with anxiety. 'I don't see how that would cause any harm,' she said.

'Good.' He picked up his fork. 'You will arrange that?'

'I will.'

'Do they have favourite foods?' he asked. 'Besides biscuits with sweet icing?'

She had to smile at his reference, and felt the strain that was filling her ease slightly. 'Yes, they do.'

He stabbed the piece of sausage he'd sliced in two with his fork and lifted it, holding it in the air. 'Such as?'

She named a few things the girls were especially fond of, trying to keep the list of desserts to a minimum, for both Fern and Ivy favoured sweets the most.

He nodded. 'See that those are served.'

'Are you suggesting they join us for all meals?' she asked, just for clarification.

'Yes, unless for some reason you feel they shouldn't.'

She nodded. 'Very well.'

He stared at her for a long, silent moment, then said, 'Nothing has changed between us. We are still partners and might as well be as comfortable as possible.'

Although she wasn't completely sure what he meant, she nodded.

'Good.' Finishing his coffee, which he preferred over tea, in one swallow, he pushed away from the table. 'I have some errands to see to, and I'm sure you have things you need to do.'

She did. Now that he'd given her tasks concerning changes to mealtimes, she felt more confident about something else she needed to do. Setting her napkin on the table, she rose. 'When shall we expect you home?'

'Not really sure,' he said as they walked towards the doorway. 'By the noon meal, I'd guess.'

Benjamin was in the hall and handed Luke a hat. Not his brown, brimmed American one, but a black top hat.

Luke looked at it as if disgusted, then plopped it on his head and, with a grin, he totally shocked her by planting a fast kiss on her forehead, before he walked down the hall and out the door.

The spot his lips had touched was tingling, and she moved to the window, watching as John Moore handed him the reins to the horse he'd bought at the stable yesterday. In one swift movement, he was astride the horse and urged him into a trot. He sat straight in the saddle, balanced and moving with the horse, as he'd told her to do.

As he rounded the corner, out of sight, Aislinn closed her eyes and momentarily remembered waking up this morning to find him smiling at her. For that moment in time, she'd known a happiness that she'd never experienced. A warmth had tickled her insides, clear to her toes. Until a moment later, when she'd remembered everything that had happened yesterday. Then reality had blasted her like a winter squall.

She had never thought about marriage in the past, but now wondered why she hadn't.

Pushing the air out of her lungs, she opened her eyes.

During her restless night, when she'd awoken more than once due to her agitated state, she had questioned what the future might hold. That, too, had been something she hadn't considered before blurting out her idea.

But the truth was, there was no use worrying about that until the guardianship was resolved.

Until then, she had other things to worry about.

Turning from the window, she squared her shoulders. Knowing the staff's routine, for up until yesterday she had been one of them, she walked straight to the kitchen. All were there, except for Claire, who was upstairs with Fern and Ivy, and John, who was in the stable, drinking a final cup of tea before continuing with their duties of the day.

They each leaped to their feet, except for Doo, who was resting a hip against the sink counter. She wanted to tell the others to stay seated, but as the lady of the house, it was conventional that they stand in her presence.

'Mr Carlisle and I would like to make a few additional changes,' she said, flinching slightly at the need to sound so superior in front of people she considered equals, friends. 'Going forward, Fern and Ivy will take their meals with us in the dining room, unless otherwise instructed.'

There were slight bows of acknowledgement, but only Gabe spoke. 'Yes, my lady.'

'There is no need for formal addresses, for either Luke or myself, unless guests or visitors are present.' She and Luke hadn't discussed that, but she knew his preference. 'It's our most ardent hope that the Court of Chancery will accept the late Duke of Havenbrook's final wishes, as stated in his will, in which he requested Luke to be guardian of Fern and Ivy. I firmly believe that each of you have that hope, too.'

She waited for them to silently agree. They all did. Filled with a competency that she hadn't known was inside her, she continued, 'I want you all to know that there was no coercion in our decision to wed. We both entered into our marriage willingly. I believe that all of us, either those who knew him before he left for America, or came to know him through his letters, have great affection for Luke. I certainly do, and I'm convinced Fern and Ivy will have the best life possible under his care.'

Again, she gazed around the room, meeting each person's gaze and holding it for a moment. All she'd said was true, and each person in the room gave a nod in agreement with her. It was quite remarkable how easily the words were coming to her. 'As you know, Percy and Hazel are challenging Luke, and I have a suspicion that they may arrive in London soon. They are using everything they can against Luke and may have recruited others to seek out additional information. Therefore, I want this house known as a loving, caring place, in all aspects, and am imploring each of you to assist me.'

'Of course,' Mary Ann said, glancing at the others as they nodded.

Mary Ann, along with Gabe, had been at the house long before anyone else, and Aislinn had determined that she would need the housekeeper's help the most. She stepped forward and laid a hand on Mary's Ann's arm. 'I will need you to teach me everything I need to know about running this house, because you all know that I've never been trained for such duties. But I can't let Luke down. I can't fail him.' Tears formed, because she was speaking earnestly. 'I just can't.'

Puffing her plump bosom like a hen, Mary Ann's wrinkled, yet kind, face grew even more tender and sincere. 'You won't fail him. None of us will let that happen.'

Over the course of the next several hours, Aislinn became educated in domestic responsibilities, including overseeing daily activities, household accounts, menus and other matters that would require her attention. All of which she felt confident in her ability to master.

She was also provided with interesting bits of family history that she made mental notes to retain, so she could someday tell Fern and Ivy.

By the time she was informed that Luke had arrived home, she was convinced that no one would find fault in the household or its management.

In the front parlour with Mary Ann, for they had been inspecting the condition of the rugs, Aislinn took a deep breath and pressed a hand to her breast to calm the increased beat of her heart.

Mary Ann touched her arm. 'The most important thing for a lady to remember about running a house is that she's doing so for the right reasons. To make her husband proud and love him through thick and thin.'

A sudden, dreadful uneasiness struck Aislinn directly in the pit of her stomach. Managing a household was one thing, something she could learn, but no one could teach her how to pretend their marriage was real. She'd seen the way the old Duke and Duchess had looked upon each other, how they'd responded to each other in conversations. There had been love between them. Though she had great admiration for Luke, and affection, as she'd admitted to the staff, he didn't feel the same way. Nor could she expect him to.

With parting words about seeing that lunch was ready to be served, Mary Ann left the room, and moments later, Aislinn heard the housekeeper greet Luke and inform him that she was in the front parlour.

She lifted her chin and pulled up a smile as she faced the doorway.

Her smile slipped, then disappeared entirely, at the stern set of Luke's lips when he appeared.

Chapter Ten

Try as he might, Luke couldn't control the reactions inside him as he set eyes on Aislinn. One look had the ability to scramble his thoughts, make him unable to focus on anything but her. He'd thought about waking up next to her several times while completing his errands and couldn't deny the effects the memory had on his body.

Those same effects were kicking in right now.

The sombre silence that had filled the room at breakfast this morning had nearly been his undoing. He knew they wouldn't be able to live like that for any length of time. Including Fern and Ivy at meals seemed like an easy solution.

If only he could find other solutions so easily.

Mr Watson had stated that a date had been set for a hearing but didn't know if there might be any stipulations, nor had he discovered why Percy had petitioned to become Aislinn's guardian. In fact, he'd claimed that he and Mr Gaines had spent hours last evening, reading though law books for some obscure decree that Percy may have been informed of, only to come up empty-handed. Luke had refrained from sharing his belief that

Percy had simply wanted to prevent him from marrying her.

However, the solicitor had provided him with other information and suggestions that he would need to share with her. Things that, like it or not, they needed to do.

'Lunch will be served shortly,' she said. 'Fern and Ivy are excited to join us.'

'That's good.' He unbuttoned his coat, just for something to keep his hands busy. For half the morning he'd questioned why he hadn't stopped himself from kissing her forehead this morning. The desire had been too strong to ignore and was approaching that point again.

Undoing the last button, he twisted his shoulders to ease the tension in his muscles. The new clothes fit fine, but his old ones, the ones he wore at the ranch, were more comfortable. These ones made him feel like an imposter. For good reason. That's what he was. But he had no choice except to get used to it, because this was his life now.

'Did you complete your errands?' she asked.

She was nervous. The way she laid a hand upon her stomach was a clear sign. He didn't want her to feel uncomfortable around him. Truth be, he'd like things to be as easily as possible for her and would try his best to make that happen.

Childish chitter-chatter coming from the hall filtered into the room. 'I will tell you about them after lunch,' he said.

Fern and Ivy shot through the doorway. The bright blue bows in their hair that matched their frilly dresses bobbed on their heads, and their faces were as bright as sunshine as they ran towards him.

'We get to eat with you,' Fern said, skidding to a stop.

'In the dining room,' Ivy added, sidling up beside her sister.

'Just like when we were in the coach, coming to London,' Fern further explained.

His heart had warmed at the sight of them, and he knelt down to their level. 'That's right, and I'm happy about that.' He touched a cheek on each one of them with a single finger. 'I like looking at these happy faces while eating.'

They giggled.

'I have a surprise for you two,' he said.

'What is it?' Fern asked.

'If I told you, it wouldn't be a surprise.' He lifted one with each arm and settled them on his hips while walking towards the doorway. 'But I will show you after lunch.'

'Give us a hint,' Fern said, holding on to his neck.

'Yes, a hint,' Ivy said, also holding on to his neck.

'Well, let's see,' he said, as if he had to think about a clue. 'It's big, but also little.'

'That can't be!' Fern insisted. 'Nothing can be big and little!'

'How big?' Ivy asked, warily.

He glanced at Aislinn, once again recalling her initial description of the girls, about Ivy being cautious. She hadn't lied about that.

Pulling up a smile for Ivy, he said, 'Not too big.'

The pony that would be delivered shortly had been a thought that came to him while thinking about Aislinn and the girls, of things he could do for them to make this time as normal and fun as possible. There was plenty of room in the stable, and the backyard was big enough for a pony to be led around. The one he'd bought was pure white, with blue eyes, and the man, the same one who'd sold him the thoroughbred, guaranteed it was as tame as a dog. In fact, it had been his daughter's pony, until she'd outgrown it.

Questions, and his vague answers, continued throughout the meal, making it very enjoyable. He was nearly as excited as the girls when it was finally time to see their surprise. At the doorway of the dining room, he handed Gabe his jacket, then rolled up his shirtsleeves while leading everyone through the house and out the back door.

'Where is it?' Fern asked, running in front of him.

Ivy grasped a hold of his hand as she asked, 'How big is it, Uncle Luke?'

Her nervousness melted his heart, and he stopped to pick her up. 'It's bigger than you, but smaller than me.'

Her tiny brows were furrowed between her big eyes.

He touched the tip of her nose. 'You see how big I am?' He waited for her nod, then continued, 'Very big, and I'll always protect you, from things big and small.'

She wrapped her arms around his neck and buried her face in his shoulder. 'I love you, Uncle Luke.'

He hadn't said that to anyone in years, but knew exactly what he felt right now. 'I love you, too, Ivy. Very much.'

His heart did an odd flutter when his gaze caught Aislinn's. The shimmer in her eyes made his throat go dry. To the point that he had to cough slightly, so he could swallow.

Collecting his wits, he set Ivy back on the ground and directed them all to the stable.

The pony was in a stall that John had prepared for her, as Luke had requested upon his arrival home. Riding equipment had been delivered along with the pony, but Luke just took down the lead rope.

'She's so adorable,' Fern said, petting the side of the pony.

Both girls, along with Aislinn, who was keeping a close eye on them, were in the stall with the horse.

'Does it have a name?' Ivy asked, running a hand down the centre of the pony's face.

'She does,' he answered. 'It's Half-Pint.'

Fern giggled. 'That's a funny name.'

'I like it,' Ivy said, wrapping her arms around the pony's neck. 'I like you, Half-Pint.'

'I think Half-Pint likes you, too,' Luke said. 'Both of you.' The pony was soaking up the attention. He pointed out how they needed to keep their feet away from Half-Pint's hooves and a few other things, then hooked the lead rope around the pony's neck. 'Shall we take her into the backyard, so you can ride her?'

Both girls readily agreed, and he looked at Aislinn, remembering her fear of Old Bones.

The smile on her face and the shine in her eyes hit his heart all over again. He knew the appreciation she silently displayed was because he'd made the girls happy. That was the way to her heart. He wasn't trying to win her heart, but his own felt as if it had been arrested.

He led the pony into the backyard and settled the girls on its back, with Ivy in the front so she would feel more secure. 'Do you feel comfortable leading Half-Pint?' he asked Aislinn. 'She's gentle, leads well. I'd like to walk beside them, to help them keep their balance.'

'Yes,' she replied, taking the rope.

'Just walk slow,' he instructed, 'she'll follow you.'

Aislinn nodded and began walking at his direction.

Half-Pint was indeed well trained. Her gait was slow and smooth, as if she fully understood how precious a load she carried. He'd examined the pony before purchase, and again in the stable before putting the lead rope on her. She was a stout animal, healthy, and he was more than satisfied with her personality. The perfect first horse.

Fern and Ivy were naturals, if he said so himself, and he could see them riding Half-Pint by themselves in no time. He liked that idea. Everyone should know how to ride a horse, be comfortable around them, for they were an integral part of life. Even here in London.

They remained in the backyard for the better part of an hour, until he said that it was time for Half-Pint to rest.

Claire was waiting for them near the back door of the house, and as she ushered Fern and Ivy inside, he looked at Aislinn. 'I understand it's warm out, but we do need to talk.'

She lifted her chin. 'Wherever you wish is fine by me, but I can assure you that no one will be listening at any door inside the house.'

He had sensed a change in her interactions with the other servants since this morning, and he hoped she was correct, for he had no desire to be concerned about disloyal servants. He gave a single nod and followed her inside the house.

She led the way to the study, where he closed the door and waited until she was seated on the sofa before sitting in an adjacent chair. It was somewhat of a mystery as to how he could feel so comfortable in her presence, while his senses were also so heightened.

He cleared his throat, just for something to do. 'Mr

Watson informed me this morning that the court has set a date for when they'll make their final decision on the guardianship petition.'

The knuckles on her fingers, clasped tightly in her lap, turned white. 'When will that be?'

'Two weeks from tomorrow,' he replied. 'Between now and then, Mr Watson suggested that you and I attend the theatre and other such social outings.'

'The theatre?' she questioned, almost as if appalled. 'Why?'

He nearly chuckled, for he too had been appalled when Mr Watson had made the suggestion. Frequenting social venues had never been high on his priority list. In fact, he'd attended very few. Only those his mother had forced him to go to. 'Because attending such outings are not about the performances or events, it's about seeing who is there and being seen by others.' That's what his mother had told him. The next part was his own thought. 'It's what the privileged do, part of the lifestyle.'

'Mr Watson believes that will help your case?'

'He believes it will demonstrate that I'm embedding myself, that we are embedding ourselves, into our new life.'

Aislinn pinched her lips together. She fully understood that the upper class found importance in attending events, but Luke didn't. He was clearly willing to do whatever it took for Fern and Ivy, the fact that he'd married her—a woman well beneath him—had proven that, but he shouldn't have to change who he was. That defeated the purpose. Rowland wanted Luke to have guardianship over his daughters because he knew Luke would care more about them than anything else.

'This is our life now,' he said. 'It's not one we would have chosen, given different circumstances, but it is what it is. I have a friend, whom I hadn't seen in years, Michael Cunningham, the Earl of Chatsworth. I stopped by to see him this morning, and Michael is very much the good chap that I remember. He and his wife, Eugenia, the Countess of Chatsworth, have invited us to attend the theatre with them tomorrow night, and I have accepted the invitation.'

Her heart thudded near the back of her throat, blocking her airway. The theatre? With the Earl and Countess of Chatsworth? How on earth had she ever imagined that she could do this?

Luke leaned to one side and dug into his pant pocket. 'In light of all that, I purchased this today.'

Curious, she leaned across the table separating them to take the small box that he held out. Lifting the lid revealed a shimmering ring nestled atop a small square of black velvet.

'Everyone will expect you to have a wedding band,' he said.

It wasn't merely a wedding band; it was a jewelled ring. The gold band was wide, with a square-shaped diamond in the centre, a rectangular ruby on one side, and a rectangular emerald on the other. She had never imagined owning jewels of any sort. The ring was beautiful, and clearly expensive. Just holding the box made her nervous.

'If it doesn't fit, we can have it resized,' he said. 'It fit on my pinkie, so I thought it might be close.'

Her mouth was dry, yet she had to speak. 'It's beautiful…' Nothing more would come out.

'Try it on,' he said.

Still nervous, and thinking she should insist such a thing wasn't necessary, her fingers shook as she picked it up. The sunlight coming in through the window made the entire ring sparkle.

'Put it on,' he said. 'Does it fit?'

Both hands trembled as she slid it on the ring finger of her left hand. 'Yes, perfectly,' she replied. 'But, Luke—'

'It caught my eye as soon as I walked in the store,' he said. 'The ruby is in honour of Fern, the emerald, Ivy, and the diamond, well, that's for you.'

She glanced up, and though they had been out in the sun for an hour earlier, she wasn't certain the red tint on his cheeks was from that. He was as nervous as she was, and she couldn't make him feel bad by rejecting the ring. 'Thank you,' she said. 'It's truly beautiful.'

He nodded and glanced around the room, as if not wanting to meet her gaze.

She lowered her eyes to the ring again and couldn't help but think that if things were different, as he'd said, if by some impossible event they had met and married for love, just how overjoyed she would have been at this moment. It was a silly thought, an impossible dream, but she couldn't imagine ever meeting another man like him. A man so dedicated to those he loved that he would do anything for them. Give up his own life for them. It would be prudent of her not to create false hope that she would ever be someone he loved. Thoughts like that would do nothing more than cause heartache.

'There is one more thing we need to discuss,' he said.

She lifted her head, nodded.

'When—' He scratched the side of his neck. 'When we are in public, we'll need to, well, hold hands and things like that. Act like we are, uh, in love.'

A fiery zip of something she couldn't quite explain shot about in her stomach. It was much more forceful than butterflies. Trying to ignore it, she said, 'All right.'

'We don't know who might see us and say something to Percy.'

Not trusting her ability to speak, she nodded.

'All right, then, that should cover it.' He stood. 'I have a few more errands to see to.'

She wondered if that was true, or if he just wanted to be gone, away from her. Acting like a truly married couple couldn't be any easier for him than it was for her.

'I'll be home in time for supper,' he said.

He was gone almost instantaneously, and she looked down at the ring on her finger. This was all her fault. She'd come up with the whole marriage idea. An idea that had forced him into a life he'd never wanted. Fake or real, it didn't matter.

Not wanting to face anyone, she left the room and made her way upstairs, to *their* room. Another thing that was all her fault.

She walked to the door that led to the small personal balcony, opened the glass paned door, and stepped outside. It overlooked the backyard, and she sighed at the wonderful event that had taken place out there just a short time ago.

The pony had been a wonderful surprise. One Fern and Ivy would never forget. Nor she, for whether Luke realised it or not, he'd found something that Ivy fully embraced. From the moment she'd seen Half-Pint, Ivy's usual wariness had disappeared. She would still be out there, on Half-Pint, if he hadn't suggested the pony needed a rest.

Aislinn rested both hands on the waist-high railing. That shouldn't surprise her. He'd done the same thing for her. She kept telling herself that she needed to change, needed to become stronger and more assertive, for the girls. But the truth was, she was doing it for him.

The letters he'd written had been fascinating, exciting, had endeared him to her, but they didn't compare to being with him in person. He was big, strong, and bold, yet equally gentle, kind, and caring. A living, breathing hero. And having him ask her—her of all people—for help had made her feel like more than just a governess. Or perhaps it had made her want to be more. Not necessarily more than a governess, but more of a person. A bolder, stronger person, like him.

She drew in a deep breath and slowly released it.

Heaven help her, for she didn't know how, but she would convince the entire world if necessary that they were in love. She would do anything to make sure that he fulfilled Rowland's wishes.

She had no idea why Percy didn't want that to happen, other than he and Hazel had taken control over everything and everyone from the moment Rowland had died.

He'd taken his final breaths in the middle of the night, in a room just down the hall from where she stood. Percy had been present, had awoken the entire house and told her to pack, that she and the girls were returning to Havenbrook. Leslie had died two days before, her body had already been sent to Havenbrook, for that was the final resting place for both of them.

Following orders, it had still been dark when she and the girls had left for Havenbrook, and when they arrived, they found some of Percy and Hazel's servants already in the house. They had cleared away Rowland's and Leslie's personal items from their rooms, and replaced them with Percy's and Hazel's.

Arriving the following day, and insisting that they were now to be addressed as the Duke and Duchess, Percy and Hazel had made it clear that anyone opposed to the changes they implemented could leave, including her. She'd never have willingly left Fern and Ivy, even though it had been evident that she was disliked.

The back door of the house opened and closed, and her heart somersaulted as, from the balcony, she watched Luke walk towards the stable. She stepped inside so she wouldn't be noticed if he looked behind him, looked up.

He didn't, but she stood in the doorway, obscured by the drapes, until he exited the stable on his new thoroughbred, then mounted the animal and rode away.

She pressed a hand over her thudding heart. He was willing to do anything because of his love for Rowland. She knew that, but she also knew that Rowland had loved Luke unconditionally and wouldn't want him to have to completely change his life.

Somehow, she had to make sure that didn't happen, because she was the only one who could. There was no one else.

But she wasn't alone.

After checking her image in the mirror, she left the room. A quick check in the nursery showed it was nap time, and Millie was sitting in a chair with a basket of mending.

Aislinn then made her way to the kitchen.

Claire was in the far corner, washing clothes. Doo was peeling potatoes at the sink, and Mary Ann and Gabe were sitting at the table, drinking tea. They rose and she waved at them to sit, collecting a cup and sitting down to join them at the table.

The silence was thick. It was up to her to break it. 'I need your help again,' she said.

Every set of eyes turned her way.

'Luke and I will be attending the theatre with the Earl and Countess of Chatsworth tomorrow night, and I have no idea what to expect.'

Mary Ann let out a sigh. 'For a minute there, you had me worried, but this…' She shook her head. 'This is nothing to worry about.'

Aislinn couldn't agree with that.

Chapter Eleven

Luke was sorely disappointed. He'd wanted a ride that would unclutter his mind, so he could think clearly, but such a ride did not exist in London. Not even in the park. There were too many people. Too much noise. What he wouldn't give for the wide-open range right now, where he could just ride.

Like he'd done for years.

This was different, though. He wasn't looking for his next adventure, he was running from the one he was in the midst of living. There was no denying that.

He knew why, too.

Aislinn.

Something had happened inside him when he'd seen that ring on her finger. His ring. The ring he'd purchased just for her. It was ridiculous to compare her to a cow, even for him, but the feeling inside him was the same one he'd felt the first time he'd seen his brand, the C Bar H brand, on a cow.

He'd owned other things in his life, but that first cow he'd branded as his own had struck a chord in him. He'd known at that very moment that he'd found exactly what he'd always been looking for his entire life. He'd been proud of that.

He sure as hell had never been looking for a wife, so feeling that same thing for Aislinn was beyond ridiculous.

Sure, he cared about her.

Had since he'd seen her puffy, teary-eyed face on the road. Hearing how Percy had sent a slip of girl out into the world, with nothing more than the clothes on her back had angered him. But he'd already been mad at Percy by that time.

He should probably be mad at Percy over this, too, but he was reasonable enough to admit that Percy hadn't forced him to marry Aislinn. He'd done that all on his own. Even though he still didn't know why Percy had wanted guardianship over her, that hadn't made or broken the deal. He'd already cared about her by then, cared what happened to her.

She wasn't the first person that he'd cared about. Besides family, there was Raf. Hell, he'd even cared about the dance hall gals he'd pulled out of the river. Hadn't wanted to see them drown. He'd cared about that little lost boy, too.

Aislinn was different, though. Right from the start, he'd wanted more than just to save her. He'd told himself it was because he needed help. Needed a partner. Fact was, he'd wanted to keep her safe.

There was another truth he had to face. He'd agreed to marry her partly because he didn't like the idea of her marrying anyone else. He just couldn't admit that. Not even to himself. Hell, his own selfishness had created a mess.

More truth rained down on him, concerning how

self-serving he'd been for years. He'd been glad that he was born last, so he wasn't obligated to do anything except what he wanted to do. Even the plan he'd come up with while travelling back to England, to find someone to take care of Fern and Ivy while he returned to America, had been selfish.

He needed to grow up, face the facts. His years of being foolish, selfish, were over. He'd had his fun; it was time to settle down and accept the lifelong commitments that were now his burden to bear.

Damn it, he'd be proud to bear those burdens. Proud to fulfil Rowland's wishes, and God willing, if he gave her enough time to get used to it, maybe one day, Aislinn would be proud to be his wife.

'Imagine that. I don't see you for years, and now it's twice in the same day.'

Luke looked up, saw Michael Cunningham reining in the coal-black horse approaching.

Pulling up a grin for his friend, Luke said, 'Must be your lucky day.'

'Hope so. I'm on my way to the club. Join me?' Michael lifted a dark brow. He had a long face, with a straight nose and deep-sunk eyes, which only looked deeper with his brow raised. 'I won't be there but a couple of hours. Promised I'd be home before the dinner hour. You know what married life is like. Keep the wife happy, and she'll keep you happy.'

Although Luke knew full well that didn't begin to compare to his marriage, he figured there was a good amount of truth to it. The other truth was that he wasn't ready to face Aislinn. Yet. She'd ended up married to him through no fault of her own, and he had to remember that. 'Thanks for the invite,' he told Michael as he turned his horse around, so they were heading in the same direction. 'Sounds good to me.'

'Excellent.' Michael nudged his horse forward. 'The men there are going to be glad to meet you. The Duke—' Michael shook his head. 'Your brother Rowland talked you up higher than the hills. Made you into some sort of fable. Even read parts of your letters aloud.'

Luke chuckled. His brother had been proud of those letters. 'He wrote me about you, too. Told me he went to your wedding.'

'He was there, and I know I already said it, but I'm sorry about his death. He was a good man, and is missed by many.'

'He was,' Luke agreed.

'You'll see plenty of faces that you remember,' Michael said as he nudged his horse into a trot. 'I guarantee it!'

Luke took the challenge of a race and urged the thoroughbred into a run.

Minutes later, he waited for Michael to dismount and tie up his horse next to the thoroughbred, before they strolled through the door of the gentlemen's club. Luke scanned the area filled with tables, tall wingback chairs, and men. Nearly every one of them had a cigar between their fingers, and a heavy haze of smoke hung below the ceiling.

Their entrance had gone relatively unnoticed, until Michael stuck two fingers in his mouth and let out a sharp whistle.

'Hear ye, hear ye,' Michael shouted good-naturedly. 'The long-lost Carlisle brother has retuned and has agreed to grant us his presence.'

To Luke's surprise, laughter and applause erupted.

Good thing he hadn't had his heart set on playing cards, because that didn't happen. The next few hours were spent catching up with names and faces, though they all looked older than he remembered, as well as meeting new ones. He joined in on a couple of toasts in Rowland's memory and heard some outlandish renditions of the letters he'd written. He also accepted congratulations on the marriage proclamation that had been printed in the paper that morning. Some questioned if his wife had sailed from America with him, while others jokingly declared that she had to be the one he left behind, his true reason for returning.

His response, that they'd have to see for themselves that her beauty compared to no other on either continent, made the men laugh and elbow each other as if he jested. He knew that was the solemn truth. Aislinn's beauty was incomparable.

When Michael proclaimed that it was time he leave, Luke agreed. Once they finally made it out the door, for every table had stopped them to say a few parting words, both he and Michael jogged to their waiting horses.

Their parting gestures were simple, quick waves, because Michael didn't want to be late for dinner, and Luke was ready to be home. Ready to see Aislinn.

She was in the front sitting room, along with Fern and Ivy, playing a counting game on the table in front of the sofa. The girls quickly rose as he entered the room and raced towards him.

'I apologise,' he said. 'I do hope I haven't kept dinner waiting too long.'

'No, not at all,' Aislinn said. 'I requested the final preparations wait until your arrival.'

Her transformation from governess to lady had not only happened overnight, it had been flawless on her part. Another validation of her underlying courage and aptitude. She should be proud of herself. He was proud of her, proud to call her his wife, as he had done for the past several hours. But that didn't change the fact that he'd pulled her into a life she hadn't wanted.

He'd been there and knew how that felt.

Meeting her gaze directly, he gave her an appreciative nod that wasn't related to delaying dinner. 'Thank you.' Then he knelt down, and scooped up both girls.

'I rode Half-Pint again,' Ivy said. 'By myself.'

'You did?' he asked, while carrying them across the room.

She nodded with great pride.

'So did I,' Fern said. 'Aislinn walked beside us and Mr Moore led Half-Pint.'

'When can I ride your horse?' Ivy asked.

Surprised, yet catching the smile on Aislinn's face, he said, 'Well, I'm sure we could arrange that soon.'

'How soon?' Ivy asked.

'Perhaps tomorrow,' he answered, happy to see that she was speaking up for herself, rather than following in her sister's footsteps.

'Time to put away your game,' Aislinn said, rising to her feet.

He set the girls on the floor, and as they hurried to collect the pieces off the table and put them in a basket, he moved closer to Aislinn.

'I believe you found something that Ivy adores.' Her head tilted slightly as she added, 'Horses.'

'It appears so.' He touched the side of her face with

one knuckle, thinking to himself that he'd found something that he adored, too.

She looked at him quizzically.

The want to kiss her was damn near overwhelming. He dropped his hand. 'I'll go change my jacket. I smell like cigar smoke.'

A smile formed as she nodded. 'Yes, you do.'

'I met up with some old friends,' he said, heading towards the door. 'I'll tell you about it later.'

Besides changing his coat, Luke washed his hands and face, and also added a quick splash of cologne, before he headed back downstairs, just in time for the dinner announcement.

As they had at the noon meal, Fern and Ivy and their conversations enhanced the meal with a glow of enjoyment. After they finished dessert, a rich chocolate cake that the girls had gobbled up as if they hadn't eaten anything else, they retired to the drawing room, where he taught the girls how to play checkers. They were quick learners and were soon playing a game between them.

'I can't believe you haven't taught them to play checkers,' he said to Aislinn.

A pink blush covered her cheeks. 'I didn't know how to play.'

'You didn't?'

Aislinn's breath stuck in her throat. Luke was looking up at her with such astonishment in his eyes that she should have laughed. Would have, if she'd been able to breathe. He was so handsome, and the way he was sitting on the floor with Fern and Ivy, the checkerboard set out on the short table in front of them, was so endearing.

He'd been so patient in explaining the game and showing them how to play, that her heart felt as if it had swelled inside her chest. Swelled with something strong and powerful.

He laid a hand on her knee. 'You can't be serious. Everyone knows how to play checkers.'

She forced air to enter through her nose and let it out slowly. 'I never learned.'

'They didn't have games at the orphanage?'

'Yes, they had some, but I was too old for games when I arrived.'

'Too old? You were only seven.'

She was surprised that he remembered that. 'Which was old enough to look after the younger children.'

He frowned. 'You've been taking care of children your entire life?'

'Yes, but it's what I love to do.' That was the honest truth. The other truth was that the touch of his hand on her knee was sending a swirling warmth throughout her system. Her mind was aflutter with thoughts, and she couldn't have moved if the house was on fire as he slowly rose off the floor and sat down on the sofa beside her.

She couldn't say what was in his eyes, because she didn't recognise what was there, but it caused her breath to lodge in the back of her throat again.

He took a hold of her hand, his touch tender yet firm, and stared at her for what felt like an endless amount of time.

'You're good at it, too,' he said quietly. 'Taking care of children. Very good at it.'

Then, before she knew what was happening, he learned forward and placed a kiss upon her forehead. A kiss so gentle and tender that she grew light-headed enough to swoon.

The woodsy, manly scent of his cologne, and the way his fingers wrapped around hers a bit tighter, added to the already heady sensation encompassing her.

'But,' he said quietly, 'if that's all you've ever done, how do you know there's not something you'd love just as much?'

'I just do,' she whispered, before she completely lost her senses, as well as her ability to speak. Her mind had suddenly become focused on one thing. His lips. How it would feel to be kissed by him. Really kissed. On the lips.

His eyes were looking at her lips, and that alone was making them tingle. It was making her heart race, too. When he licked his lips, such a crazy flip happened inside her stomach that she had to bite down on her bottom lip to hold in a gasp.

Aislinn wasn't sure what she heard, perhaps one of the girls did something, or made a sound of some kind, but it was enough to make her turn to the table and suck in a deep breath, hoping to settle her insides.

'Forgive me, but I have a bath ready for the girls.'

Aislinn heard Claire's voice, but it was yet another moment before she could respond. By then, Luke had already reacted.

'Off you two go,' he told the girls, while gathering the black and red chips into a pile. 'We'll be up to say good night after you're spanking clean.'

'What's spanking clean?' Ivy asked.

'He means sparkling clean,' Aislinn said, giving Luke a quick glance.

'That is exactly what I mean,' he said. 'Sparkling clean. I'll pick up the game. Off you go.'

The girls agreed to that and hurried towards Claire.

Once they were out of sight, Luke stretched his arms over his head, with his fingers threaded together.

She heard his knuckles pop and looked his way.

'Ready?' he asked.

'Ready for what?'

'To learn how to play checkers.'

She shook her head. 'I already know.'

'You said you didn't.'

'I didn't, until you taught the girls.'

'Oh, no. You don't learn by watching, you learn by doing.' He slid off the sofa and onto the floor. 'Red or black?'

'Red,' she said, tucking her dress tight beneath her so she could slide off the sofa to sit on the floor beside him.

He won the first two games, but by the third one, after listening to his suggestions, she'd caught on to the strategy and won. Although she did wonder if he let her win.

'You said you saw some old friends today,' she said while they both set their chips on the back squares again.

'I did. I ran into Michael Cunningham again, and he was on the way to a gentlemen's club. I went along and saw people I'd completely forgotten about. Rowland frequented the club regularly and had read excerpts of my letters there.'

'He had?' A feather of hope tickled her insides. 'More than just the beginnings?'

'Yep.'

More than one feather tickled her, turning hope into

excitement. 'So other people know the truth. The entire truth?'

'They do. Any member of the courts who visited that club, and there are several, would know the truth.'

She laid a hand atop one of his. 'That's wonderful.'

'Yes, it is.' He clasped a hold of her hand, then pushed up off the floor and sat on the sofa, tugging her hand so she would join him.

She did so.

He still had a hold of her hand, and softly kissed the back of it, an action that once again played havoc with her insides, although she was getting used to it and was finding it to be pleasurable.

'They had also read the announcement in today's newspaper about our marriage,' he said. 'And I'm afraid that we now have a somewhat lengthy list of invitations to a variety of social events.'

Her stomach dipped. 'I'm sorry.'

Frowning, he asked, 'Sorry for what?'

'The list of invitations. I know you don't like social events.'

He looked at her for a moment before his grin grew. 'Perhaps that was because I never went to any with the right person. That makes a difference you know. The right person can make all the difference in the world.'

She nodded, because that was true, but the way he said it made her wonder if he'd only said that to make her feel better, if he truly still didn't like social events.

He gave her hand a squeeze, then released it and stretched his arms across the back of the sofa as he leaned back. 'I wish that I could have been a mouse in the corner when Percy learned about our marriage.'

She leaned back against the sofa, too, as a real sense

of dread washed over her. 'Do you think he already knows?'

His arm behind her dipped down around her and his hand grasped her shoulder, tugging her up against his side. 'Probably. Whoever he has on the inside at the courts would have read the announcement in the paper today and sent him a message. I expect him to arrive in London within a day or two.'

Although she probably shouldn't, she liked the comfort of being next to him, the feeling that she wasn't alone in all of this. 'What are we going to do about that?'

'Live. We'll attend the events just as Mr Watson suggested, but other than that, we've done all we can do. It's up to the courts now.'

A pit formed in her stomach.

He rubbed her upper arm. 'Mr Watson has requested that only complete letters be used as evidence. After today, when I confirmed what Rowland had read to patrons at the club, even if Percy alters the letters to make them look complete, others will already know the entire truth.'

'You're sure?'

'I am.' He leaned his head towards hers, until their temples touched. 'Now that we are married, Percy doesn't have a leg to stand on.'

Chapter Twelve

Later, as she prepared for bed, Aislinn was filled with a nearly overwhelming bout of nervousness at the idea of sleeping next to Luke again. They had sat on the sofa, talking about a variety of topics, some serious, some just downright silly, before Gabe had informed them that Fern and Ivy were asking to bid them good night.

Together, they had gone to the nursery and had spent an extended amount of time reading stories to the girls, two books each. He was as talented at making stories enjoyable as he was at writing letters, changing words and adding his own thoughts into the story, which at times were very comical.

Upon leaving the nursery, Luke announced that he was going to take a bath. With cheeks heating at the image that had spontaneously formed in her mind for no good reason, she'd excused herself and ended up in the study, where, ironically, she'd found a book about America. It was one she'd already read and had enjoyed, so she forced herself to become engrossed in the pages. Which she had done, namely because images of Luke seeing the things described in the book had formed in her head.

Smelling amazingly clean, with his hair still damp and wearing his American pants and shirt, he'd found her in the study, where he'd informed her that he was going to read for a time, but she could go on up to bed.

So here she was, in the dressing room, where she'd shed her gown, petticoat, and chemise and donned a nightdress, wondering if she should have left on more. He'd slept in his clothes last night, and she questioned if that had been something he'd wanted her to do, as well.

Though their new kinship and the bond she'd felt growing stronger as they'd sat on the sofa were wonderful, she couldn't help but question if it would lead to more.

The thought embarrassed her, for she should not be thinking, nor wishing, for such things. He had married her for one reason. They'd agreed that their marriage was in name only. Married but not being married. That's what she'd said.

Fully trained in all aspects of being a governess, along with living amongst staff where every subject was whispered about behind closed doors, she knew the full details of procreation. Some particulars had always made her quiver with disdain, but quite the opposite was true right now. The idea of Luke touching her, kissing her, didn't repulse her in the least.

Truth was, it filled her with quite unusual sensations, and a yearning she couldn't deny.

It was foolish, utterly so, to imagine they would have marital relations, yet she found herself wondering if not being married, while being married, could last. He'd said marriage was for ever.

But they wouldn't be together. He would return to Montana after the guardianship was settled, and she'd live here with the girls. That's what they'd agreed to, and she wouldn't go back on her word. He belonged in America.

'Oh, dash it all,' she uttered. She was driving herself mad with her own thoughts, and unless she wanted him to catch her standing in the dressing room like some ninny, she needed to go to bed.

Opening the door slowly, she peered into the bedroom. There had been no noise, but she wanted to make sure he hadn't entered yet.

Thankful the room was empty, she quickly scampered to the bed and slipped beneath the covers. Moments later, realising she'd left all the lamps lit, she flipped back the covers to leap off the bed and quickly blew out two, then turned down the wicks on the one next to the bed on his side and the one in the dressing room.

Back in bed, she wished she'd brought the book with her, but rapidly decided it would be better if she was asleep when he entered. She closed her eyes, only to have them pop open, claiming she wasn't sleepy.

Flipping onto her side, she nestled her cheek deep in the pillow, but then realised she was facing the empty side of the bed. Rolling onto her other side, and crowding the edge of the bed, she pulled the covers up over her shoulder to try again.

That's when the door opened. 'Good,' Luke said with his permanent grin in place, 'you aren't asleep yet.'

Her throat went dry.

Luke headed straight to the changing room, tossing the book on the bed en route. 'I'll be right back.' He'd thought ahead tonight. After his bath, he'd put on a pair of his old pants. They were roomy and would be more comfortable to sleep in than the ones he'd worn to bed last night.

That was a ridiculous thing for a man to worry about, especially a married man. It might not always be that way for him, but it was for now. Would be until after the guardianship hearings were completed. Then, he'd ask Aislinn what they should do about their marriage.

Strike that.

Then he'd ask her what she wanted to do about their marriage.

Until then, he'd be sleeping in his britches.

With his boots, socks, and shirt removed, he blew out the light in the changing room and entered the bedroom. 'I want to show you something.' He turned up the wick on the lamp before climbing on the bed and picking up the book. 'This is the book you were reading downstairs.'

She nodded.

He pushed the pillow behind him up against the headboard, leaned back, and flipped open the book, looking for the page he wanted. 'Scoot over here, where the light is better.'

She moved her pillow next to his and leaned back against it, staying under the covers from the waist down. Her nightdress was again buttoned clear to her chin and the sleeves went down to her wrists.

He held the book open wide, so they both could see the page. 'See this drawing of a tornado? It's exactly like the one I saw.'

'It is? Did you write about it? I don't remember that.'

'Yes,' he answered. 'But it was a long time ago. Fern and Ivy hadn't been born yet. I was travelling across Oklahoma Territory, on my way from New Orleans to

Colorado. There were places that the land was so flat, it was like looking over the sea, all the way to the horizon. They call the covered wagons in the wagon trains prairie schooners, because their canvas covers waved in the wind like the sails of ships on the ocean. There were four of us heading for the gold towns in Colorado.'

'Was one of them Raf?'

'No, I didn't meet up with him until Colorado.' He couldn't help but wonder how things were going back at the ranch. Branding should be done by now. Pushing those thoughts to the back of his mind, he pointed to the top of the picture. 'See how the artist drew these clouds? See how they look like boiling water?'

'Yes, they resemble that.'

He shook his head. 'I tried to explain to Rowland what the tornado looked like. I'd told him it was massive, but I couldn't describe it, couldn't get the words right. This person did. See right here, they say that the clouds looked like a pot of water that had been heated to a rolling boil. That's what I saw. Within a matter of minutes, the blue sky had turned grey and the clouds started churning. Then they hit a boil. If I'd have thought to explain it like that, it would have described it better.'

The memory of what he'd seen that day would stay with him for ever, but now he had the words to describe it. Thanks to this book. 'The clouds were all shades of grey and green, from dark to light. I'd never seen anything like it. The other men jumped off their horses and took cover in the grass, holding onto boulders. I couldn't. I couldn't do anything but watch the sky. Then this tail dropped down out of the clouds, whipping around like rope. The more it whipped, the bigger it became, until it was a big cone shape, just like this picture. The wind had been blowing, because it always blows there, but when that big funnel formed, it was like it sucked all the wind into it. Everything around me was still. Not a blade of grass moved. There was a moment of eerie silence, until the noise of the funnel hit with a roar like a train.'

'Weren't you scared?'

'I was too fascinated to be scared. It wasn't coming at us. It was moving across our path, a distance ahead of us. See how the artist drew the dirt and dust where the tail touched the ground?'

'Yes.'

'That's exactly what it was like. Everything that tail touched was sucked up inside that funnel. After it was over, and we rode through where it had been, it looked like someone had swept the earth with a broom, leaving nothing but hard-packed ground. Then we came upon the debris it spit out as the tail got sucked back up into the clouds. There were tree limbs, big ones, and we hadn't seen a tree for miles.'

'The tail got sucked back up?' she asked. 'It just disappeared?'

'Yes, as quickly as it had appeared. Within no time, the sun was out and the sky was blue.' He studied the picture again. Downstairs, when he'd seen it, it had reminded him of the first time he'd seen her. How both sights had mesmerised him. He couldn't tell her that, but he'd never forget it.

She was quiet for a moment, then asked, 'Can you turn to another page?'

'Sure. Sorry, didn't mean to scare you.'

'You didn't. I just want to know about the mountains. It's closer to the front of the book.'

He knew the page. It had reminded him of home. Strike that. This was home now.

'Is that what it looks like at your ranch?' she asked, pointing at the picture of the mountains he'd found.

Again, it was a drawing, a good one. 'Yes, but this is black and white with some grey. Colourless. The one thing the Montana Territory is not, is colourless.'

'Tell me about it.'

He did, all about the mountains and foothills, the rivers and lakes, the ranch, and that big Montana sky that went on for ever. About the Northern Lights and the hip-deep snow, the fields of flowers in the summertime and the colourful trees in the autumn.

They sat there for hours, with her picking out other pages in the book, and him answering all her questions When she was struggling to keep her eyes open, he set aside the book and blew out the light. Taking her pillow with her, she scooted over to the other side of the bed. He thumped his pillow and lay down. She was lying on her back, not her side with her back to him, and he reached down, taking a hold of her hand.

'Good night, Aislinn,' he said.

'Good night, Luke.'

It was amazing how wonderful her softly whispered words made him feel.

When Luke had practically dragged her into the dress shop, Aislinn had believed she'd never wear the dresses and gowns that he'd approved for purchase. Now, standing in the lobby of the theatre, with a glass of champagne in her hand and surrounded by silk wallpaper, tiled mosaic floors, ornate woodwork, and sparkling chandeliers, not to mention the people dressed in their finery, she was very grateful for the beautiful dusty-rose-coloured gown she was wearing.

She was also grateful for the schooling on current events from the household staff, which made her confident in responses if needed, But she was most grateful for Eugenia Cunningham, the Countess of Chatsworth. Genie, as she'd asked to be called, was as delightful as she was beautiful. Her hair was a golden-yellow, and her blue eyes were as light in colour as her silver-blue gown, but it truly was her personality that shone.

Aislinn had never been to any social events, not even balls that had been held at Havenbrook. She'd always remained in the nursery with the girls, but between Mary Ann, Genie, and Luke, she wasn't even nervous.

Not even when a hush had filled the room upon their arrival. It hadn't lasted long, nor had the whispers. An elderly man, whose name she couldn't recall, the Duke of somewhere, had been the first one to approach them.

With a slight bow, the man had introduced himself, and said to Luke, 'No other on either continent is correct.' The man had then said to her, 'I am honoured to make your acquaintance, my lady. I am now convinced that every paragraph your husband wrote in his letters is one hundred percent true.'

'He does have a way with words,' Aislinn had said while glancing up at Luke, who winked at her.

Other introductions had quickly followed, and during a pause, Genie had whispered, 'Don't even try to remember all the names. It's useless. I still don't know half of them, and believe me, it has made no difference.'

Luke had collected a glass of champagne for both of them from a uniformed attendant, and when Michael had waved him over to a group of men, Genie had told him to go, that his wife was in good hands.

Aislinn had agreed and was enjoying visiting with Genie, talking about her son who had just turned two and was learning to talk.

Luke wasn't far away, only a few steps, and each time she glanced his way, their gazes met. The warmth that filled her was reminiscent of last night, of falling asleep with him holding her hand.

'Now, there is a man who only has eyes for his wife,' Genie whispered.

Heat rushed into Aislinn's face.

'Don't be embarrassed,' Genie said. 'Be proud. For believe me, others would give up the jewels around their necks for a love like that.'

At that moment, Aislinn knew she would give up everything, anything, for Luke to truly love her. That was an outrageous thought for a person who'd never wanted to get married to have, but Luke made her have all sorts of outrageous thoughts.

He and Michael joined her and Genie, and the evening proceeded. The performers were most likely excellent, their colourful costumes undeniably gorgeous and the overall performance well deserving of the applause, but Aislinn was too engrossed with the man beside her to give the production the attention it deserved.

Luke was clearly here because it was expected of him.

No one but her would have noticed, but it confirmed that she couldn't let his life change any more than it already had.

Last night in bed he'd been animated, jovial, excited to tell her about things and places in the book. She'd felt his excitement, and that had increased her own as she'd listened to his numerous adventures. Many that she'd never heard about in the letters.

It was clear how much he loved Montana, and how much he needed to return to the life he loved.

Over the next few days, the theatre wasn't the only time she sensed weariness in him. The dinner parties, balls, and other events they attended that week were a nuisance to him. He didn't say that. In fact, he was his charming self the entire time. She simply knew. Like him, she was willing to do whatever was needed for Fern and Ivy, so said nothing, but would much rather be home with them each evening and knew Luke felt the same. That was where he was the happiest, when they were home together.

Even after the girls were in bed, he was happy. Each night, he carried another book upstairs and they would read through it together. They weren't all about America. It didn't seem to matter what the subject was, they enjoyed talking about whatever was on the pages. Although, none of the others instilled the enthusiasm in his voice as that first one had.

It was a full week later, when they were attending an opera, that Aislinn determined enough was enough. Luke shouldn't be tortured, and that was exactly what was happening. She could tell by the way he kept shifting in his seat and flinching every time a singer hit and held a high note that, in her mind, should have shattered the chandeliers.

When the intermission arrived, and they proceeded down the marble steps with the ornately carved banister, she suggested they leave.

'Are you sure?' he asked, with a gleam of hope in his blue eyes.

She smiled up at him. 'Very.'

He kissed her temple right there on the steps. 'Thank you.'

He did that more often than not, and though she loved those tiny kisses on her temple or cheek, her lips quivered with jealousy each time his lips touched her skin.

At the doorway, he asked, 'Will you be all right here for a moment? It's raining, I'll just step outside to ask the attendant to have our coach brought around.'

'Yes. I'll be fine.'

He was gone less than half a minute, but in those few seconds, her heart had come to a stop.

Arriving in front of her, he grasped her arm. 'What's wrong?'

'Percy and Hazel.' Pushing the dead air from her lungs, she continued, 'At the top of the stairs.'

He touched her cheek with his other hand. 'Good for them.'

He'd never taken his eyes off her, so she repeated, 'They are at the top of the stairs. Probably walking down them now.'

His grin grew. 'Maybe they'll trip.'

She had to smile, yet asked, 'Aren't you even going to look?'

'Why would I want to look at them, when I can look at a face more beautiful than all others on all continents?'

Then, before she had time to think of a response, he kissed her. On the lips. A soft, warm kiss that lasted no more than a still moment, but would live with her for ever.

'It's raining pretty good.' He shrugged off his black,

tailcoat and draped it over her shoulders, before leading her out the door to where their carriage was pulling up.

Once inside the carriage, with her thoughts slowly returning, she asked, 'Did you know they were there?'

'No, but considering they've been in London for several days now, I assumed we'd encounter them sooner or later.'

Later would have been totally fine with her.

'Is that why you wanted to leave?' he asked.

They were sitting side by side, and she laid a hand on his knee. 'No. I wanted to leave because you were miserable.'

He covered her hand with his. 'I was trying to hide that.'

She giggled. 'I know.'

'Now I know why my father was so averse to the opera and didn't make me attend one when my mother suggested it. He said music shouldn't hurt your ears, and I agree.'

She agreed, too, and knowing they had opera houses in America, asked, 'You never attended one in America?'

'No.' He laughed. 'I had all the music I needed.'

'How so?'

'Raf plays the guitar, and he taught me.' His smile grew. 'I'll have to buy one here, play some real music for you.'

'I'd like that.'

'So would I.'

She would like another kiss, too, and half-afraid he'd be able to read her mind, she looked the other way. 'Raf must be talented.'

'Not as talented as his dog,' Luke said with a laugh.

'Banjo, that's his name. He can dance on his hind legs while Raf plays guitar. It's a sight to see.'

She laughed at the image in her mind, but it didn't chase away the one of Percy and Hazel on the stairway. 'Do you think Percy and Hazel have told others that I'm—I was Fern and Ivy's governess?'

'Probably.'

Others knew. Genie and Michael, and of course Mr Watson and Mr Gaines.

'I'm not embarrassed about that, and you shouldn't be, either,' he said.

'I'm not, I just worry that—'

'Don't.' He caught the side of her face and tugged it so she had to look at him. 'Don't worry. It doesn't matter.'

If only that were true.

She tried to smile or nod, but he was leaning closer, and the next thing she knew, his lips were touching hers. The warmth and pleasure of their lips melding together filled her very soul with satisfaction. It also thrilled her beyond belief.

Responding to his lips, the way they moved across hers, didn't take any thought. Meeting each caress was natural. As natural as breathing.

His arms were around her, and he leaned her back in the seat as the intensity of the kiss increased. His lips parted and his tongue slid along the seam of her lips. A great desire rose up inside her and she parted her lips, not in surrender, but in unity.

This was exactly what she'd wanted. What she'd thought about over and over again. The desires that had lived inside of her were satisfied, in one way, and increasing in another. For the first time in her life, she felt as if she was embarking upon a thrilling, life-changing adventure, and she was more than willing to fully participate in it.

Their arrival home brought an end to their kissing, but she wasn't disappointed. Not with the way Luke looked at her. He had the same excitement in his eyes as when he talked about America and all his adventures.

It was raining hard, a complete downpour, and though he held his coat over her head as they ran from the carriage to the house, they were soaked by the time they entered.

'Forgive me,' Gabe said, hurrying towards them. 'I didn't expect your arrival so soon. I would have met you at the carriage with an umbrella.'

'No harm done,' Luke said, handing over his wet coat with one hand and wiping at the water dripping from his hair onto his forehead with the other.

'I'll collect each of you a towel,' Gabe said.

'No need,' Luke said, putting pressure on the small of her back with one hand. 'We'll go change.'

With her heart beating erratically, Aislinn hurried towards the stairway, with Luke at her side. The wet hem of her gown slapped against her shins, and she had no doubt she was leaving droplets in her wake. She didn't care. The idea of continuing to kiss him was filling her mind. The shine in his eyes said that's what he was thinking, too.

Penny was in the hallway and dipped into a quick curtsey. 'The lamps have been lit in your room. Will you be needing anything else?'

'No. Thank you,' Aislinn replied, barely pausing.

Luke opened the door to their room. She quickly stepped inside and, perhaps because of the prominent four-poster bed, she suddenly became unsure. Would their kissing lead to something more? Dare she hope? She shouldn't, but it was impossible not to. Not to want more.

His hand clasped hers and he stepped around her, so they were face-to-face. 'I'm fully aware that things have not been resolved with the guardianship, nor do I know what will come after that decision, but I do believe that our marriage will continue. I'm curious as to your opinion on it continuing in name only.'

Her opinion. He was giving her the choice. Things were unresolved, and when those resolutions were determined, it would affect their marriage, whether it was in name only or not. Because she knew one thing for certain—he didn't belong in England. He'd never be truly happy here. He belonged underneath that big Montana sky he loved so much.

Her true choice was whether she loved him enough to allow him to have the life that would make him happy, not the one that had been thrust upon him by responsibility.

Chapter Thirteen

Aislinn knew her answer, and her choice. She also knew that she did love him. It was there, a love that consumed her day and night. This was her moment, her chance to experience a grand adventure that would help her live with her choice for the rest of her life. She stepped closer, looped her arms around his neck, and stretched on her toes to kiss him.

She felt the smile on his lips, and that cemented her decision. Whatever the future held, she would never regret this moment. She'd fallen in love with him, with who he was, and didn't want him to change.

In the midst of their kiss, a passion-filled kiss that had every part of her throbbing and tingling with anticipation, Luke lifted her into his arms as if she weighed no more than Fern or Ivy.

'You need to get out of these wet clothes,' he said against her still parted lips.

She didn't hesitate in her response, 'You, too.'

Their kissing barely slowed as he carried her into the dressing room and then lowered her feet onto the floor.

Alas, they both needed to draw in a full breath of air,

and as they did, standing there, staring at each other, Luke asked, 'You're sure about this?'

She had never been more sure of anything in her life. 'Yes. Very sure.'

His gaze was so tender, so amorous, that for a heart-stopping moment she thought he was going to say something. He didn't. Instead he covered her lips with an exceptionally affectionate kiss. She wasn't disappointed, for she had no delusions that he'd fallen in love with her. Her love for him was strong enough to last her a lifetime.

He released her and sat down in the chair to use the bootjack. She sat on the bench and removed her boots, then her garters and stockings.

Although she was trembling with anticipation, she was hesitant as to what her next move should be.

He'd already relieved himself of his vest and shirt and stepped closer, hands out. 'Let me help you.'

She placed her hands in his and stood.

He unbuttoned the top button of her dress, the one right beneath her chin. The one thing she'd insisted upon while picking out the dresses he'd purchased was that they button down the front. She'd never had assistance in dressing herself and saw no reason for that to change.

His assistance, though, was very different.

It felt as if it took an eternity for him to reach the final button just below her waist. Her heart was thudding inside her chest, and her toes were curled inside her shoes from the sensations swirling inside her. Especially her breasts, which felt heavier, fuller, and overly sensitive.

If she'd had a mind to, she might have told herself that

she should be more self-conscious, for she would soon be baring herself to a man. But he wasn't just a man. He was Luke. He was the man who lived in her head and her heart, always.

He slid the dress from her shoulders, down her arms, until it pooled on the floor around her feet. Her chemise and petticoat were made of soft, white linen and silk. She didn't own a corset and had declined to purchase one, even though the dressmaker had suggested it.

Perhaps she should have taken the suggestion. Her chemise was wet and clinging to her breasts. The thin material had become translucent.

'Your beauty knows no bounds.' With a mischievous glint in his eyes, Luke cupped both of her breasts as he leaned forward and captured her mouth in an open-mouthed kiss.

When the kiss ended, his deft hands caressing her breasts were filling her with intoxicating sensations. She leaned her head back, sucking in air. He kissed the length of her neck, the line of her shoulder, as his hands untied the string of her petticoat, then her drawers.

A moment later, she was relieved of her chemise, and he lifted her again, carrying her back into the bedroom, where he laid her on the bed.

Lying there, completely naked, she had no thoughts of being embarrassed, for she was too busy watching him undress until he wore nothing but the leather strap around his neck.

It was her first sight of a naked man, but she knew what she looked upon was not the norm. Bared to the flesh, it was even more evident that he was taller and broader than most. He was all man, from head to toe, and she held no shame in appreciating his masculine splendour.

She sat up, touching the bear claw as he climbed onto the bed. 'This describes you. Big, strong, bold. A fierce contender.'

His chuckle was deep and throaty. 'You, my dear, are the fierce contender,' he said, while lifting the leather strap over his head and slipping it over hers.

The bleached-white claw hung much lower on her, down between her breasts. He dipped his head and kissed each of her breasts, then took one nipple in his mouth, teasing the overly sensitive bud with his tongue. She clutched onto his head as a wonder of delicious sensations, as pleasing as they were torturous, overtook her.

Lost in a world of feeling, touching, kissing, and overwhelming pleasure, she joined him on what became far more than an adventure. It was a journey into an entirely new world, where she realised that all the training and whispering behind closed doors had not taught her all she'd needed to know about the marital bed.

She also discovered he was a gifted teacher.

Their coupling, the union of their two bodies, turned out to be exactly what her body had been craving. Even the quick snap of pain when he'd entered her hadn't quelled her desires. He was gentle and caring, eased her into a motion that enhanced the friction between their bodies and increased the pleasure into new heights.

Nothing had ever felt so right, so wonderful, as lying beneath him, skin to skin, united as one. Until later, when an unknown, internal force, driven by his masterful rhythm, sent her reeling into a pinnacle, feeling like she was suspended in time. Then it exploded into a burst of pleasure that was absolutely indescribable.

'Dash it all!' she gasped as waves of pleasure washed over every part of her body, over and over again. Nothing had prepared her for anything close to what she'd just experienced.

Luke let out a low chuckle as he kissed her. 'Does that mean you enjoyed becoming my wife in all ways?'

She smiled and wrapped her arms around him tightly. 'Yes. Very much.' Her entire being felt wonderful. 'I had no idea it would be so amazing.'

'Would be?' He kissed her. 'My darling, it's far from over.'

'It is?'

He kissed her, then began to move again, and she quickly learned that it hadn't been anywhere close to being over.

It wasn't for a very long time.

With Aislinn sleeping soundly within his embrace, her cheek nestled on his shoulder and one of her legs draped across his thigh, Luke couldn't have washed the smile off his face with the harshest lye soap on earth. He'd just experienced the most satisfying adventure of his life.

He leaned down, kissed the top of her head, then nuzzled her hair, relishing the fresh, floral scent. There had been so many times tonight, from the moment she'd said she was sure about becoming his wife in every way, to the last moment before she fell asleep, that he'd wanted to tell her that he cared about her.

Cared very deeply.

It had been hard, but he'd kept those words to himself, because the things he felt for her scared him. If there ever was a woman he could love, it would be her, but there were miles between caring and love.

Miles that he was incapable of travelling. He knew himself too well.

When you love someone, you are willing to give up everything for them. Though he was here now, willing to do whatever he had to for Fern and Ivy, and Aislinn, he knew he wasn't ready to give up his ranch. Wasn't willing to give up his desires to return there at some point.

He also knew he couldn't ask them to return with him. It was nothing like life here. It was rough and wild, no place for women and children. Not daughters of a duke. Fern and Ivy needed to be raised here, where they would have all the opportunities afforded by their birthrights.

Aislinn belonged here, too.

She'd easily conformed to the role of a lady of the ton. Like her beauty, her grace and poise were incomparable. He was proud of her, proud to say she was his wife. She fit right in everywhere they went.

He was the one who didn't fit in. The one who didn't belong here.

He never had.

His return to Montana wouldn't happen right away. That was a given. He was convinced that guardianship would be granted to him, but if by some minuscule chance it was granted to Percy, he still couldn't return to Montana. He'd have to stay here to make damn sure that Fern and Ivy, and Aislinn, were not mistreated in any way.

He was trying to immerse himself into this life that that he had right now, but the more parties, the more social activities he attended, the more shallow this life felt to him. He couldn't live this way.

Not long-term.

Aislinn shifted slightly, snuggling closer, and her hand caressed his chest, right over his heart. The warmth that spread through him was uncanny. It was also real, very real. This part of living here would be very easy to get used to.

Something in his mind clicked. Maybe he'd been thinking about this in the wrong way. He was here, and would need to remain here, at least for the time being. Therefore, why couldn't he create a life that didn't feel shallow?

There was no reason he couldn't.

He laid his hand over the top of Aislinn's. Learning to love her, travelling those miles he thought he couldn't, might turn out to be the easiest thing he'd ever done. For she was loveable.

Very loveable.

He lifted her hand to his lips, kissed the back of her fingers.

His desire for her was renewing itself all over again, which wasn't new. He'd wanted her long before last night. The other truth was that if it had been any other woman who had suggested marriage, he wouldn't have agreed. No matter what was at stake.

Starting tomorrow, he'd put a new plan in place. One that wasn't born of his own selfishness, but of his intention to provide a good life for his wife.

Before noon the following day his plan was off to a good start. He'd found not one, but two buildings to buy. He had money in several banks, as well as his holdings from his father, and could simply manage those to provide a financially stable life for them, but that wasn't him. He needed to have something to do. Something he could physically participate in growing and changing.

Both of the buildings he'd purchased were in disarray. One had been repossessed by the bank, the other had been suggested by Mr Watson. Luke's plan was to refurbish both. He knew little about construction, but that's why he chose this venture. He liked learning new things.

The repossessed building was downtown and would become office and business units, or sold if the right buyer appeared. The other building was on the north edge of town, and the current tenants would remain in occupancy, just in a more modern facility. He was excited about that project and anxious to tell Aislinn about it.

As he rode his horse up the street towards his house, excitement made him grin. His morning had gotten off to a great start, too. Waking up next to Aislinn, and what had ensued before they'd climbed out of bed, was responsible for that. He was excited to see her, even though it had only been a few hours since they'd parted.

She was in the stable, along with Fern and Ivy, visiting Half-Pint in her stall.

'The three faces I like seeing the most,' he said, leading his thoroughbred inside.

'Uncle Luke!' both Fern and Ivy exclaimed, running towards him.

He handed the reins to John in order to capture one niece, then the other, in his arms, giving them each a kiss on the cheek and a tickle on the belly, before setting them back down.

'Aislinn said you'd be home soon,' Ivy said.

'And that we could wait for you out here,' Fern said.

He lifted a brow while walking towards Aislinn. He'd told her that he'd be home before noon and still had a good half hour to spare.

She grinned, and shrugged.

He kissed her on the lips. A fast one, considering the company, but heartfelt nonetheless. This plan he was putting in place was growing on him more and more.

'How was your morning?' she asked.

'Very productive. How was yours?'

'Uneventful,' she replied.

'Really?'

Her cheeks pinkened. 'Since you left, that is.'

He laughed, draped an arm around her shoulders, and tugged her closer to his side as they walked out of the stable. The sun was shining, the sky blue, and life here wasn't bad. Not bad at all.

His optimism continued to grow day by day, night by night. Aislinn was overjoyed when he told her that the second building he'd purchased was the one that housed the orphanage where she'd grown up. At first, she'd been confused, but when he'd explained that, although the other building was being renovated to most likely be sold, the orphanage building would be renovated only to improve the lives of the occupants. His way of thanking the group for providing her a home when she'd needed one.

She'd thanked him, not only with her words, but her actions. What had started out as a kiss of gratitude had quickly turned into a night of passion. Every night with her was filled with passion.

The days rolled from one to the other, and though he normally went to check in on and work with the men he'd hired at both buildings, the morning of judgement day, he remained home. He assumed Mr Watson would send a messenger as soon as the decision was made, so when Gabe announced that the solicitor had arrived at the door, Luke had his first moment of doubt for the outcome.

Standing beside him, Aislinn grabbed hold of his arm. They were watching Fern and Ivy ride Half-Pint around the backyard. Both girls had learned to ride by themselves, but it was Ivy who was the natural. She would spend all day on horseback if allowed.

Luke patted Aislinn's hand. 'Perhaps he wants to share the good news in person.'

'I hope so,' she whispered.

'I showed him into the front sitting room,' Gabe said, as genteel as ever, but also boasting a few extra worry wrinkles on his face.

'Thank you,' Luke replied, and then nodded at Claire, who had followed Gabe outside and hosted her own concerned expression.

He rested a hand on the small of Aislinn's back to urge her forward and didn't miss the way Claire lightly touched Aislinn's arm as she passed them to take over watching the girls.

'Don't fret,' he said to Aislinn as they approached the house.

'I'm trying not to,' she said. 'It's just that I was expecting a messenger.'

'I know.'

They walked the rest of the way in silence. Mr Watson was waiting just inside the door of the sitting room, near a side table, where he'd set down a large envelope.

'I thought I'd deliver the news myself,' the solicitor

said, laying a hand on the envelope and curling his lips into a smile. 'It's all here. Congratulations.'

Luke hadn't realised he'd been holding his breath until the air gushed out.

Aislinn gasped, too, and covered her mouth with one hand.

He tugged her closer to his side while asking, 'I've been granted guardianship?' He wasn't sure if he wanted clarification, or simply wanted to hear it said aloud.

'Yes, you are the legal guardian of Miss Fern Carlisle and Miss Ivy Carlisle, until they reach the age of twenty-one,' Mr Watson replied. 'And, I've brought along your new will and testament as requested. I, of course, will secure a copy in possession once signed.'

Luke was so exuberant, he let out a whoop, the like of which he hadn't shouted since scaring maverick cows out of the brush.

His excitement lasted long after Mr Watson left. He told Doo to cook all of Fern's and Ivy's favourite foods for the evening meal and said that everyone in the house was going to eat in the dining room tonight.

Though Fern and Ivy had never known the disorder that had been going on, they easily joined in on the gaiety filling the house. They were also overjoyed about the meal that included an ungodly number of sweets.

After they ate, Luke insisted that everyone join them in the large sitting room near the back of the house. With the help of the other men, the furniture was moved out of the centre of the room, then he collected the guitar that he had bought and had played for Aislinn more than once.

He wasn't at all bad, if he did say so himself, and every member of the household joined in dancing to the music he strummed. Doo, who had always had a creative mind, made up words to go with some of the chords, which had everyone laughing as they danced a Scottish reel, hooking each other by the elbows and dancing in a circle before letting go and hooking elbows with the next person.

Luke was keeping time with the music by tapping a toe and had every intention of playing until his fingers bled, when a screech not only stopped his strumming, but stopped every single dancer.

'Well! I never!' a female voice declared.

Luke had to stand up to see over the dancers, who had become statues. The happiness that had filled him for hours was doused like a campfire getting hit by the remnants of a coffeepot.

He should have recognised the screech. Though he'd seen Percy and Hazel a few times at social events, he hadn't spoken to either one of them since leaving Havenbrook. 'Ever hear of knocking?' Luke asked.

'We did knock,' Percy replied.

'It couldn't be heard over that atrocious music,' Hazel hissed, shifting an evil glare to the room's occupants.

The room emptied, as staff members slipped past the newcomers and out of the doorway, including Claire, who ushered Fern and Ivy from the room.

Luke set his guitar on the chair behind him. 'I'm assuming you are here to congratulate us.'

Hazel let out a muffled growl, while glaring at Aislinn.

Luke glared back, putting his arm around Aislinn's shoulders and pulling her closer to his side, then he turned to his brother and waited.

Percy tugged at the lapels of his black tailcoat.

Hazel elbowed him.

Percy puffed his chest out a bit further.

Luke opened his mouth, ready to tell Percy to spit out whatever it was he wanted to say, but held silent as Aislinn laid a hand on his chest.

She was staring at Percy, how he'd turned to Hazel and shook his head. The air seemed to seep out of his brother slowly, like the wind had been knocked out of his sails, even as Hazel pursed her lips.

'Congratulations,' Percy said to him.

His brother's tone was far quieter than Luke had heard him speak in years.

'Percival!' Hazel hissed.

Percy shook his head again. 'It's done, Hazel.'

Luke could have thrown a barb. The old him would have, but the new him had an understanding of the lengths a man would go to for the woman he loved.

With steam nearly blasting out of the top of her head, Hazel grabbed Percy's arm as she spun around and tugged him towards the door.

He could let them leave, but he was tired of it all. 'You just don't get it, do you?' Luke asked.

Percy stopped, which forced Hazel to stop, too, but they didn't turn around.

'Rowland asked me to oversee the care of his daughters if anything was to happen to him, and I agreed. Promised I would.' He laid his hand on Aislinn's, the one that was still on his chest. For years, too many to count, he'd thought he and Percy hated each other. But he didn't hate Percy. He didn't approve of some of his actions, but they were brothers, and there had been times when they'd got along. 'The truth is, if it had been you who'd asked, I would have returned to oversee the care of your son, just as I did Rowland's daughters. Not because of money or titles, or prestige or power, but because you're family. We're family.'

Aislinn looked up at him, and the gentle smile on her face, the shine in her eyes, was like a reward.

'This is it, the four of us in the room,' Luke said, willing to put an end to their fighting. 'There are also three children, and, God willing, there may be more, who need us. All four of us. They need to know that someone will always be there, ready to look out for them.'

It was an olive branch, but one that needed to be extended. It was up to Percy if he accepted it or not.

Percy turned about, looked at him, and with a half smile, nodded. 'You're right. And just so you know, we were thinking about what was best for the girls.'

Luke hadn't forgotten about the guardianship request that Percy had put in concerning Aislinn, but they were married, so that was water under the bridge. 'I promise I'll do right by them.' He glanced down at Aislinn. 'We'll do right by them.'

Percy shuffled his feet, then nodded. 'I suppose we should be going.'

'Actually,' Luke said. 'I have some business ventures I could use some advice on.'

Percy's brows lifted. 'What type of business ventures?'

Luke grinned. This time, he couldn't hold it against Percy if money was the first thought that crossed his mind. In that, they were like-minded. He too hoped his ventures would turn out profitable. They were an integral part of the new life he was creating.

Chapter Fourteen

The weeks following the proclamation of guardianship were the happiest of Aislinn's life. Her days were busy with household tasks, the evenings frequently held events and parties, and her nights... Her nights sleeping in Luke's arms were glorious.

They were also bittersweet. Despite their gratifying, passion-filled activities, which left her exhausted and the bedsheets tangled, she'd often found herself unable to sleep.

Luke had given her a life that she'd never dreamed of having and would continue to, of that she had no doubts. That was what troubled her. Luke wasn't living his life. He was living for everyone else. He was trying, trying so very hard. He'd purchased the first two buildings to be renovated and had been enjoying working on them, had even been looking at buying more. But then he stopped, explaining that a member of the ton couldn't be seen getting his hands dirty.

He was frustrated by that but tried not to let it show. She'd seen it, had said that it shouldn't matter, but he insisted that he couldn't do anything that might tarnish the family name.

Then he'd spent days in meetings, researching other businesses to invest in. He'd chosen a few, but he wasn't going to find what he was looking for. Not even with his newest idea of buying an estate. One of their own.

Letting out a sigh, Aislinn put the book back on the shelf. The one about America. She'd taken it to bed last night, hoping to see the shine in his eyes again.

Shaking her head, she wiped away the tear that formed in the corner of one eye. She'd seen the shine in his eyes, but it hadn't been because of the book. He had set that aside and focused all of his attention on her. Which had been truly wonderful.

Loving him was so easy, but it was also hard. So very hard.

The front door opened and closed, and she heard Gabe's greeting, Luke asking for her location. She wiped both eyes, making sure they were dry, and pinched her cheeks in preparation for seeing him.

He appeared in the doorway of the study, with a smile that went from ear to ear. 'I found it. Our estate. It will be perfect. I'm sure of it.'

They met in the centre of the room and he grasped her waist with both hands.

'We can drive over there later this week. Just you and me,' he said. 'You can decide what you think. It's only about five hours from London, but we'll still spend the night.'

He kissed her, and she returned his kiss with all her heart and soul. Then she pulled up a brave face. 'Sounds wonderful.'

'It will be.' He kissed her forehead, then stepped around her. 'There will be plenty of room for Ivy to ride Half-Pint in more than a circle in the backyard. And

Fern can get the dog that she wants to teach to dance. You'll be able to refurbish the entire place. Rugs, drapes, furniture, whatever will make you happy.'

What about you? she wanted to ask, because whatever would make him happy was the only thing she truly wanted. He looked happy, acted happy, but she knew deep down he would only be happy underneath that big Montana sky he loved so much. The same sky that lay over a place he'd recently, and quite kindly, told her wasn't fit for a lady or children of a duke. He'd gone on to say that there wasn't a cook there, or housekeeper, or any of the staff they were used to having. That there were no balls or fancy dinner parties or a number of other things that he thought she cared about.

She didn't, but she was expected to.

He had been talking about the estate, about moving some of the household staff there when he bought it, but had suddenly gone quiet. She turned, looking to see why.

Standing at the desk, he was staring at an envelope.

'What is it?' she asked.

'Oh, just some mail that must have arrived today.' He tossed it on the desk. 'I'll read it later.'

She walked to the desk, picked up the envelope and, recognising the postage, said, 'It's from America.'

'Yes. From Raf.'

Her hands shook. She had never dreamed of getting married, of having a family of her own, because she'd lost all that as a child. Now she had it again and didn't want to lose it. But she would if she had to. For him. He had a right to be happy. 'Read it.'

He grinned. 'It won't be all that interesting. Raf's a man of few words.'

'Unlike you,' she said, teasingly, to lighten the mood. 'Prove it.'

Chuckling, he took the letter, broke the seal, and opened the flap. While pulling out the letter, he leaned a hip against the desk so they were side by side. 'I'm not good at writing like you,' he started to read, but paused to glance at her with a quick grin. 'You could have knocked me over with a feather when I read your last letter about you getting married. She must be one heck of a gal to have lassoed you.'

She giggled at the way he winked at her.

'I can see why you're staying in England,' he continued to read. 'Maybe I'll visit you there someday. Miss that ugly mug of yours. The cows and cowboys are doing fine, but I have some questions for you. You know I'm not good with the money and the Army is wanting to buy some beefs. I'm wondering if you want me to sell—' He stopped reading and his back stiffened.

She looked at him as he stared at the letter, reading silently for a moment, before he looked at her, shaking his head.

'The rest is boring,' he said. 'Raf just wants to know how many cows to sell, and for how much. I'll write him back.'

It was more than that, but she chose not to pry. 'I'll leave you to do that.' She kissed his cheek and left the room.

The letter hung in her head throughout the afternoon, especially as Luke remained in the study right up until mealtime. He was his entertaining self during the meal and the evening hours, but she caught him frowning when he thought no one was looking.

As she prepared for bed, dropping her night rail over

her head, a somewhat useless act because, more often than not, the gown was removed long before she fell asleep wearing nothing more than the leather strap necklace he'd slipped over head over two months ago, Aislinn told herself that she needed to be strong. To act.

Luke was already in bed, reading through the stack of papers that had been delivered earlier concerning the estate he'd mentioned. He smiled as she exited the changing chamber. 'I'm sure you'll like this place.'

She didn't answer, nor did she walk to her side of the bed. Instead, she went to his side and flipped back the covers, exposing his bare loins. Then, she hitched up her night rail and climbed on, lowering herself while straddling his hips.

He set aside the papers as their bare skin made contact. Smiling, he gathered the material of her nightgown, which was bunched up around her waist, with both hands.

She raised her arms over her head, preparing for him to lift the gown off. Before losing her nerve, she said, 'We both know you need to go to Montana.'

His body stiffened, and his hands released the material of her gown. 'No, I don't.'

She kept her arms up, as if more interested in their actions than their words. 'Yes, you do. You call Raf your partner, but only you own the ranch. The land and the cattle.'

Luke remained still. 'He is my partner. Owning something is only a part of what it takes to make it successful. Raf has my permission to do whatever is necessary.'

She lowered her arms and cupped his face with both hands. Kissed him softly. 'The girls and I have everything we need here, and people who will come to our aid if needed during your absence.'

He grasped her wrists and pulled her hands off his face. 'Why are you doing this?'

There was no giving up. She couldn't. 'Because I know how committed you are to seeing things through to the end.'

His gaze shifted, avoided meeting hers, as he said, 'I already have, as far as the ranch is concerned. That part of my life has come to an end. I wrote to Raf this afternoon. Told him to sell the ranch and cattle.'

That was exactly what she'd feared and had to be cautious. 'I imagine that's not a responsibility he expected.' She kissed his chin. 'Or wants. But being your friend—' she kissed him again '—will do as you ask, whether he's comfortable with it or not.'

He let out a tiny growl.

She could feel a particular body part that she was sitting on growing hard. Despite the seriousness of their conversation, her own wants and needs were swirling inside her.

'Are you trying to get rid of me?' he asked.

Reaching down, she grasped the hem of her night rail and pulled it over her head, dropping it on the floor. 'Do I look like I'm trying to get rid of you?'

He cupped her breasts and teased her nipples with the pads of his thumbs. 'No. You look like you're trying to tempt me with this gorgeous body of yours.'

She wiggled against his hardened member, showing him how ready she was for him. 'Oh?'

'Yes.' In deft, swift movements, he flipped their positions so she was on her back with him above her and his member deep inside her.

'It worked,' he claimed.

Hooking her legs around his, she arched her hips upwards, taking him in even deeper. 'Indeed.'

Hours later, snuggled up against his side, where she'd dozed but not really slept, she stated, 'You're still awake.'

'As are you.' He kissed her forehead. 'Because we both know I need to go to Montana.'

She blinked back the tears and kissed his chest, knowing she now had to live with the consequences of her actions. 'I will miss you.'

His arms tightened around her. 'I don't want to leave you.'

It was a moment or two before she could speak around the lump in her throat. 'It won't be for ever.'

'No. Six weeks at the most.'

He was committed to her and the girls, he would return, but she wasn't so naive as to believe that selling his ranch would relieve his desires to live the life he so loved. The life he'd created for himself. 'When will you leave?'

'As soon as possible. Within the next couple of days. It would behove me to be there to negotiate the deal with the Army. If I can sell the herd in its entirety, that would just leave the land and homestead.' His sigh sounded ragged. 'That will take a lot off Raf's shoulders.'

She was sure it would, and attempted to brace herself for the hardest day of her life. Saying goodbye to him was going to be so hard, so sad.

Luke put every provision in place for Aislinn and the girls for every possible scenario that he could think of and tried to make the trip sound like a grand adventure.

He showed them his route on a world map. How he'd take a train to Portsmouth, then a passenger ship to Baltimore, Maryland. From there, more trains would take him to Chicago, Illinois, another to St. Paul, Minnesota, and a final one to Bozeman, Montana Territory. Given a variable or two, he explained that he'd be travelling for nearly two weeks, but would write to them as soon as he arrived at the ranch.

None of that was making the trip more exciting for him, nor the idea of leaving any easier.

Which would happen tomorrow morning. He considered not going too many times to count, even considered taking Aislinn and the girls with him, but the trip was long and not overly comfortable. He was better off going alone. Getting his business done.

Luke climbed off the thoroughbred, half wondering why he had yet to name the animal, and walked up the walkway to Percy's town home. His brother had agreed to oversee the completion of the renovations on the buildings he'd purchased and anything else that might come up in his absence, and Luke was grateful for that. Actually, he and Percy had been getting along well the past few months. Better than ever.

His knock on the door was answered by the butler, who informed him that Percy wasn't home.

'I don't need to see him,' Luke said. 'Just wanted to drop this off.' He handed the butler the final inspection papers for the orphanage. Percy knew about the changes but would need the actual papers, which had just arrived at the house that afternoon. 'Just give these to him, please.'

'Very well, sir.'

With a nod, he turned and walked towards his horse. He had one foot in the stirrup when he heard his name.

He was surprised to see Hazel walking out of the doorway.

He removed his foot from the stirrup. While Percy had remained in town for Parliamentary duties, Hazel had returned to Havenbrook over a month ago. 'I was just dropping some paperwork off for Percy. I know he's in session today.'

'Yes, he is.' She stopped before him and glanced about as if making sure they were alone. 'I was going to burn it, because, well, it's all over now, but when I heard you were making a trip to America, I felt as if I should give it to you. I only arrived in town this afternoon and well...' She lifted an envelope and handed it to him.

'What is this?'

'That was discovered in Aislinn's room after you left Havenbrook. Percy and I knew about it. That was why he petitioned to become her guardian, so she wouldn't marry some blackguard who would take all of her money.'

Luke's spine shivered.

'We don't have to worry about any of that now, but if something were to happen to you, she might need that.'

Totally confused, he asked, 'What is it?'

'A provision of Rowland's will. Aislinn's inheritance.' Hazel patted his arm. 'You have a safe trip now, and tell Aislinn that if she needs anything, to let us know.'

Luke watched Hazel walk back inside, then looked down at the envelope. Aislinn's inheritance? That didn't make any sense. Unable not to, he lifted the flap on the envelope and pulled out a single sheet of paper. Handwritten, and brief, it stated that if Aislinn remained with the girls until they were of the age of twenty-one, she would receive a lump sum of monies—a substantial lump sum. It was signed by Rowland and witnessed by someone named Stockholm, dated two days before his brother had died.

Luke's hand shook.

His entire body shook.

And his mind conjured up a dozen memories all at the same time.

She'd said she had no idea why Percy would want guardianship over her. Said she wanted to remain with the girls until they were old enough that they no longer needed her. Said she'd never thought about marriage, until meeting him. Him. Who she agreed to marry, but not *be* married to, so he could return to America as soon as the guardianship was settled.

She'd said other things, too. So many things that were flying through his mind like bullets shot from a revolver.

No wondered she transformed from being a governess to the lady of the house so easily. That had been her plan all along.

The paper crinkled as he balled his hand into a fist.

All that time he'd been mad at Percy, thinking his brother was trying to make a fool out of him, when it had been her the entire time. The only reason she'd married him was for herself. For money. She'd wanted him to gain guardianship so she could fulfil the terms of her inheritance. Now that she'd secured that, she wanted him out of the way, telling him to go to Montana—for the sake of others. The only *other* she was thinking about was herself.

It felt as if barbed wire was wrapping itself around his heart. He'd spent his entire life avoiding any kind of commitment, yet here he was, willing to give up a life he'd loved, for *her*, and it was all an act on her part. She'd lied about not knowing why Percy would petition for guardianship over her. Lied about everything.

The pain inside him felt explosive. She didn't care about him. Didn't care about the girls. She'd been so convincing, acted so innocent and naive. It had all been a ruse.

He mounted his horse, and during the ride home, it was as if pieces to a puzzle all came together, forming one very clear picture.

Damn! He'd been so stupid. Had done the one thing that he'd sworn he'd never do. More than one. He'd married her. Cared about her, *loved* her. He'd known better, but had still walked straight into her trap.

The anger inside him was hot and cold at the same time, as was the pain in his chest. She reminded him of a tornado the first time he saw her, and that was exactly what she was. She'd spun her lies around him, sucked him in, all of him, and now that she had what she wanted, she was spitting him back out on the ground, broken and damaged beyond repair.

Oh, no, he wasn't broken. No one would ever break him. She might be like a tornado, but he was a wild horse, destined to run free. Remain free.

Upon arriving at the stable, he told John to leave his horse saddled. As usual, Fern and Ivy were riding Half-Pint in the backyard, and his heart constricted in his chest.

Damn her! Damn her for... He shook his head. There

were too many things for him to start naming them one by one.

Ivy brought the pony to a stop beside him. 'Are you mad, Uncle Luke?' she asked.

He took control of his expression, smiling at her. 'No, just sad.' He took a hold of one of her hands and one of Fern's. 'I'm sad, because I have to leave tonight for America, instead of in the morning. But I will write to you, and I will be back in six weeks.'

'I'm going to miss you,' Ivy said.

'Me, too,' Fern said.

'I'm going to miss you both, very much.' He gave them each a hug and a kiss on the cheek, then walked to the house.

Once inside, he went straight upstairs to the bedroom.

He was in the midst of stuffing the clothes he'd thrown onto the bed into his saddlebag when the door opened.

'I was in the kitchen,' Aislinn said. 'Doo is making all of your favourite foods for supper and—'

Her words faded as her gaze met his. The muscles in Luke's neck ached as he kept his cold glare on her, still jamming his clothes inside the dual leather bags.

'What are you doing?' she asked.

'I'm leaving tonight.'

'Why? What's happened?'

The anger mounting inside him went beyond anything he'd known. Her betrayal not only angered him, it *hurt*. He'd falsely believed her to be authentic and genuine, but that was all a ruse. In fact, her audacity was unmatched. Yet, he had to give her credit. She was one hell of an actress.

'Luke?' She walked closer. 'You're scaring me. What's wrong?'

'Wrong?' He shook his head. 'I'd say just about everything.'

She stopped near the foot of the bed. 'Excuse me?'

He picked up the saddlebags. 'You got what you wanted, Aislinn, but you overlooked one thing. Once married, a husband has control over all funds.' He tossed the bags over his shoulder. 'You will never get that inheritance.'

She frowned, shook her head. 'I have no inheritance. My father delivered flour for the mill and he died when I was seven.'

Luke pulled the balled-up paper out of his pocket and tossed it towards her. 'Maybe that will refresh your memory.'

'What is it?' she asked, without picking it up.

'The reason you married me.'

Questioning her hearing, Aislinn repeated, 'Excuse me?' She had never seen him so angry. So cold.

'You know,' he said, 'that idea that just popped into your head. Did you think I would never learn the truth?'

The tone of his voice, the glint in his eyes, made her entire body tremble. She would never lie to him, not ever, and having him believe that she was a liar hurt. Was so hurtful, that she wasn't sure if she wanted to cry or scream.

Choosing somewhere in between, she let out a tiny growl. 'You know the truth! It was for you and the girls.' His anger was making her angry. 'Do you suddenly think that I wanted to get married before that day? Wanted to have to learn how to become *the lady of the house*?

Wanted my life to turn into something completely different? Because, I assure you, I didn't. None of that ever crossed my mind.'

The disgust on his face sent a shiver rippling up her spine.

'You have six weeks,' he said, 'When I return, I will petition the courts for a divorce.'

She grasped a hold of the bedpost to keep from collapsing. 'A divorce?'

'Yes, a divorce. That is one benefit that the privileged, the wealthy can obtain, and I *will*.'

Chapter Fifteen

The sheen of tears blurred her vision. Everything just seemed useless, completely useless. She knew there was no sense following him. All that would do was expose the entire household to an argument that she didn't even know the cause of. He was so damn stubborn.

Her entire being hurt beyond any pain she'd ever known, yet she couldn't stand there like a ninny hugging the bedpost. He was leaving for America!

No! Not like this!

She started for the door, but then remember the paper he'd thrown across the bed.

Snatching it up, she ran all the way to the back door. But he was already gone. The group of household staff who stood there staring at her told her that much.

Mary Ann put an arm around her. 'Come into the kitchen, have a cup of tea.'

It was either that or collapse onto the floor, which wouldn't help. It wouldn't even make her feel better.

She sat at the kitchen table and used a linen napkin to wipe at the still steady trickle of tears with one hand, while flattening out the paper with her other.

'I remember writing that,' Gabe said. 'Such a sad day.'

Aislinn wiped both eyes again and blinked, hoping to clear her vision enough to read the paper. 'This?'

'Yes,' Gabe said. 'After the Duchess died, and the Duke was certain of his fate, he made a request. I penned it for him, and Dr Stockholm signed it as a witness and said he would see that Mr Watson received the script.'

Aislinn read, and was shocked to discover that the note stated that if she remained with the girls until they were of age, she was to receive a substantial sum. She was also confused about why Mr Watson had never mentioned it, nor Luke before today.

There was only one way to find out. 'Please have Benjamin bring around the carriage.'

Less than an hour later, she and Mr Watson were on their way to Dr Stockholm's residence, both curious as to why Dr Stockholm had never delivered the note to Mr Watson.

Dr Stockholm was a tall, wiry man with a full moustache as black as his thick brows. Aislinn had never met him, because during the days of the Duke's and Duchess's illnesses she'd kept the girls sequestered in the nursery, to prevent them from catching whatever had befallen their parents.

The doctor invited them into his office and quickly read the note that Mr Watson handed him. 'Yes, I remember this. That is my signature. After his wife died, and understanding his failing condition, the Duke of Havenbrook requested Mr Houghton pen this. Is there a problem?'

'I was not aware of this letter until today,' Mr Watson said.

Dr Stockholm rubbed his forehead. 'Let me see. As

I recall, I had promised to deliver it to you, however the Duke's brother, Percy, collected the envelope from the room. I saw him take it and did not question it. I assumed, since he would be seeing to your family's affairs upon the Duke's death, that he would deliver it. I clearly recall your name was written on the envelope.'

'Well, we thank you for the explanation,' Mr Watson said.

'You have my sincere apologies,' Dr Stockholm said. 'It never occurred to me that the bequest had not been delivered. The Duke's and Duchess's deaths were such a tragedy. So many attendants of that party became ill, and nearly all perished. Irritant poisoning. Although parliament continues to pass laws and regulations, food adulteration is still a serious matter.'

'Thank you for your time, Dr Stockholm,' Aislinn said. There was only one person Luke could have gotten this note from. She'd hoped the feud was over between the two brothers, but Percy had obviously told Luke that she'd known about this. A shiver tickled her spine. Luke and Percy had been friendlier lately, but Hazel's attitude hadn't changed. The pain over Luke leaving was still there, but the anguish was quicky turning into anger. She nodded towards Mr Watson. 'We must be going.'

Outside, as they walked to their carriages, Mr Watson said, 'Now we know why Percy petitioned for your guardianship. Would you like me to retain this with your husband's other papers?'

She didn't care what happened to the document, it was the trouble it had caused that she wanted fixed.

Strike that. She *would* fix it. Luke had taught her a lot, and it was time to use it.

'That would be fine,' she said, 'and thank you very much for your assistance.'

'It was my pleasure. I told your husband that I would be at your service during his absence. Please don't hesitate to contact me at any time.'

She thanked him again and then requested Benjamin to take her to the train station, just in case.

Luck failed her there. Benjamin's enquiry discovered that Luke had already boarded a train to Portsmouth, and John had already retrieved his horse.

Saddened, but undeterred, her next stop was Percy's town home, where she was told that he wasn't home.

She said she'd wait.

The butler showed her into a room that was completely blue, from the furniture to the draperies, to the walls and the rugs. It was a bit overwhelming. She sat on a chair and folded her hands in her lap, fully prepared to wait as long as it took.

'Hello, Aislinn,' Hazel greeted, as she strolled into the room less than a minute later. 'I was just informed of your visit.'

Aislinn knew the rules and almost stood, almost addressed Hazel formally, but she didn't. The smirk on Hazel's face was all the confirmation she needed to know who was behind the letter not being delivered to Mr Watson and who had given it to Luke.

A new bout of anger boiled in her stomach. 'I just wanted to say thank you,' Aislinn said.

'Oh?' Hazel sat on the edge of the sofa.

'Yes.' Aislinn nodded. 'About my inheritance. I hadn't been aware of it, but Luke's solicitor has it now.'

Hazel rolled her eyes. 'It doesn't matter. Now that

you're married to Luke.' She sighed and shrugged her shoulders.

Aislinn nodded. 'Which made me wonder why you would reveal it now, when Percy and Luke are getting along so well. But then I remembered something.'

Hazel leaned forward with knitted brows. 'Remembered what?'

'That this isn't about Luke, or Percy, or even me. It's about you. This has all been about you.'

Lifting her chin, Hazel said, 'I am the Duchess of Havenbrook and—'

'You've made that perfectly clear,' Aislinn interrupted, not concerned with being polite.

'I've earned that title! Not like you. Thinking you can become a lady of the ton.' Hazel let out a humph. 'I fired you because you were nothing but an orphan. Not fit to raise the daughters of a duke. You still aren't.'

Aislinn didn't let the insults strike her. In fact, it amazed her that she hadn't considered how jealous Hazel was before now. Thinking about things that Luke had said, she shook her head. 'A title alone will never give you the esteem or reverence that you are seeking, Hazel. That needs to be earned. The matriarch of a family understands the importance of the entire family's reputation and works to build it up, not tear it down. That's what Leslie did. She never said a disparaging word about you or Percy.'

Hazel shot to her feet. 'How dare—'

'I dare,' Aislinn said, slowly standing up, facing her sister-in-law eye to eye, 'because I love my husband with all my heart. I didn't marry him for money or prestige, or simply for guardianship of Fern and Ivy.' Admitting all that aloud was a relief. Though she loved the girls and had wanted Luke to obtain guardianship, deep down she knew why she'd married him, why she wanted to stay married. Love. It was as simple as that. 'I married him because he is a wonderful man, and I refuse to let you interfere in his life any longer.'

'You have no power,' Hazel hissed. 'You're nothing but a governess.'

That would always be true, and in that moment, she *felt* the reason why Luke had wanted a different life from the one he'd been born into. She was also still spitting mad. 'I was a governess. I am now Luke Carlisle's wife, and if you think I'll ever stop defending him, ever stop wanting him to have the best life, you are sorely mistaken.' A sense of power rose up inside her. 'I suggest we put an end to this now. You have what you wanted. You're the Duchess of Havenbrook. You should have been happy with that.'

Hazel didn't say anything, just stared at her with narrowed eyes.

Though Hazel's jealousy was pitiful, Aislinn was done letting it affect her life. 'I'll show myself out.'

Moments later, as she walked towards her carriage, Aislinn knew exactly what else she had to do. 'Take me to the House of Lords,' she told Benjamin. No one was going to take away her family.

It was midday when Luke stepped off the train in Bozeman. He was glad to be off the train, to see Raf and Buck, but he was downright miserable. Two weeks of reliving the worst day of his life was enough to make any man miserable.

He was an even bigger fool than he thought. That right there summed up fourteen entire days and nights of thinking. He missed Aislinn far more than he'd ever have imagined. It wasn't just the fun they had between the sheets, it was all of her. The hours spent together, being peppered by her questions about all topics, listening to her voice, her laugh, seeing the way she smiled. Just everything.

The next four weeks were going to be torturous. That's how long it would be before he saw her again. At every stop along the way, he'd considered turning around, going back, but hadn't, because when he saw her again, the only commitment he would have would be to the girls. That's what he kept telling himself and would continue to do so, despite how his mind kept trying to deceive him by telling him he didn't really want a divorce. What he really didn't want was to have been lied to. Over and over.

'How do?' Raf greeted. 'Your telegraph surprised me. I was expecting a letter.'

Luke settled the saddlebags he'd hauled to England and back behind Buck's saddle, and took the reins Raf handed over. 'You got me instead.'

'Can't say I'm sorry,' Raf said. 'I was afraid you'd write me back and tell me to sell the whole kit and caboodle.' Raf swung into his saddle. 'Had me sweating bullets, I tell you.'

Luke swung into the saddle, figuring he'd wait to break that news until they got to the ranch. 'Took a dislike to razors again, I see.'

'I've told you before,' Raf said, as they settled their horses into a slow walk, 'I shave, and the women start falling at my feet. I've been too busy taking care of your ranch to let that happen.'

As they rode, Luke took in the various wooden buildings lining both sides of the packed-dirt main street, housing stores that provided the general necessities. The town boasted a population of a little over a thousand people, but only when all the farmers and ranchers were counted. All in all, it was as different to London as a town could get.

He glanced at Raf. 'I do appreciate you taking care of things.'

Raf laughed and urged his horse into a gallop, now that they'd hit the edge of town. 'You might not once you see the place.'

Luke wasn't worried and urged Buck into a gallop that quickly overtook Raf's horse. The freedom that struck him at that moment was like an old friend. One he'd missed. The lush, green grass that stretched out for miles in front of him, the mountains cresting the horizon, topped with their white peaks, and the sky, a brazen blue and dotted with slow travelling clouds filled him with an inimitable wholesomeness.

He wished Aislinn could see all of this, the beauty of it, in person. What the hell? No, he didn't wish she could see it. He wished the woman he'd fallen in love with was who he'd thought she was, not some imposter. It was going to be good to be so busy the next few weeks. Hopefully he wouldn't even think about her. Not a single thought.

The miles between caring and love that he'd thought he couldn't traverse had turned out to be a short, quick trip. One he'd trekked without even realising it, because he had fallen in love with her. Lock, stock, and barrel. Selling the ranch didn't scare him, living the rest of his life without her was what was doing that. Actually, it was the idea that she didn't want to spend the rest of her life with *him* that really gutted him.

Damn it! He had to get her out of his mind. He let Buck run until the horse had enough and then waited for Raf to join them in a slow walk. It didn't take long for Raf to get him caught up on the comings and goings of the ranch, including that an Army spokesperson should be arriving in a few days. That would give them time to round up the cattle, since most of them were on open range, eating their fill of the lush green summer grasses.

The ride to the ranch took close to an hour, and Raf, being Raf, wanted to know more about Aislinn, and Fern and Ivy, than he'd mentioned in his letters. Luke obliged and tried to make it sound like they were one big happy family. That was easy. He was used to elaborating.

When the homestead, a cluster of buildings and corrals situated in a placid, flat-floored valley, came into sight, he pulled up on Buck's reins and took a moment to appreciate it all. His thoughts went to Aislinn again.

She had taken everything from him, left him empty.

He urged Buck into a gallop for the last trek of the journey. The quicker he got things done here, the better off he'd be.

Everything was just as he'd left it, including all the cowboys. A total of six lived in the bunkhouse, all except for Wayne Cardin. He lived in the log cabin the original owner had built, a short distance behind the bunkhouse, with his Native American wife, Doli. They'd worked for the previous owners and had stayed on when he'd bought the place from Mrs Brings. So had two of the cowboys, Jake and Buster, who doubled as cooks most of the time. Ted, Tad, and Andy had been hired later. All were good men, and upon greeting them,

he wondered if they'd want to stay on with the new owners, or if he'd be putting them out of jobs.

They'd all heard about Aislinn, and Fern and Ivy,
via his letters to Raf, and once again, Luke obliged
and told them more. Much more, including how Ivy
had taken to Half-Pint and learned to ride in a heartbeat. He even told Banjo that Fern wanted a dog who
could dance like him.

He spent the remainder of the day in the bunkhouse,
ate supper there, and then made his way into the main
house. The two-storey stone and wood structure was
used to being unused. He slept, bathed, wrote letters,
and not a whole lot more.

It was solidly built, as was the furniture filling it,
and hopefully the new owners would use it as it was
intended. To house a family for generations to come.

That's what he'd thought he'd gained in England. A
family. He had. The girls.

With that thought in mind, he sat down at the roll-
top desk in the room he used as his office and wrote a
letter to them, trying to make his trip sound exciting.
That's what he'd been doing for years. Writing, making
his life sound like the one he'd always wanted.

He balled up the paper, tossed it onto the desk. The
action reminded him of the paper he'd tossed on the
bed back home.

Disgusted with himself all over again, he got up to
heat water for a bath in the water closet down the hall
from the kitchen.

Every single one of his footfalls, each noise he made,
echoed off the silence filling the house, the silence inside him. He'd never felt so lonely in his life.

That ache and loneliness remained, even as he fully

immersed himself in the work that needed to get done. By his third day back at the ranch, a good portion of the cattle had been rounded up and brought closer to the homestead. Posts for temporary fences to keep them there and to separate out the breeding stock were being cut and pounded into the ground. So far, the count looked good.

They were some good-looking, healthy critters, and he was sure to get top dollar from the Army. The spokesperson was scheduled to arrive any day, and as he rode into the yard, he questioned if the wagon sitting near the barn was the visitor he was expecting.

It looked more like a freight wagon from town, but the Army had freight wagons, too.

No one was about. The only person who'd stayed behind at the homestead was Doli. The others were out working on the fence, in the foothills searching for cattle, or tending to the ones being corralled.

It wasn't yet quitting time, but he'd ridden home to collect the letter he'd written to Aislinn and take it to town to post. It was a simple one, stating he'd arrived at the ranch. He knew the girls would be waiting on a letter and didn't want to disappoint them.

That wagon threw a wrench in his plans. It was strange that there were no horses hitched to the wagon, and Luke was perplexed as he rode Buck straight to the house. Whoever that wagon belonged to was probably waiting for him there.

He was just reining Buck to a stop by the hitching post when the front door opened.

Luke's entire body froze, except his heart. It pounded so hard, it echoed in his ears.

He had to be hallucinating. There was no conceivable way it could be her. Yet, a single word, a single thought, came out of his mouth. 'Aislinn?'

She stepped further onto the porch, to where the afternoon sun was no longer blocked by the wooden overhead awning of the porch and lit on her face. 'Hello, Luke.'

His feet barely hit the ground before they flew up the steps.

Still questioning reality as his feet landed on the porch floor, he stopped so quickly, his body rocked from his heels to his toes by the sudden change of movement. For a still, unbroken moment, they stood there, gazes locked, his heart pounding against his ribcage like it was trying to get out. A dozen things to say crossed his mind, but he settled on just one. 'What the hell are you doing here?'

Lifting her chin, she said, 'I don't want a divorce.'

He balled his hands into fists, refusing to admit that he didn't, either. In fact, he'd give anything to have her in his arms right now, to be kissing her breathless. 'You shouldn't be here.'

'Well, we are,' she said. 'Fern and Ivy are taking a bath, which they greatly need, considering the last one they had was at the hotel in Baltimore.'

He could smell the scent of soap, the kind she used in London.

Her cheeks pinkened. 'I took mine first.'

Why was he having such a hard time finding the anger he'd harboured for weeks? He was digging, but it just wasn't there. 'How long have you been here?'

'A few hours. Doli offered to go get you, but I said we'd wait, put our things away.'

'Your things away?' Of course, they'd have luggage, and—'This is no place for you.'

She looked over her shoulder, at the house. 'You mentioned that before, so I brought along a cook and a housekeeper. Doo and Millie are inside. We purchased some supplies in Bozeman and rented a wagon. Mr Williams at the emporium says hello, as does Mr Kemp at the livery.'

He shook his head in a mixture of disbelief and something he didn't want to feel. Love. Admiration. They were there, though, and strong, pushing their way into his heart.

She touched his cheek. 'Don't be mad, please. I knew nothing about the inheritance. Neither did Mr Watson. Dr Stockholm was present when Rowland had Gabe write it, and he saw Percy take it from Rowland's bedroom. That was the last time anyone saw it until Hazel gave it to you.

That couldn't be true. It had to be another one of her lies, but then why was she here? What more was there for her to gain?

'Mr Watson has it now, and I have a letter from him, for you.' She blinked several times, yet a tear trickled from the corner of one eye. 'Explaining what Dr Stockholm said.'

His heart was hammering in his chest. Could it be that simple? Could he have been the one in the wrong? Been so stubborn that he never thought that maybe he didn't know the full story? Had he truly been that afraid of love? Of loving her? A woman who had just travelled halfway around the world for him?

'I'll go get it, so you can read it,' she said. 'Perhaps then you'll know that I didn't lie to you. That I've never lied to you.'

He grabbed her arm. In part because he didn't need

to read the letter, and in part because he'd already waited too long to admit the answers to all the questions that he'd just asked himself. It was yes. He'd been wrong and afraid, and…

In the next instant, she was in his arms. He kissed her, held her tight. There was so much he had to tell her, but he settled for, 'I don't want a divorce, either.' Truer words had never crossed his lips. Nor had anything tasted sweeter than her lips.

'Uncle Luke!' Two voices shouted in unison, as Fern and Ivy bolted out of the door together.

He released Aislinn in order to hoist both girls into the air, one at a time, hugging them tightly and planting kisses on their cheeks before setting them back down.

'Are you happy to see the three faces you like looking at the most?' Fern asked.

His gaze locked with Aislinn's, and in that earth-shattering moment, he fully understood just how deep his love for this trio of females went, clear down to his very soul. The soul he'd thought he knew so well, but hadn't. Not until now.

Looking down, he touched the tip of Fern's nose. 'Yes, I am very happy to see the three faces I like looking at the most.'

'I like your ranch, Uncle Luke,' Ivy said. 'So does Half-Pint.'

He opened his mouth to respond, but stopped and looked at Aislinn. 'Half-Pint? You brought the pony?'

She grimaced and shrugged. 'We couldn't leave her behind.'

'She would have missed me too much,' Ivy explained. 'Look, see how she likes it?'

He followed the direction that Ivy was pointing to

the corral beside the barn. Indeed, the white pony was there, prancing about the pen as if quite happy with her new home.

'Benjamin took very good care of her the entire way,' Aislinn said. 'Each time the train stopped, he unloaded her for some exercise so she wouldn't get overly stiff. Mr Kemp at the livery said she was in excellent shape, even after all the travels. He also said that the wagon and team could be returned the next time someone goes to town.'

Luke waited until she stopped talking before he asked, 'Benjamin is here, too?'

'Yes.'

'Did you leave anyone in England?'

'Don't be silly. It was just the three of them that travelled with us.' She laid a hand on his arm. 'They wanted to come. Even offered to pay their own way, though I couldn't let them do that. I used some of the money you put in the account under my name.'

Ivy tugged at his pant leg. 'Is this Buck?' she asked. 'Can I ride him?'

He couldn't leave Buck standing in the sun and needed time to process everything, to decide what to do about them being here. 'That is Buck.' He hoisted Ivy up again. 'Yes, you can ride him.'

Luke walked down the steps, put Ivy in the saddle, then lifted Fern up and set her behind her sister. Then he took a hold of Aislinn's hand, and as he led Buck to the barn, his nieces proceeded to give him an earful about their voyage across the sea and the train ride.

His heart was in his throat over the idea of them travelling such a distance, yet he gave Aislinn credit. If he'd had to choose anyone to travel with them, it would have been Doo.

But, damn it, none of them should have made that trip. None of them should be here. They should be in England, where they belonged. Where they all belonged.

Chapter Sixteen

Aislinn felt as if she'd been holding her breath since the moment Luke had ridden into the courtyard, or homestead, as the others referred to the area where all the buildings were located, including the lovely two-storey house, painted white and hosting a huge front porch that looked out over the mountains, which were exactly as Luke had described them.

Huge, with white snow-capped tops. Majestic was what he'd said, and they truly were. Everything about this place was grand. The entire ranch was wonderful. Beautiful. It was all just as Luke had described it, so much so that she felt as if she'd already seen it. That everything was familiar. She hadn't been fearful of any part of the trip, because she'd known what to expect.

Even the beauty.

And the ranch. Besides the house, there was a huge red barn, the bunkhouse where the cowboys, Ted, Tad, Andy, Jake, and Buster, lived, the log cabin where Doli lived with her husband, Wayne, the chicken coop, the corn crib, the machine shed, and three other buildings that she didn't know the names of, or what they were used for, but she'd learn.

She would learn everything there was to know about living here.

That's why she felt as if she was holding her breath, because, though he appeared happy that they were there, Luke was troubled by their presence.

She wasn't convinced that he didn't want them here, he just didn't feel as if it was the right place for them. What he didn't understand was that wherever he was, was where they belonged. They were a family. Her family.

She also had to tell him the entire truth about what she'd done before leaving England.

The sound of the door opening made her heart flip, but she remained still, looking out of the bedroom window at the sky that looked like black velvet, and stars that shone as brightly as the diamond in the ring on her finger when light hit it just right.

The hands that slipped around her waist from behind her were familiar, and the firm touch of them was one of the many things she'd missed that last couple of weeks.

Luke pulled her back against him and nuzzled the side of her neck.

'The stars look almost close enough to touch,' she said, rubbing his forearms folded around her waist.

'It's you I want to touch,' he whispered.

She twisted around, ran her hands over the skin of his shoulders. 'Should I check if you washed behind your ears? It took longer to heat your bath water than for you to wash with it.'

His chuckle was low and husky, and his hands roamed down her back. 'This evening was already the longest I've ever had to endured.' He kissed her ear, then the side of her neck.

'It was nice to meet everyone,' she said, tilting her

head to give him more access. 'They were all so friendly and welcoming, and I believe everyone enjoyed the meal Doo prepared. Including you.'

He lifted his head, looked at her. 'I admit his cooking beats the heck out of Buster's cooking, but why are we standing here, discussing food, when we could be in the bed, right over there!' He picked her up on the last word and carried her across the room.

With her arms looped around his neck, she said, 'I remembered something recently.'

He paused next to the bed and lifted a brow. 'What's that?'

'When Mrs Hall was teaching me everything that I needed to know to become a governess, she told me to stay away from the charming ones.' She trailed a finger from his chin to his chest. 'Meaning men. She said they would charm me right out of my clothes and into their bed, and then I'd lose my job.'

He fell backwards onto the bed with her in his arms. The bed creaked and the mattress bounced. So did they. She ended up lying atop him, and her entire body tingled in anticipation of what was to come.

'Well,' he said, inching her night rail upwards. 'I guess she was right.'

'Are you saying you're charming?' she teased. 'Or that I lost my job?'

'Both,' he said, his lips almost touching hers. 'And I really like your new job. That of being my wife.'

She did, too.

It took far less than a minute for her night rail to be discarded, and his pants. Then their reunion fully began, with him kissing her into a state where nothing existed except for the two of them.

* * *

The following morning, Aislinn determined there was no time like the present to get things in order. Doli, who was, beyond a doubt, the most beautiful woman Aislinn had ever seen, with her bronze complexion, dark brown eyes, and long, straight black hair, had shared a variety of information yesterday. Yet, there was much more that Aislinn would need to know, so shortly after the men rode off to take care of the cattle, she knocked on the door of the log cabin, armed with a pen and paper.

Within an hour, she had a full list of domestic matters that needed immediate attention and another list of accounting matters that she would need to discuss with Luke. She did not know the financial situation of the ranch and hoped the addition of Doo, Millie, and Benjamin wouldn't be a burden.

They wanted to come here as much as her. Upon returning to the house with her list, and Doli in case others had questions, she sat everyone down to designate duties.

During her conversation with Doli, Aislinn had become aware of all the duties the woman had been completing, and asked her if she would like assistance. Not because she wasn't doing a good job, but because there were now enough people to share those duties.

As sweet as she was pretty, Doli had expressed with sincerity that she would enjoy having others to share the work with, especially with a baby arriving in a few months. She also expressed how happy she was to have more women in residence.

Doo was in full agreeance about cooking for all, stating that it was only a couple more than he was used to cooking for, and agreed to create a weekly menu. Benjamin said the cowboys took such good care of the horses and tack themselves, he'd have plenty of time to help in other areas after completing his stable duties.

Millie said the house was half the size of the London house and would take only a fraction of her time to clean.

The house was smaller than their London home, but larger than what she'd expected. That was the only thing Luke had never fully described. The house. There were four bedrooms upstairs and two downstairs. Millie and Benjamin had each taken a room upstairs, and Fern and Ivy shared the one near Millie's room. Doo had taken the downstairs bedroom that was off the kitchen. Her and Luke's room was down the hall, past the dining room and water closet. There was also a large front parlour that had a massive rock fireplace and a smaller room that Luke used as his office. Below the house, accessible by a door in the kitchen, and down a set of stairs, was a large root cellar.

The one thing Aislinn was worried about was that not having a designated governess might be unseemly, but she was certain that between she and Millie, someone would always be on hand to see to the girls' needs, including schooling.

With everyone in agreeance, she started with the most prudent issue. Doli had said that the men rarely ate a noon meal. They would simply take biscuits, or bread and bacon, or jerky with them when they left in the morning to eat later in the day.

With Doo and Benjamin working on a meal that Benjamin would deliver to the men to eat at noon, and

Millie busy with household chores, Aislinn and Doli entered the bunkhouse.

'Luke said the men could clean up after themselves,' Doli said, 'but as you can see, they aren't very good at it.'

Kicking at a chunk of mud on the floor, Aislinn said, 'I can see that. I suggest that they clean up after themselves daily, but we'll give it a good cleaning once a week.' Walking past beds that were built up against the wall, two high, she added, 'And wash the bedding.'

'I agree,' Doli said, pointing out with one hand that the room also had cobwebs in the corners. 'I've wanted to suggest that, but Luke said that I already did enough.'

Aislinn's heart warmed. 'The only person he over-works is himself.'

'I will get a broom, mop and bucket,' Doli said.

'Thank you. I will find a nanny for Fern and Ivy.'

'Who?' Doli asked.

'Half-Pint,' Aislinn replied.

The girls were outside the bunkhouse, playing with Banjo. The shaggy, grey and white dog had taken to the girls as quickly as they had to him.

Having watched both Luke and John bridle Half-Pint numerous times, Aislinn completed the task in no time. She led the pony into the centre of the courtyard and lifted both girls onto Half-Pint's back. 'You can ride all around the yard, but not past any buildings, promise?'

'We promise!' Ivy shouted. 'I've missed riding so much!'

Aislinn returned to help Doli and easily kept an eye on the girls while cleaning. By the time Benjamin left with the meal for the men, the bunkhouse was clean, including the dishes, pots, and pans that had been in need of a good scrubbing, and the bedding and curtains were hanging on the clotheslines stretched between the bunkhouse and a building that housed the buggies and wagons.

The C Bar H ranch, she discovered, stood for Carlisle's Haven. The closeness of the name Luke had chosen for the ranch to the name of their family estate, Havenbrook, wasn't lost on her.

After lunch, while the girls were napping, the beds were made in the bunkhouse, and Aislinn neatly printed a sign and tacked it up on the back of the door. It explained that washday was Wednesday and any clothing needing to be washed, should be left on the cowboy's respected beds. She also wrote the weekly menu on a sheet of paper and left it on the table.

Fully satisfied with the work they'd accomplished, she closed the door of the bunkhouse. As she walked towards the house, she thought how lovely it would be to have a few rose bushes planted along the front of the porch and added it to a growing mental list of other ideas she'd had. Like a child-sized table for the girls. She'd brought along books, games, and toys, including their beloved tea set, but there was no table for them to use.

There had been so many of them eating last night that Tad and Ted had found some barrels, laid some boards between them, and carried chairs from the bunkhouse and kitchen for everyone to sit on. It would be nice to have a table like that out in the yard, so they could eat outside whenever they wanted. She was more like Luke than she'd known, because there was something about that big sky overhead that she just couldn't get enough of.

She was in the parlour, where Fern and Ivy were using the short table in front of the sofa for their tea party, which included Banjo alongside their dolls, when Benjamin announced that the men were arriving.

'Thank you, Benjamin. Will you please inform them that their supper will be delivered to the bunkhouse as soon as it's ready?'

'Yes, ma'am,' Benjamin replied. 'Doo said it'll be about half an hour. The men will need that much time to take care of their horses.'

'Perfect, thank you.' She stood and told the girls. 'Time to put away your tea set. Uncle Luke is home.'

Excited to see him, they quickly obeyed and carried the box containing the set, as well as their dolls, up to their room. Followed closely by Banjo.

Aislinn waited for them in the front entranceway, by the foot of the stairs, and upon their return, they walked out onto the front porch to wait for Luke to emerge from the barn.

He emerged from the bunkhouse instead. The girls raced down the steps to greet him, and she followed more slowly, though was just as happy to see him.

After each of his nieces received a hug, kiss on the cheek, and a tickle, he approached her. With a frown. 'Madam,' he said, 'could we speak for a moment?'

'Of course.' Her stomach hiccupped. He'd never called her madam, nor had he ever spoken to her so formally.

He gestured to the house, and once inside, escorted her into his office, where he closed the door. Removing his hat with one hand, he ran his fingers through his hair with the other. Then, using the hat as if it was a pointing stick, he gestured it towards the window. 'Those men are cowboys, not schoolboys. That is a bunkhouse, not a prep school.'

His expression said she should completely understand. She did, and also fully understood that when he got pushed, he pushed back with all he had. That's why he and Percy had been like two rams butting heads. It was also why he was so successful. Well, in a very short time, she'd been taught to do the same. By him. 'Your point is?' she asked.

'My point is…' He let out a tiny growl and slapped his hat on his leg, spewing dust into the air. 'My point is, are you trying to spoil them?'

She planted both hands on her hips. 'I do not consider a clean floor and bedding *spoiling*.'

'You hung up a note on the door telling them to put their laundry on their beds!'

'To make it easier for Doli to know what belongs to whom. Right now, they throw it all in a pile. After washing, she puts it on the table and, at times, they don't get the right socks.' Having learned how important socks were to cowboys, she asked, 'Would you want to wear someone else's socks?' He momentarily closed his eyes, and she continued, 'No one has complained to her, but it makes her feel bad. This will be easier for everyone.'

He rubbed his forehead. 'You had food delivered to us, and—and put a menu on their table.'

'You can't expect men to work all day on empty stomachs. Doo said he didn't mind cooking for everyone. It's only a few more people than in London, and not close to as many as Havenbrook. If they don't like what is on the menu, Buster can cook something else for them.'

Luke was trying his damnedest to be mad at her. He'd already spent the day listening to the men sing of her beauty and courage, which he hadn't minded, because he agreed. Praise for her had increased after she'd sent the hot meal out to them. Add in a sparkling clean bunkhouse, freshly laundered sheets, and an evening meal ready to eat, the men wouldn't ever want her to leave. Hell, they might try to stop him from taking her back to London.

She was looking at him, arms now crossed over her bosom. Her mighty fine bosom, which he couldn't wait to touch, to taste, again tonight. Hell, but he was losing his steam and tried desperately to find it again. 'Buster's not going to make something different for them,' he growled.

'Would you like me to have them approve the menu before I confirm it with Doo?'

'Hell no.' He slapped his hat on his head. 'They'll eat whatever is put in front of them.'

'Then, my lord,' she said, 'I do not see the problem.'

Her *my lord* was payback for him calling her *madam*, and that almost made him grin. But she'd even washed the windows and curtains in the bunkhouse. Which had been needed. The entire place had needed to be cleaned, but he hadn't wanted to impose on Doli. And the cowboys, well they'd been too busy with round-up, branding, and then planting, so the cattle would have grain next winter, to bother with cleaning. Damn it to hell. He couldn't find a single issue with what she'd done.

She stepped closer, touched a button on his shirt. 'I simply saw things that needed to be done.'

'I know.' He did realise that.

'I was only thinking of the best interests for you, for your ranch. If you never doubt me, I'll never doubt you.'

He was reminded of when he had thought she'd lied

to him, and the lesson he'd learned. How he could have lost her for ever, if not for her determination. 'I don't doubt you,' he said, earnestly, because she was capable of far more than anyone could imagine. 'I don't doubt anything about you.'

She stretched on her toes so her lips were near his. 'Nor do I doubt you. I never have.' Her kiss was not only sweet and tender it was full of promises of more to come.

Before that thought overrode all others, he said, 'I'm selling this place, Aislinn. It's not fair for the men to think everything will be like it is today, when in a couple of weeks, it'll all be sold, and we'll be on our way back to England.'

She let out a long sigh. 'You can't sell this place. It's where you belong.'

'Yes, I can. We belong in England.' He wasn't going to argue. 'I'll go get washed up for supper.'

The next few days brought about more changes. Nothing major, just little things that had the entire place running like a well-oiled machine.

The cowboys appreciated all of her efforts, and they let her know that through their actions. After hearing that she'd like some flowers near the front porch, Tad had ridden ten miles to the Rocking B Ranch and came back with sprigs of roses, lilacs, and clumps of several other flowers. Aislinn had immediately planted them in various places around the yard.

Buster, Ted, Andy, and Raf had spent a couple of evenings building the girls a child-sized table and chairs set, which Fern and Ivy loved, and Jake and Wayne had built two large picnic tables, along with benches, which were just outside the back door of the house and used every evening.

There were other changes, too, things she'd done for him. Organising his office and books. Whatever he needed, when he needed it, was always close at hand, including her.

Life was as perfect as possible, and he knew why. She was attempting to make him believe there was no need to return to England. There was. He could think of a thousand reasons. Summertime in Montana was wonderful, beautiful, and that's all she was seeing. Winters were cold, harsh, brutal, on man and beast.

There was also the isolation that would set in. More people lived here than before, but the lack of social activities hit everyone at one time or another. Dinner parties and dances didn't happen daily as they did in London. Here, months went by between events.

He had admitted to himself that he loved Aislinn. He did. He couldn't even remember why he hadn't wanted to fall in love with her. But when you love someone, you want the best life possible for them, and that's what he wanted for her. A life where her worries were little more than what gown to wear to what party.

When he'd left home all those years ago, Rowland had told him to live every adventure to its fullest, because a day would come when the right woman came along. Whether that happened when he was young or old, his life would change. The love that they would hold for each other would consume him. Everything he did from then on, would be for her benefit. She would be his haven in life.

He'd paid little heed to those words then, had thought

it had been Rowland's way of explaining why he was satisfied with his lot in life.

Luke knew differently now, and as usual, Rowland had been right.

Fern and Ivy, though happy right now to ride Half-Pint around the yard and play with Banjo, needed more. In London, there were museums to visit, exhibitions, and when the time came, the most prestigious schools that would prepare them for adulthood. He was responsible for them receiving all of that, and none of it would happen here.

Every morning, when the sun came up, he wondered if it would be the day that the Army spokesperson arrived, so he could learn the fate of the herd and then move on to the sale of the property. Aislinn may have a plan, one she was executing without flaw, but he had one, too. The same one he'd formed before leaving England, and it hadn't changed one iota. Rowland's daughters would be raised in England.

He'd read, and re-read, the letter from the Army that Raf had written to him about. There weren't a lot of details in it, just stating the Army was interested in buying a significant number of standing beefs to feed the soldiers, and that a spokesperson would visit the ranch before the end of the month.

The end of the month had been two days ago, and he was questioning if they'd chosen another ranch to purchase from. There were plenty of other ranches between here and the closest fort. That was also why he'd thought they might like the whole herd. His cowboys could drive it to them, and they wouldn't have to purchase any more beef for a significant amount of time, could even use some in their negotiations with the reservations.

Of course, he would have to let his regular buyers know as soon as the deal was done. Since purchasing the ranch, he'd sold a goodly amount of cattle to the stockyard in Bozeman every fall, to be shipped out across the territory to the meat processing facilities in the larger cities. There were also the local butchers, who purchased a few head monthly to keep the town fed.

Those sales, large and small, had kept the ranch profitable. There had been a time when he'd imagined his herd growing, the number of cattle shipped out larger, until his ranch was the largest producer of prime beef in the territory.

'Boss!'

Luke turned to Jake, who was up on top of the ridge. The two of them were looking for a maverick that Jake had got a glimpse of earlier this morning.

'Rider coming!' Jake yelled.

Luke waved his hat to gesture that he'd heard and then pointed it towards a cluster of thick sagebrush, where he was sure the maverick was hiding.

As he rode up the ridge, Jake rode down it.

'Looks like Benjamin,' Jake said, as their paths crossed.

Luke nudged Buck to reach the top faster, instantly concerned that something had happened at the homestead. The dangers were endless; that's what caused the fear that lived inside him daily.

'Mrs Carlisle sent me to collect you,' Benjamin shouted, upon seeing him. 'You have visitors. Army men!'

Relief struck Luke, but he'd be lying if he didn't

admit there was also some remorse. He would miss working every day until he was bone tired. But not too tired to enjoy his wife, and missing her had been far worse than missing anything else would ever be.

He met up with Benjamin and listened as the young man explained that Aislinn had sent him out to get him. Two Army men had arrived.

Chapter Seventeen

It took a good half hour to ride to the house, and during that time, Luke worried that Aislinn was afraid. Once again, he was grateful that she'd brought Doo with her from England. He and Doo visited every morning, while others in the house were still sleeping, and Doo prepared breakfast that would then be carried out to the bunkhouse.

One thing was clear about his childhood friend— Doo had no intention of ever returning to England.

At the house, Luke found Aislinn and two Army men, with yellow Cavalry chevrons on their blue uniforms, in the parlour. The empty cups and plates showed tea and sweet cakes had been served and consumed. After introductions, she graciously excused herself, and Luke noted his weren't the only eyes watching the swish of her blue skirts as she left the room.

They could only wish they had what he had. He knew that as the gospel truth.

Both Major Huckabee, a tall, middle-aged man with greying sideburns, and Sergeant Hill, a young, blue-eyed man with orange peach fuzz on his chin, had thanked Aislinn for her hospitality and repeated the same to him.

Luke accepted their praise with pride, then questioned if the men cared to ride out and see the herd.

'That won't be necessary,' Major Huckabee stated. 'Our enquiries led us to your ranch for quality beef to feed the occupants of the fort. I do apologise. Things were delayed in Washington that affected our deployment. It remains our hope to obtain a contract with the C Bar H. Once the fort is fully reinstated, our order will increase significantly.'

'Reinstated?' Luke asked, confused.

'Yes, sir, in order to assist with the territory becoming a state.' Major Huckabee pulled an envelope from his pocket. 'I have the contract here and, upon signature, can provide you with a payment voucher from the government for a dozen head. Eventually, there will be more than five hundred soldiers assigned to the fort. At that point we'll be buying cattle regularly.'

A dozen? Luke held back his disappointment that selling the entire herd was no longer an option. Not today at least.

He took the contract, which was succinct and to the point, and read it. The amount listed was fair, more than he'd figured. 'I can have a couple of cowboys drive a dozen head to the fort tomorrow,' he said. 'Leaving by daybreak, the cattle will arrive by nightfall.'

'Thank you, Mr Carlisle,' Major Huckabee said, his smile as large as his companion's. 'We can help with the drive, as well.'

The nodding of the younger sergeant confirmed what Luke had imagined. These men had travelled a long route to get to the fort and were in need of a substantial food source. 'I'll get a pen to sign this,' Luke said. 'We'll ride out to the herd and you can pick out the dozen steers. Then you're welcome to spend the night, eat supper with us.'

The deal was completed that easily, yet Luke felt as if he was being thwarted around every corner, just as he had been in England.

Aislinn had found the Army Major and Sergeant very nice, and the idea that an entire troop of soldiers were only twenty miles away kept her smiling well after they'd left. Luke would never be able to deny that they made living here safer. Their safety was one of his reasons for claiming they had to return to England. That they didn't *belong* here.

He didn't understand that when you love someone, you belong with them, wherever that might be, and he truly belonged here.

Footfalls on the front porch made her smile, for she even knew the sound of his boots, but it also made her frown, because she hadn't expected him home this soon. She set aside the cloth and tin of beeswax she was using to shine the banister of the stairway, and moved to meet him as he stepped inside the house.

'Is something amiss?' she asked.

'No. There's a meeting of the Stockgrowers Association in Bozeman this afternoon that I'm going to attend, in order to find a buyer for the herd and the ranch.'

Her heart dropped.

He walked past her. She followed, all the way to their bedroom, where he began to unbutton his shirt. There had been times when she could have told him, before now, but hadn't, because she was afraid. She'd given him the letter from Mr Watson, but had never told him what she'd done.

'You're not going to talk me out of this, Aislinn. It's too dangerous here. The weather is fine now, but it won't be for long. The winters are brutal. Cold. Snow. Wind. People freeze to death. Cattle freeze to death. A doctor can't make it out here for days.'

She wanted to tell him that if a doctor was needed, he'd find a way a way to get one. She had complete belief in his abilities, but remained silent because he was talking again.

'Think of the things the girls need,' he said. 'Schools. Prestigious schools. Social outings. Friends from their same class. Clothes. Shopping. You saw the stores in Bozeman when you arrived. The emporium is nothing like the stores in London.' He removed his shirt and tossed it over the back of a chair. 'Fern and Ivy were born privileged and they will live a privileged life. That can't happen here.'

She picked up the discarded shirt and dropped it in the basket near the door. 'There is one thing about your reasoning that I don't understand.'

He opened the closet door. 'What's that?'

'I don't understand why you would impose a life you clearly disliked upon your nieces. You couldn't wait to escape it.'

He took out a clean white shirt. 'It was different for me. I was the third son. There were no expectations that I would one day take over the title, become the head of the family.'

'There are no such expectations for Fern and Ivy, either. They were born to a duke and duchess, but are now the nieces of a duke. Tell me exactly what that will provide them with?'

'Privilege. Prestige,' he said, while putting on the shirt.

She didn't blink an eye as she stared at him. Waiting for him to say more.

'The opportunities to marry well.'

'So, that's your goal? To have them marry well?'

'No.' He ran a hand through his hair. 'There are also schools. The best schools.'

'You already mentioned schools. I don't even want to think about those days,' she said. 'We'll never see them, except for school breaks, which will be short and far between. You remember that, don't you? Being a child and separated from your family for months on end.'

'I remember, but why are you so against it?'

'I'm not against them having an excellent education. I want them to have that, but I want them to have other things, too. I want them to be prepared in all aspects of life. To be independent, self-assured, and bold enough to know what they want, when they want it. I imagine you do, too.'

He nodded.

'I would think you'd want them to explore things and places,' she said, 'be left afoot a time or two, so they know the importance of staying in the saddle. Learn the importance of respecting people for what they do, who they are, titled or not. To accept responsibility, but to also stay true to themselves. Isn't that how you'd raise your own children? For you will be the only father they remember. Will ever know.'

He stared at her for a moment, then shook his head. 'Fern and Ivy can learn all that in England.'

'I've no doubt of that.' She crossed the room and

closed the closet door he'd left open. 'They can learn those things anywhere in the world, because places don't teach things, people do.'

'Some places are safer than others.'

She'd been beating around the bush and was getting nowhere, which left nothing but the truth. 'I did something before I left England that I'm quite ashamed of.'

'You?'

She wasn't afraid of his anger, for he had every right to be upset with her. Swallowing, she nodded.

He stepped closer, rubbed her upper arms with both hands. 'What did you do?'

Her stomach was churning hard. 'After I discovered the truth from Dr Stockholm about Rowland's request, I was mad. So very mad that I went to see Percy. He wasn't home, but Hazel was, and I, well, I told her that she needed to learn how to become a duchess. Then I went to the House of Lords, and waited until Percy came out.' She had to draw in a breath, hoping to settle her nerves. 'I met him on the steps and told him that I was done with his wife interfering in our lives, and that he needed to learn to become a duke, or at least a man whose wife didn't lead him around like he had a ring in his nose.'

Luke let out a laugh.

'It's not funny,' she insisted. It wasn't at all. By the time she returned home that day, she'd realised she had acted just like Hazel. Had been thinking only of herself. 'Percy wasn't alone when I said those things.'

Luke's eyes grew wide, then he let out an even louder laugh. 'You told my brother to either grow a brain or a set of—guts, in front of his peers?'

Her face burned, for that was exactly what she'd done. 'Yes, and I'm very sorry.'

'I wish I could have seen it.' He kissed her forehead, hugged her. 'Don't worry about Percy. I can handle him.'

'The two of you were getting along, and I ruined that for you,' she whispered. 'I should have gone and apologised the next day, but there was so much to do. Tickets to purchase, packing, meeting with Mr Watson to oversee the London house expenses.'

He hugged her tighter. 'You didn't ruin anything.' Then he stiffened slightly. 'Did Percy do something? Threaten you?'

'No, he didn't say anything. Just stood there. Beet red. I got back in the carriage and went home.'

He took a step back, and the frown on his face made her heart flip.

'Is that why you came here? Because you're afraid of Percy?'

'No, I'd already planned on coming here. I think that's why I had the courage to say the things I did, because I figured once we got here, we'd be staying.'

He was still frowning. Severely. 'You already planned on coming here?'

'Yes.'

'Why?'

It was time to tell him the entire truth, even though it wasn't something he'd want to hear. 'Because, ever since we got married, I wake up at night thinking I must be dreaming, but then I hear you breathing, feel your arms around me, and know I'm not. That this is my life. The life I want for ever.' She wiped away a tear from the corner of her eye. 'I know you didn't want to get married, ever, but I swear that I will try to be the best wife possible for you, the best surrogate mother for the girls. I will live anywhere you want.'

He hadn't moved. Not at all.

'I thought this was what you really wanted,' she said. 'You were so happy when you talked about Montana. I didn't want you to feel trapped in England. To be miserable. I thought if you came here, you'd be happy. Even before you left, I planned on following you.' She shook her head. 'I knew you'd never agree to us coming with you, and I couldn't risk losing you. I lost my family once before, as a little girl, and I was afraid that might happen again.'

Luke's heart dropped to his feet thinking of how he'd left her with his demand for a divorce. He'd regret that for ever. Stepping forward, he wrapped his arms around her. 'I will never leave you ever again. I promise. I love you.'

She went completely still. 'You do?'

'Yes, I do.'

She made a tiny sob sound. 'I love you, too. So much, But I didn't—I don't—expect you to love me in return.'

The rejoicing inside him made him chuckle. 'You should have, because I do. That's how it works.'

She leaned back, looked at him with bewilderment in her shimmering brown eyes. 'Are you sure? Sure that you love *me*?'

'Yes, you.'

'He touched his forehead to hers. 'I've never been more sure of anything, and I plan on spending the rest of my life loving you.' He lifted his head, kissed her forehead. 'I was never miserable in London. The very idea that I could ever be miserable with you near is impossible. I'm sorry you thought that.'

'But the businesses you bought,' she said, 'the frustration about a member of the ton not getting their hands dirty.'

'I admit, I was frustrated, but not with you. Never with you. I was frustrated with how shallow life felt doing nothing but attending parties, balls, and the opera.'

She grimaced. 'That was excruciating.'

He touched the side of her face. 'For you, too?'

'Yes.'

'I'm sorry I put you through that. I just wanted to make the best life for you. I still do.'

She stretched on her toes, kissed his lips softly. 'You've already done that.'

In that moment, he understood that loving someone wasn't about giving things up for them, it was about sharing. Sharing life. All parts of it. The depths of emotion filling him would be there for a lifetime, of that he had no doubt.

He ran a finger along the side of her face. 'I'm going to ask you a question, and I know you won't lie to me. That you'll never lie to me.'

'I won't.'

'Where do you want to live?'

'Wherever you are.'

He brushed the hair away from her face, but never took his eyes off hers. 'I feel the same. I want to live wherever you are, so I'll ask again, where do you want to live with me? Montana or England?'

She pinched her lips together.

'Don't worry about Percy and Hazel,' he said, still wishing he could have witnessed her putting Percy in his place. 'This is about us. You and me, and a decision we need to make together. This is our life.'

She let out a tiny sigh. 'We do have the girls to think about.'

'Yes, we do, so let me ask this, where do *you* feel at home?'

She closed her eyes and sighed. 'You are so stubborn.'

'I, my dear—' he kissed her cheek '—am merely asking a question. Where do you feel at home? Montana or England?'

She looked at him, for a long quiet moment. 'In England, though I was your wife, I was easily reminded that I had been a governess. A servant. Whereas, here, I've never been anything except your wife. I can't even begin to explain what that feels like. How different I feel here. How free I feel.'

'You don't need to explain it,' he whispered. 'I know.'

'And I know how you felt, wanting a different life.'

He kissed her, then held her close in a long hug, filled with a great sense of contentment. Yet, he knew he would have been just as content if she'd said London. 'We will visit England, yearly, and when the girls are older, they will have a choice as to where to go to school,' he said. 'We will teach them to think for themselves, to follow their dreams, and we will support them in whatever they choose. They may not have been born to us, but they are our children and will be raised as our children.'

She lifted her face, looked up at him with shimmering eyes. 'Luke Carlisle, you are a wonderful, amazing man, whom I love with all my heart.' Kissing his chin, she added, 'I fell in love with you while listening to your letters, but the real you…' She sighed. 'Is even more than I ever dreamed.'

He kissed her, a long, slow kiss. 'Rowland once told me that when I met the right woman, my life would change. That the love I felt for her would consume me.' He kissed her again. 'If he were here today, I would tell him that he was right. That I found my haven.'

Epilogue

Aislinn stood at the top of the porch steps, breathing in the subtle aroma of the rose bushes in full bloom, and smiled at the sight before her. Fern and Ivy were riding into the yard on their horses, a pair of matching black and white paints. At nine, they were quite accomplished riders.

Between them, riding Half-Pint, was Rowland Lucas Carlisle, affectionately known as Rowdy, because he certainly was that at times. Their four-year-old son was never far from his sisters. He adored them as much as they adored him.

Following the trio was their father. Handsome, proud and, as always, keeping a watchful eye over his children.

Her heart fluttered and she rubbed her stomach, where another Carlisle was growing, due to arrive in the fall, when the entire landscape would be ablaze with colourful shades of red, yellow, gold, and green foliage.

She loved how the seasons were each so unique, beautiful in their own ways. Luke had been right about the winters. They were cold, snowy, and windy, but also wonderful—and fruitful. During some of those long winter nights, both of their children had been conceived.

While the children rode their mounts to the barn, where Benjamin and Millie, who was now married to Jake, were waiting, Luke rode Buck straight to the house. Benjamin had moved into the bunkhouse when Jake and Millie had moved into a small house that had been built for them near the log cabin.

It was a good thing there was more room in the house. Not just for their growing family, but for regular visitors.

She walked down the steps as Luke dismounted. 'How did that go?' The cowboys had corralled several wild horses earlier in the week, and all three children had been begging to see them.

'Fine.' His smile shone with pride as he looked towards the barn. 'Rowdy picked out one that he wants.'

There was no need for her to voice caution or concern. He never put any of them in danger, and never would. 'I'm sure he did.'

'How was your afternoon?' Luke asked, kissing her cheek while laying a hand on her stomach.

'Fine. We received a telegraph.'

He frowned. Telegraphs arrived regularly, but she rarely mentioned one.

'From Percy.' With a shrug, she added, 'They'll be here by the end of the month.'

'Again?' Luke chuckled. 'Between our trips to England, and theirs here, I see him more now than when we were kids.'

'Caldwell wants to spend his school break here.' She explained what the message had stated.

'He's turning out to be a pretty decent kid.' Luke grinned. 'Not as good as ours, but pretty good.'

She slapped his chest. 'Even when the two of you are

getting along, you can't help but outshine your brother, can you?'

'Me?' Luke kissed her. 'I'm just a rancher. He's a duke. A real one, ever since he took that advice you gave him.'

She had apologised to both Percy and Hazel when they'd came to Montana the first time, within weeks of receiving Luke's letter than he and his family would be staying in America. Percy and Hazel had changed, for the better, and visiting with them here and in London was always pleasurable. But she had to correct her husband. 'Just,' she scoffed, then leaned against him. 'You, my love, will never be *just* anything.'

The prime beef produced by the C Bar H was very well known and widely sought. He was the president of the Stockgrowers Association, and had turned the ranch into practically a small city. Besides adding additional cowboys and employees, when the girls had become school-aged, he'd built a schoolhouse, hired a teacher, and invited all the neighbouring ranches and farms, who felt Bozeman was too far away, to send their children to the school. He was the king of his own kingdom, his haven, and made her feel like a queen every day of her life.

With excited squeals, Rowdy, Fern, and Ivy ran towards the house, and told her all about the horses as they walked inside. The smile on her face demonstrated her happiness, but it truly lived in her heart. She'd thought she couldn't love her husband any more, yet day by day, her love grew deeper and stronger.

From a governess to a queen…now, that had been an adventure. And it wasn't over.

Far from it.

* * * * *